FROM
CANADA
TO
PHILIPPINES

FROM
CANADA
TO
PHILIPPINES

NONSENSE NOVEL

JOE REMESZ

iUniverse, Inc.
Bloomington

FROM CANADA TO PHILIPPINES
Nonsense Novel

iUniverse books may be ordered through booksellers or by contacting:

iUniverse
1663 Liberty Drive
Bloomington, IN 47403
www.iuniverse.com
1-800-Authors (1-800-288-4677)

ISBN: 978-1-4759-9128-4 (sc)
ISBN: 978-1-4759-9129-1 (ebk)

Library of Congress Control Number: 2013908961

Printed in the United States of America

iUniverse rev. date: 05/24/2013

ONE

Jose and Pasita Ramos, hardy Filipino Canadian citizens, loved Canada, but after 25 years of living and working in Edmonton, Alberta, because of the long and cold winter nights, with their teenage son Eduardo (Ed), decided to retire in their native Philippines and to live in the industrial port city of Batangas City.

Once they arrived in the city, they often traveled throughout the Philippines to spend a weekend in a different region. On a January morning while having breakfast and the city was basking in sunny weather, Jose posed the question to his family, "Where shall we spend next week weekend?"

Ed suggested, "Let's travel to Manila." He had recently been reading about the city, the Pearl of the Orient, and was interested in seeing how the construction boom would affect the most densely populated city in the country."

Ed's parents agreed.

"First, however, we better find out if a hotel in Manila which will accommodate our poodle, Fido," Pasita suggested and asked Ed to write a letter to enquire if their poodle was allowed at the hotel. Within several days the Mall of Asia Hotel manager wrote back:

> Dear Ed Ramos,
>
> I have managed the Mall of Asia Hotel for 20 years and never have I had to call the police or eject a disorderly dog during the small hours of the night.

Never has a dog set our hotel on fire because of a cigarette or have I found a blanket, towel, glasses or a *Bible* missing.

Never have I found liquor rings staining the desktop from a dog's bottle or a television busted or the remote control missing. And I never missed a key to a room at checkout time. Certainly your pet dog Fido is welcome to stay at the Mall of Asia Hotel.

PS: If Fido will vouch for your parents, bring them too.

Crescencio Actuel
The Mall of Asia Hotel Manager

The distance from Batangas City to Manila is approximately 115 kilometers and accessible by land or sea. As a prime tourist attraction one can view the nearby spectacular Tall volcano.

The Ramos's arrived at the majestic Mall of Asia Hotel on a Friday evening, registered and before going to sleep went for a swim in the hotel swimming pool. Actually there were three pools—one filled with warm water, the second with cool water and the third was empty.

When Ed asked the receptionist, "Why the empty pool?" she graciously replied, "Simple. Some visitors who come to Manila and stay at our hotel can't swim."

That Saturday and part of Sunday the Ramos family toured the 2nd largest mall in the Philippines and the 4th largest in the world and then, Ocean and Rizal parks.

On Sunday evening, the Ramos's returned home and Ed's close friend, Jephony Banko, asked what Manila was like.

In reply Ed said, "Aside from traffic jams, the city is littered with cranes. There's a building boom. Eventually I would like to live permanently there and become a real estate salesman."

To accommodate their son's passionate dream, Ed's father listed the Ramos home in Batangas City for sale with a real estate agency.

After the listing expired, he tried to sell the home independently by inserting ads in newspapers and on shopping mall bulletin boards but it did not sell, so Ed then said, "Dad, let me try to sell our home."

"Go ahead try," his father replied and the following, day Ed marched back and forth in front of the City Hall. Ed used creative showmanship by wearing a Raggedy Anne costume which was used for Halloween, advertising the home on a sandwich board. The spray-painted sign read: FOR SALE BY OWER A BEAUTIFUL HOME. Ed accidentally misspelled the word Owner in the for Sale by Owner sign. At the bottom were the address and phone number.

A week later, Ed's mother said, "Ed, this is like a zoo. My head is spinning. People are looking at our house every day."

That particular day, two prospects were touring the upstairs, two more downstairs and another two waiting in the living room for their turn.

Like many home owners, Mr. And Mrs. Ramos were selling their home by themselves, hoping to avoid an agency fee that would cut several thousand pesos of their profit.

But while selling their home in Batangas City, they had to buy one in Metro Manila. The payoff was that within a week the Ramos's received a fair offer with a deposit, but before they felt like prisoners in their own home constantly fielding phone calls, answering questions, giving directions and tours. Prospects would call for an appointment only with the caller say, "We are standing outside in the driveway. Can we see your home now?"

These calls came even if it was already dark outside.

Ed perused his passion to be a real estate salesman and in order to get his foot into the industry, sent a letter to the Best Realty Ltd. in Madaluyong City to sponsor him. Within a week Ed received a reply from Rogelio Best, the manager and owner, asking Ed to answer the following question.

In order to become a salesman with our company—Are there any significant experiences you have had or accomplishments you have realized which will help you to become a successful realtor?

In essay form Ed wrote back.

Dear Mr. Best:

I helped my parents to sell our home by using a sandwich board. Unfortunately I can't swim but eventually intend to take lessons. I enjoy playing golf and eating adobo, pancit and lechon but not balut, recipe # 5 and dinuguan, and to smoke a cigarette once in a while.

I have an insatiable thirst for knowledge and enjoy reading books. My favorite authors are William Shakespeare, Jose Villa and Stephen Leacock who happens to be a Canadian.

When I'm bored, I compose poems or turn hydrogen and oxygen atoms into water. The laws of physics do not apply to me. I'm an abstract artist, a philosopher and fashion conscious.

I have a haircut once a month. People trust me. I know the exact location of every shopping mall in Batangas City and some in Metro Manila.

I balance, I weave, I dodge. I frolic and have my own skate board, bicycle, credit card, cell phone and a driver's license. I'm also computer literate. All my bills are paid on time. On weekends I let off steam by going to concerts. I enjoy listening to Sara Geromino, Charice Pepango, Lea Solonga and Christian Bautista.

I enjoy politics too, and have met and spoke to Joseph Estrada, Gloria Arroyo and 'Noynoy' Aquino111. I translate documents into Pig Latin and wow women with my guitar playing. I manage time effectively. With the slap of my hand I killed twenty three mosquitoes in a rice field in Laguna. I believe in prayer, reincarnation, angels and saints and possess a slightly twisted, sarcastic and cynical sense of humor. I know a lot of adult jokes. I'm a member of the No Name Universal Church where a 7th son of a 7th son, told me about bribes, graft, corruption and being honest. I will be graduating from college this coming March. In a nutshell that's me, Eduardo (Ed) Ramos and my eventual destination is to be in heaven.

The next week Ed's application was approved subject to him finishing college and then writing a Metro Manila Real Estate Board exam.

Following a successful garage sale, the Ramos's moved to Mandaluyon City part of Metro Manila where there are more Chan's and Wong's in the phone book than there are Cruz's or Gonzalez's and purchased a home in the San Miguel district, which they initially thought was a piece of cake. To assist in the purchase Ed's father called on a realtor, Helen Chan, at Best Realty. After qualifying the Ramos's, Ms. Chan said, "I'm going to match you and your home by using the ancient Chinese *fend shui* method which is a system of geomancy used on earth and even China, to help improve your life."

Ms. Chan convinced the Ramos's to buy an older type house which did not improve their life, but made it frustrating.

There are things one should know about this particular house and it has nothing to do with an ancient Chinese ritual.

The house appeared like any ordinary house with three bedrooms, white colored and a picture window, but after the purchase was made, the Ramos's discovered that they had made several mistakes and did not read the fine print.

They shopped for a house without getting a pre-arranged mortgage. (2) Chose a lender based only on the interest rate forgetting about a balloon clause, and (3) Purchased the house without being professionally inspected.

After the Ramos's moved into the house, they went through an exhilarating experience of renovating it. To start they purchased several home improvement magazines, read through the articles and got useful tips. The first tip Jose Ramos picked up, was to have a large bank account, and the second, go to garage, liquidation sales, flea markets and Ace Hardware to purchase tools, lumber and paint.

Home renovating brought both joy and frustration and began with removing old fixtures, windows, tearing out door frames and drywalls, tonguing and grooving.

Of course everything did not go perfectly. Murphy's Law took its toll. Rain did not stop, the plumber broke his arm and the electrician fried himself while drilling through a wall. Renovation also revealed old termite damage, dry rot and the duct work was out of whack. There were glitches to numerous to mention and of course, plenty of cussing.

In the end of the renovation process, there were enough changes made in the ecological picture that it's a wonder why the Mandaluyong City Council hadn't asked for an environmental impact statement.

During the month of March, the Ramos family was sitting in the auditorium of the Asia Pacific College where Ed was graduating and growing into adulthood. To this point in life, Ed had many pluses aside helping his parents to sell their home in Batangas City. Ed also had the distinction of being the only college graduate in the Philippines to write his exam in Pig Latin believing PL should be Philippine's third official language.

Ed had a look of maturity as the principal, Ariel Sorita, presented him with a diploma and said, "Ed Ramos, congratulations. Now get rid of all the negatives and reach for the sky. The world is yours. Go and conquer it."

As soon as the graduation ceremony was over, it wasn't certain if Ed, this 5 foot/6, 130 pound, athletic-looking teenager would be arrested when in the family car, he picked up several of his class mates, cranked up the radio to full volume, and they were hollering and whooping, screaming and burning rubber, throughout the city. Ed's parents were concerned that their only son wouldn't drive sensibly to a graduation party.

Two

Fortunately Ed did drive carefully and wasn't picked up by the cops, but next day slept until noon and had the worst headache of his life when he reviewed copies of previous real estate exams at the Best Realty Ltd. office on Boulevard Avenue.

When the owner-agent Rogelio Best, took samples, one of the assignments was to write a short composition which included a murder, Philippine history and a mystery.

Ed on a sheet of paper wrote: "Holy Moses, in Manila, a senator got pregnant. I wonder who did it."

The exam paper also asked candidates entering the real estate profession, to write a short composition what each candidate would do if he/she earned one million pesos in commission. While other candidates wrote furiously, Ed instead of writing gazed out the window and handed in a blank sheet.

"Why, Ed?" Best said looking at the sheet of paper. "You've done nothing. Why is that?"

"Well," Ed replied, "That's what I would do if I made one million pesos in commission."

The following week, when Ed was called the actual exam at the Real Estate Board office he was worried, so he went to his father for his blessing, and then to his mother, to pray for him.

On his way to write the exam, Ed met a scraggly looking homeless man who said to him, "Kind sir, I swear to God, have not eaten or a place to sleep for two days.

Please, can you spare me some money so I can buy myself a cup of coffee?"

With a great deal of composure, Ed gave him several pesos hoping that God would remember the gesture, and that He would give him the correct answers in order to pass the exam.

At the Real Estate Board office Ed was nervous. As he opened the envelope containing the actual exam, the first question read, "In what part of the Philippines do most ignorant people live?" Ed wrote 'Manila', reasoning that according to geography the population of Manila was densest in all of Philippines.

The next question read: Name 3 types of cars that appear in the *Bible.*

Ed responded, "Jehovah drove Adam and Eve out of the Garden in a *Fury.* David's *Triumph* was used thorough out the land and maybe a *Honda* because all the apostles were in one Accord."

The exam also asked Ed to correctly answer the following questions.

1 Give the important characteristics of the ancient Spanish Empire with particular reference to real estate in the Philippines.
2 What kind of a room is not found in a house? If your answer is a mushroom, draw a sketch of one.
3 Why are they called apartments when they are all stuck together?
4 The statement: A realtor specializes in fabricated homes. Does that mean his/her sales are built on lies? If your answer is yes, write down in one or two sentences the greatest lie a Filipino president ever told

5   Finish this sentence: There is so much poverty in the Philippines because_____

6   Divide 6/8 by 2/3, and what do you get?

7   Name the three wealthiest families in the Philippines

8   How have the Abu Sayaff and the People's New Army affected Philippine economic growth?

9   Where is the basement located in a three-story building?

10 Besides a vacuum cleaner, fly paper and a pooper-scooper, write down what you think is another collective noun.

Ed began writing furiously, first answering the above questions, then the Essay ones, followed by Multiple Choice and finally True or False. Among the True and False questions Ed had to decide if:

1   Market value is found only at a Farmer's Market?

2   A contract for sale of real estate property is not valid if completed and signed on the day of a Fiesta or during a cock-fight

3   Objective Value is found only at Robinson's store.

4   A Bundle of Rights includes the right to slug a realtor on the head if one isn't satisfied with his/her service?

5   When the Congress passes a Rent Control Act, it's an Act of God?

6   The effect of Condition Precedent is an extreme headache?

7   The highest or absolute value right in real estate is Fe Simple?

8   A counter offer is generally made on a kitchen counter?

9   An icon of Santo Nino is considered a chattel.
10 Loss of value to a building is due to any cause known as graphite vandalism?
11 The difference between an investment banker and a lawyer is a pizza?

Ed also had to pick the right answer in a series of fifty Multiple Questions. Here are copies of ten:

1   The basic distinction between a salesman and an agent are:
    (a) The agent must have a bald head
    (b) The agent usually is older than the salesman
    (c) The agent is responsible to the vendor
2   Which of the following is a designation that can apply to people who have completed a prescribed course of studies in the real estate profession?
    (a) MLS,
    (b) FRI
    (c) GMA
3   Under Philippine law a person under eighteen years of age is considered:
    (a) An infant
    (b) an adult
    (c) a juvenile
4   Depending on low or high tide, how many islands are there in the Philippines?
    (a) 77
    (b) 3
    (c) 7,107
5   When an agreement for sale is granted the title is held by:
    (a) Vendor
    (b) municipal office
    (c) purchaser's wife

6   A hip roof slopes:
  (a) Towards Mecca
  (b) Towards India
  (c) Four sides

7   If the mortgage provides that it may be paid out at any time without notice or bonus, the mortgage is usually called:
  (a) A swear word
  (b) Open mortgage
  (c) Closed mortgage

8   When accepting a deposit on a real estate transaction it is payable to:
  (a) An honest Senator
  (b) The Vendor
  (c) The agent

9   Philippines economy is considered:
  (a) Mixed economy
  (b) Gone to pot
  (c) Controlled by incompetent politicians

10 In event the purchaser does not fulfill the terms of an accepted offer the deposit is:
  (a) Used by the salesman
  (b) Forfeited to the vendor
  (c) Given to the Salvation Army

RATINGS

(a) 45 out of 50—You may get your license
(b) 45 to 35—Have another exam within 2 weeks
(c) Less than 35—Find another profession

As soon as Ed completed writing his exam he turned it in to the supervisor and then went home to wait for the results and read books that dealt with real estate matters, and also watch videos on the same subject. The ten books Ed enjoyed reading the most were:

1 How to be a Superstar in Real Estate by author I. M. Wealthy
2 Amusing Incidents While Listing Homes by Mini Haha
3 Chattel or Fixture? by R. U. Upjohn
4 Real Estate as an Investment by I. C. Moon
5 Diary of a Slumlord by Ping Pong Lord
6 The Strength of the Filipino peso by Harry Scarry
7 Strike it rich in real estate by Jack Pott
8 How to Save a Listing by Les Chance
9 Sue for Damages by Jack Frost
10 Recession in the Real Estate Industry by Cardinal Sinn

Among he videos Ed enjoyed were:

1 Real Estate in Cyberspace produced by Clare Voyant
2 Real Estate in Southern Leyte produced by Ho Hum
3 Real Estate and the Environment produced by Les Waste
4 Real Estate for Dummies produced by Peekaboo Butt
5 Abroad Filipino Foreign Contract Workers produced by I. C. Yu
6 Real Estate Humour produced by Marc Joker
7 Sophisticated Real Estate Technology by Sam Sung
8 Unusual Real Estate Features produced by Al Over
9 Deceptive Real Estate Appearance produced by Jesus Saves
10 One-Of-A-Kind Home produced by Juan Holmes

THREE

As soon as Ed was notified he had passed his exam, he joined the sales force at Best Realty. As Ed began his orientation he sat down at a table with the company owner and agent, Rogelio Best. The two discussed various aspects of listing, selling and giving a house an edge on the market.

"Before a prospect arrives at a house he/she wants to see put several drops of vanilla extract in the oven and crank up the heat to make the house smell more inviting," Best suggested. He also gave other tips for successfully selling a home including:

1   Replace the light bulbs with higher voltage.
2   Remove any items in the house that may create a junkyard image.
3   Place freshly cut flowers in the kitchen and living room.
4   Tidy up the garage.
5   Make certain the toilet is flushed in case the prospect wants to use it.

Ed then took a memory improvement course to enforce his real estate knowledge. The course covered how to list properties, how to qualify a prospect; appraise a property and real estate language. Technical jargon in any profession can create confusion and misunderstanding for those not well-versed in the lingo and the real estate jargon is no exception.

Ed learned the following are commonly used real estate industry terms along with what he understood them in mean in plain English,

WORDS	WHAT ED THOUGHT IR MEANT
Abstract	First to add and then to subtract
Accord	A car cheaper than a Mercedes
Agency	A home for the aged
Agreement for Sale	A friend agrees to sail a sailboat with Ed
Appraisal	Another name for an umbrella
Block	A derogatory reference to a buyer or seller's head
Caveat Emptor	A Roman emperor
Chattel	Another name for a telephone company
Circuit Breaker	A purchaser who goes directly to the seller, bypassing a real estate salesman
Contract	To make smaller
Covenant	A home for nuns
Cul-de-sac	A bag with shredded documents
Deed	Not alive
Deposit	Something you make in the bathroom
Fixed assets	People embedded in cement
In testate	In United States
Lease	Please
Lien	A popular girls name
Listing	About to go under
Mortgage	A dead male (French)
Mortgagee	A dead female (French)
Multiple listing	More than one ship gone under

Joe Remesz

Power of Attorney	Having a big mouth
Principle	A top honcho at a school
B. S.	Better Service
CEO	Chief Embezzlement Officer
CFO	Corporate Fraud Officer
PAL	Plane Always Late
Financial Planner	A guy whose phone has been disconnected
Market Correction	The day after you buy stocks
Cash Flow	The time your cash goes down the toilet
Yahoo	What you yell after completing a successful real estate deal
Window	A place you jump through after a deal collapses
Profit	An archaic word seldom used
Real estate broker	A real estate salesman who is broke most of the time
Realtor	A real person from Toronto
Facebook	Something you look at when a deal collapses
Twitter	Treat a female realtor who gives you a referral
Closing statement	Thank God
Abandonment	Everyone present for a contract signing but the buyer
A.R. M.	Part of the body that is twisted during a real estate negotiation
RAPE	Retire adult people early
Base line	Your property is worthless
Cellular	Vendor who wishes to sell a property

Deed of Trust	Salesperson loaning the buyer a down payment
Developer	Muscle builder who converts raw land into housing
Easement	Right of one agency to trespass on another agency's exclusive property
Extension	Time elapsed between a bank deposit and the clearance of funds

When it came to advertising, Ed thought for example that *split* meant a home that was falling apart. *One of a kind* meant a cave with inside plumbing. *Reduced* meant either a house with bad tenants or one ideal for pygmies and, *Old World Charm* meant no bathroom.

Ed did not realize *Spacious Green Grass* meant the septic tank had to be changed. *Country Living* could mean India or Rwanda. *Room to Grow* meant the house had 12-foot ceilings and. *Low Maintenance* meant no landscaping or grass.

Park-like Setting, there's a tree in the back yard, *Natural Setting*, an animal will eat anything you plant. And, *Much, Much More*, meant can't think of anything else to say about the heap.

Bedroom Community, neighbor's gossip so one might as well invite them into your bedroom. *Deal Won't Last*, the house is collapsing. *Wide Open Floor Plan*, previous owners removed the supporting walls. *Hidden Away*, shrubs are so tall one can't see out the front window. *Secluded Setting* far from anything convenient.

Rustic Charm, house needs major structural repairs, and, *Handyman's Special*, another way of saying "disgusting," "rotten," "hopeless."

Unusual Features, the house has no roof. *Rare Opportunity to Buy*, No one wants it. *Asking Price*, Amount set on the property that a realtor thinks is too high, vendor thinks the price is to low and the prospect thinks the property isn't worth half the selling price.

Ed also memorized catch phrases he could use while overcoming objections, when handling indecisions, while trying to list FISBO's and qualifying prospects. He also joined the Best Realty salesmen in role playing and acted out a scene where a grasshopper kept jumping from place to place while an ant kept building a nest and saved.

Best also suggested Ed familiarize himself with economics and the routine of other salesmen employed by Best Realty but the latter wasn't a good suggestion because five salesmen: Emmanuel Crook, Ricardo Bandit, Roberto Pickles, Rommel Swindler and Elmer Cheat had unlikely surnames for a realtor and they spent much of their time enjoying themselves at a local watering hole. There was also Vernon Sled but he was totally retired and active only every four years—during the Winter Olympics.

As for real estate economics Ed discovered that:

(1) You can talk about money without ever having to make any
(2) You can say "trickle down" with a straight face
(3) When you are in the unemployment line, at least you will know why you are there
(4) If you rearrange the word ECONOMICS, you get COMIC NOSE
(5) Mick Jagger and Arnold Schwarzenegger both studied economics and look how they turned out
(6) Standard and Poor—your life in a nutshell

(7) Bear Market—6 to 19 month period when the kids get no allowance, the wife gets no jewelry

(8) Bull Market—A random market movement causing an investor to mistake himself for a financial genius

(9) Stock Split—Ex-wife and her lawyer split your assets equally between themselves

(10) Institutional Investor—Investor locked up in a nuthouse

Ed also reviewed the Metro Manila Real Estate Board forms and personal data sheet, and signed both. He then joined the Philippine Real Estate Association, which automatically entitled him to use he word *Realtor* as his occupation aside from salesman.

He pledged to abide by the Board's and Association's bylaws, covenants, undertakings, waivers claims and live up to a code of ethics.

Ed next studied how to make a market analysis, prices of properties which sold in Manila during the past three months, what a pro forma was and the proper way to conduct Open Houses.

This done, Ed discussed house hunting by prospects and about housing styles, floor plans, square footages, zoning, demographics, community leagues and neighborhoods. All had to do with determining how happy home buyers will be in a house he/she picks out.

Best also reminded Ed that a salesman in order o be successful should be able to field questions from prospects about transit zones, schools, parks, churches, shopping malls, medical facilities and a neighborhood.

"All told they can be the determining point for a home buyer," Best said. "Often its amenities and distance to work or a combination of both, that make the buyer choose one area over another."

Best went on to say that local people often have certain areas in mind as to where they want to live. But first-time buyers and people from out of town frequently need direction.

Realtors should be adept to asking leading questions to determine what are important to the prospect and where those needs can be met. It's not unusual for realtors to have first-hand knowledge of the area.

Where a kid can play basketball or soccer and how far it's from a shopping mall and a church. Best then said, "Let's not forget a school site doesn't mean a school will be built there."

Ed was told that initially, he could market residential and commercial properties but not farms and ranches, and was given a pair of grey-colored slacks, a blue jacket with a Best Realty crest on it, a matching necktie and a pair of black-colored socks. Why black socks?

The reason is because the black color looks dressy and doesn't show dirt.

Even while attending High School in Edmonton, Ed conducted an experiment during a science class where three rats wore different colored socks: black, white and red, and then posed the question to his classmates: "Which colored socks look the best?"

The students voted unanimously—the rat with the black socks.

Ed continued with his experiment a week later when he took the three rats to a meeting of the Alberta Real Estate Board held at the Fairmont Hotel in Calgary.

Ed waited until most of the executives were sitting at a table or standing nearby and there was a lull in the chatter, and then he posed the same question, "Ladies and gentlemen.

If you were inclined to hire a rookie salesperson, which colored socks would you like him/her wearing?"

The answer was practically unanimous: "A salesman/woman with black socks"

As soon as Ed was outfitted with a suit of clothing, he was told during his first day of orientation, to make cold calls and see if he could pick up his first listing. Ed recalled what the college principal said on graduation day: "Get rid of the negatives. Reach for the sky. The world is yours. Go and conquer it!"

Initially, Ed teamed up with Mr. Best and the two chose an area in the Binondo district primarily populated by ethnic Chinese and located across the Pasic River from Intramoros.

The area is well known for where Saint Lorenzo Ruiz, the Filipino protomartyr, and Venerable Mother Ignacia del Espititu Santos, founder of the Congregation of Religious of the Virgin Mary lived, but since hardly anyone spoke Tagalog or English, no listings were taken, so the next day their campaign changed to the middle class Greenfield district where Ed and his employer walked from one house to another knocking on doors and making cold calls.

At the first call Mr. Best, who had 20 years' experience as a realtor, said to the owner, "Sir, you should sell your home now while the market is hot. In addition to the hot market it appears to me that you are a heavy smoker and statistics indicate may die of cancer."

On the way to the second home Best said, "Ed, while making a pitch for a listing a realtor has to be observant and watch for clues on what subject to talk about initially, and get the prospect motivated. For example at the last home, there were cigarette ashtrays and the odor of tobacco smoke."

"I got you," Ed said and when it was his turn to approach a prospect he said to the lady of the house, "Madam, you have to cut down on your cholesterol level and stop drinking milk and eating butter and cheese."

As the two realtors were on their way to the third home, Mr. Best congratulated the rookie real estate salesman and said, "Ed, that was excellent, but tell me, what did you use for a clue to initiate a conversation?"

Simple," Ed replied, "The milkman hiding under the woman's bed."

Ed enjoyed doing cold calls and evaluating homes. Some of the reasons were:

- He could dazzle his friends with his knowledge of external obsolescence
- He could see the wonderful world of stray dogs, chickens, lizards and mosquitoes
- See spaces in people's houses that usually required a search warrant
- Take notice that some people still do hang on their living room walls portraits of Jose Rizal, Santo Nino and Pope John Paul 11
- Get attention in the neighborhood while walking around with a clip board

On August 16th, Ed had to pay attention of a different kind, when news broke that a devastating earthquake, followed by a tsunami, the largest in Philippine history, took place between the island of Mindanao and Borneo. The initial quake was felt as far away as of the central Philippine islands of the Visayas. A casualty report said that 8000 people lost their lives that included Ed's uncle Dindo and aunt, Jocelyn.

Next day, Ed put on his skateboard and helmet and went searching for a listing alone. At one the homes, a young boy answered the door and Ed said, "Hello, may I speak to your daddy or mummy."

The youngster replied, "They're not home."

"Well is there anyone else I can talk with?"

"Would you like to speak to my sister?"

"Please,"

The boy went away and returned a minute later, "Mister."

"Yes."

"I can't lift my sister from the play pen."

"That's all right I'll come back later."

And when Ed did, his first question was, "Are your mom or dad home yet?"

"No, sir."

"Can I leave a message?"

"You sure can mister, wait till I find a pencil."

Ed waited and when the youngster returned said, "Mister."

"Yes."

"I'm here but you want to know something?"

"What?"

"I can't write only print."

Frustrated, Ed didn't talk to the boy's father until much later.

On the same day, Ed got his first listing and was trying to figure out how to measure a flagpole in front of the house. Ed got a ladder and a tape measure and went up to the flagpole. However, the measurement turned more difficult than he had expected when both the tape measure and the ladder fell to the ground. The whole thing turned into a disaster. Frustrated, Ed phoned Mr. Best at the office explaining what had happened.

Best scrambled and said, "Pull the flagpole out of the ground, lay it on the grass and then measure it from end to end."

After Ed hung up the receiver he said to himself, "I'm looking for the height of the pole and he gives me instructions on how to find the length."

Ed eventually did measure the pole.

The following day, Ed rode his bicycle to find prospects on his own and came upon a home that was partially destroyed, valuables stolen and furniture ruined. Vandals had broken into the home before the owners returned home from a holiday in Bohol to see the Chocolate Hills and the tarsier monkeys. Seeing Ed, the husband said, "Vandals stuffed the drains with their socks and then turned on the taps."

Upon inspection Ed could see the ceiling collapsing and when he entered the sunken living room he was up to his ankles in water. The couple managed to salvage some of the clothes but the photos of their children were lost for ever.

To make the damage more catastrophic, the culprits spray-painted the walls and plumbing fixtures. Only the outside walls of the house and its foundation were salvageable.

"It gives me the creeps to walk into our home. Luckily we are covered with insurance," the wife said as her husbanded turned to Ed and continued, "Would you like to list this place for sale?" While Ed was making up his mind the wife said, "As is."

At Ed's next stop, a newly wed couple's home turned into a nightmare after the bride and groom had discovered that the home they had purchased a month earlier had been the scene of a grisly murder.

The couple was horrified that in the FOR SALE BY OWNER home the owner's wife had been murdered by a prospect, the body chopped into pieces and thrown into a back ally dumpster. The newly married couple was upset and reluctant to move in.

"Even our mom's say they won't come to visit us if we move in," the bride said.

"Tell me more," Ed probed.

The groom took over. "It was a week ago that we found out about the murder. The fact that the murder took place in the home we bought is a latent defect and it should have been disclosed by the owner at the time we signed the purchase agreement."

"That will teach you to buy a home directly from the owner," Ed thought but used good judgment and instead said, "So you want to list the home for sale through me?"

"No, we already spent 20,000 pesos in renovating the place. All we want is advice on what to do?" the groom continued.

"My advice is finding a lawyer who specializes in real estate matters."

And while continuing searching for more listings, Ed came to a home which was partially destroyed. Valuables stolen and furniture ruined. Vandals had broken into the home before the owners returned from a holidaying on Palawan Island.

Seeing Ed with a clipboard the owner said, "The vandals stuffed the drains with clothing and turned on the taps."

Upon inspection Ed could see that the ceiling was collapsing and when he entered the sunken living room he was up to his ankles in water. The couple managed to save some of the clothing but photos of their children were lost for ever. To make the damage more catastrophic the culprits spray painted the walls and plumbing fixtures.

Only the outside walls of the house and the foundation was salvageable.

"It gives me the creeps to walk into our home." The owner continued. "Luckily we had insurance and would like you list this house for sale while we move into an apartment."

A week later, Ed got another listing on a small, older—two bedroom house on a large lot and the vendor, Theodor Cruz, made an offer on a larger three bedroom bungalow. The offer on the bungalow was subject to Cruz selling his home within seven days. Ed evaluated the tiny home based on recent comparable sales in the area and then said to Mr. Cruz, "Your home needs major repair. On the other hand one can never tell who is in the market for a fixer-upper like yours that needs work."

"What work does it need? Cruz asked.

"Like the living room walls, the bathroom and the roof. Take a day or two to paint the interior and then I'll start bringing prospects."

Cruz, his wife Jessa and their two daughters, Cherry and Mary, stayed up all night painting the kitchen and removing mildew from the bathroom tiles. Cruz then installed a lovely toilet seat he had purchased earlier at a flea market for one 100 pesos.

On the 2nd day, the first potential buyers were scheduled to arrive so Cruz said to his two teenage daughters, "Listen, our home won't sell unless we impress the prospect with neatness. Your mother will tell you what that means.

"No more underwear left on the stairs or the floor of your bedroom," Mrs. Cruz explained. "Or drops of toothpaste left in the bathroom sink. You will make your beds the moment you get up and better still, why don't you sleep on the floor in your room so that the beds won't be messed up?

Your father will have to smoke and take his naps in the garage, but first, he has to haul the junk away."

At 11:00 a. m. Ed phoned to say that he was on his way with Mr. and Mrs. Gonzalez. In that time the Cruz's placed themselves in position with Mary in the living room standing on the cigarette burns in the carpet and Cherry near a window with her back against water stains on the wall. Jessa meanwhile, sprayed the entire house with a herbal scented air freshener and Cruz tied the two dogs to a tree in the back yard which had come down with Dutch elm disease

The Gonzalez's viewing was so fast that Cruz didn't have time to tell them that the house was only a block away from the offices an oil company and across the street from the planned site of a gas station.

On the 3rd day, Ed phoned and said that the Ayuban's were coming and, "Let's spread some leaves over the bare spots on the front lawn."

"That's an excellent idea," Cruz replied and quickly led his wife and daughters with the camouflage. As soon as the Ayuban's arrived at the front door, a gust of wind blew the leaves away.

The Ayuban's stayed longer than the Gonzalez's, but they hadn't found a dream home either, although they had found yellow patches on the lawn.

On the 4th day, Ed phoned and said, "Your home isn't suitable for the Ayuban's. They want something bigger, but loved the aroma of the air freshener, so don't air the place, out because I'm bringing the Mandapat's. By the way, why don't you light the fireplace so the home looks lived in?"

Not many homes in the Philippines have a fire place but this one did.

"I'll have the fireplace going by the time the Mandapat's arriving."

The Mandapat's arrived on schedule, equipped with a measuring tape. Mrs. Mandapat dropped to her knees and began measuring the living room carpet which would need to be replaced.

She was so engrossed in measuring that she didn't notice smoke billowing from the fireplace. Then she began coughing and screamed, "Hey is the house on fire!"

Cruz said the house would never catch on fire because it was built mostly of concrete blocks.

The Mandapat's seemed so gracious that Cruz felt sorry he could not help clear their lungs.

On the 5th day, the phone rang again and Ed said to Cruz, "Forget the Mandapat's; they made an offer on a larger house with new carpets and a fireplace that did not send out smoke signals."

"What are we going to do? We have only two days left before the *subject to* clause is to be removed on the bungalow? Cruz asked.

"I have an idea," Ed said.

Curious, Cruz said, I'm listening."

"Let's reduce the price by 50,000 pesos"

This time Cruz did not say '*It's an excellent idea*' but gave Ed permission to lower the price. During an Open House prospects came but no offer was made. Most of the prospects that came to see the home said, "We're just looking."

By now Cruz found his tiny home so attractive that he was inclined to take it off the market until it began to rain and the ceiling went drip, drip and drip.

On the 6th day, Ed arrived with Mr. And Mrs. Navarro but they didn't make an offer because their dream retirement home didn't mean taking a shower in the living room where the ceiling went drip, drip, drip.

There was one consolation, however; the Navarro's wouldn't have to water their house plants.

As soon as the Navarro's left, Cruz crawled into the attic and patched the roof from inside with a silicone gun. On the way down, he slipped off a beam and punched a hole in the ceiling. He immediately called a carpenter and pleaded, "We re trying to sell our home. Can you please repair the ceiling by midnight?"

The carpenter managed to repair the ceiling on time, and Ed was able to bring Ms. Galope through at 11.00 on the 7th day.

"We are ready for her," Cruz said.

To Ms. Galope house hunting was as exciting as an Olympic event. Her enthusiasm for the house was filled with warmth, so much so, that Cruz began to confess about its defects.

Cruz was making his way to the repairs he had done, when Ms. Gallope made an unexpected offer which Cruz accepted, and then, had the subject to clause, removed on the offer he had made on a three bedroom bungalow in a another neighborhood.

A week after the Cruz's took possession of their home; they drove by their former residence and were surprised that it had been demolished.

But that did not matter, what ultimately did, was that both Cruz and Ms. Galope were satisfied customers and Ed made his sale.

Ms. Galope had the tiny home torn down so that she could build a larger one on the huge lot, which had a panoramic view of a valley and the Pasig River flowing through the middle of the city.

The home-building project for Ms. Galope began with a bulldozer driving smack into the middle of the house.

The sound of a bulldozer was music to Ms. Galope's ears, as she said to anyone who questioned her, "I've been planning to build a custom-built home for months but couldn't find a large enough lot with a view."

Ms. Galope didn't salvage much from the house before it was torn down. She, however, saved the antique bathtub, living room chandelier and the toilet seat, which she donated to the National Museum of the Philippines.

The following day, Ed kept an appointment with an elderly prospect by the name of Ernesto Campo who had a beard large enough for small birds to make a nest in, and dressed in shabby clothing.

The man's belt buckle sank 2 inches into his stomach and his black shoes and yellow jacket were in need of repair. Ed showed Mr. Campo a low-priced home, a medium priced and finally a more expensive where he said to the prospect after viewing, "This home may be too expensive for you."

With a twinkle in his eyes his eyes, Campo took off his hat, as soon as Ed said, "Too expensive for you."

Believing there is no substitute for experience the prospect then asked, "Ed, how long have you been selling real estate?"

In jest Ed replied, "There's a little know fact about my career that Moses brought three tablets from the mountain. There were the Ten Commandments and the other was my real estate license."

Campo then asked Ed if he had sold a high-rise condo.

"I have."

"Please tell me about the experience."

"Well, I sold a high-rise condo in Makati City that is so high one can touch the stars. One can also tickle the feet of angels as they fly by."

After pausing for several seconds the shabbily dressed Campo put his hat back on his head and said. "Ed, do you want to know something."

"What?"
"Kid, I have free advice for you."
"What kind of advice?"
"Never judge your prospect by the size of his beard or clothing he or she is wearing. You have underestimated my intelligence and that is why I will not buy a house through you but another salesman."

Ed talked himself out of a listing and the following day had difficulty in negotiating others. In the first, Rabbi Abe Libowitch, and his wife arrived in Manila from Israel, and was trying to find an apartment to rent. Because of the construction boom, this was difficult.

As soon as Ed did find a rental for the Rabbi and his wife, he introduced the couple to Pastor Atupan of the No Name Universal Church and Father Napoleon Bajo from the Perpetual Help Catholic parish.

It so happened that Father Bajo's church and Rabbi Libowitch's synagogue were across the street from each other, their schedules intertwined and since their parishioners weren't generous, they decided to pool their resources and buy a car. After they bought a used Nissan, they drove it home and parked it on the street between the two places of worship.

A few minutes later, the Rabbi looked out the window and saw Father Bajo sprinkling water on the car. It didn't need a wash so the Rabbi ran out and asked Father Bojo what he was doing.

"I'm blessing it."

Rabbi Libowitch said, "Oh", and ran back to the synagogue reappearing a few minutes later with a hacksaw, ran to the car and cut off the last two inches of the tailpipe.

That did not bother Father Bajo who said, "It's a perfect example of ecumenism."

As Ed had a good rapport with the local clergy he hoped that eventfully they would provide him with leads who wanted to buy or sell.

Father Bajo enjoyed caribao racing so on a weekend evening, Ed took Father Bajo to the carabao races where the priest blessed the animal he bet on with holy water. Following a similar blessing a caribou won races 2, 3 and 4. Seeing this Ed placed his money on the next caribou that Father Bajo sprinkled with holy water, but half-way around the track the caribou fell and died.

That is when Ed said, "Look Father, I lost a bundle of money on the carabou in the 5th race."

"Are you Catholic?" the priest asked politely.

"No, I'm a member of the No Name Universal Church."

"Ed," Father Bajo replied, "If you were, you would have won had you known the difference between a blessing and the last rites."

Since Father Bajo's parish was a poor one, he asked Ed for suggestions as how he could raise money in order to renovate the parish rectory. Ed told him that farmer Carlo Joson, near Batangas City, was having a caribou auction and he could buy a caribao to race.

Unfortunately Father Bajo made a poor buy. Instead of buying a caribao he bought a donkey also known as an **ass,** and entered the animal during next race day. The donkey placed third.

The headline in the local newspaper read: "*Father Bajo's Ass Shows.*"

The archbishop saw the article in the newspaper and was greatly displeased. Next day the donkey placed first and the headline read: "*Father Bajo's Ass out In Front.*"

This was too much for the archbishop. Something had to be done, so he forbade Father Bajo from entering the donkey in anymore races.

The headline next day, read: "*Archbishop Scratches Father Bajo's Ass*".

Finally the archbishop ordered Father Bajo to get rid of the animal but he was unable to sell the donkey so he gave it to Sister Mary Grace as a pet.

The archbishop ordered the nun to dispose the animal at once. She sold it on e-Bay for 10 American dollars.

Next day, the headline in a newspaper read: "Sister Mary Grace Peddles Her Ass for $10.00."

Ed soon gained enough experience listing and selling, he was allowed to deal with international clients but not farms and ranches. Ed's first prospect was a financier from Hong Kong who was searching for a home to purchase. This occurred after Ed and the prospect, Chung Lee, had a drink of gin and tonic at the Hyatt Hotel and Casino. Ed had driven the multi-millionaire throughout Metro Manila and came to a wonderful home beautifully landscaped overlooking Manila Bay.

Ed finally asked, 'What you think of this fine piece of property?"

"I don't care for it." Mr. Lee replied, "Take away the sunset and what have you got?"

Ed also had difficulty dealing with a Chinaman from Hong Kong but also with an Arab-speaking rice farmer near Santa Cruz in the Laguna province named Mustafa Ayad who wanted to cash-in on the real estate hot market and sell his farm and purchase a fast food restaurant.

Through an interpreter Ed asked Ayad how much rice his farm expected to yield that year.

Ayad became agitated. In order to soften the reply the interpreter said, "Ed, he says he doesn't' know."

Ed realized something had gone wrong but had no way knowing what. Later he learned that that Arabs regard anyone who tries to look to the *future* as slightly insane. When Ed asked about the future yield the Arab was highly insulted since he thought Ed considered him crazy. To an Arab only God knows the future and it's presumptuous to ask.

Ed had a different experience however, when he met with an executive representing a major oil company that was searching for sites for a service station in Mandaluyong City.

The executive cross-examined Ed on the merits of various potential sites and finally said to him "All right. I'll give you a letter of introduction to the CEO of our company."

Ed met with the CEO and negotiated a multi-million peso order. In his zeal Ed forgot about the letter and did not present it.

Back at home several days later, Ed found the letter in his suit pocket. Curious, he opened it. The instructions inside were, "Learn all you can from Mr. Ramos but don't purchase any land through him if you can help it."

A month after the oil company purchased the landmark; it altered its architectural plans for the service station to include a restaurant and a car-wash thus needing more space. The company asked Ed to present a fair offer on the adjacent lot with an old brick house on it and owned by an 82 widow by the name of Teofista Menor saying that he was acting for his client but no identifying the client. Ed came to see Mrs. Menor and in current terms made a fair market offer on the property.

"I'm sorry but this house isn't for sale," Mrs. Menor said, "But please come in and have a cup of tea with me."

While having tea, Ed indicated that the client may pay a bit more but Mrs. Menor shook her head and said, "Definitely not. My home isn't available for any price. It's part of my Filipino heritage and I intend to spend the rest of my life right here in my home."

Meanwhile, the oil company applied for a building permit showing a service station, a restaurant and a car-wash and a large parking area.

Across the street residents signed a petition charging that the service station would congest local traffic, disturb the neighborhood peace and lower property value.

As a champion of commercial development, the Mayor of Mandaluyong City, called a special council meeting and after reading the petition, cautioned his council members, "The service station means taxes and jobs. This is a progressive step council has to support otherwise the oil company will build its service station in Quezon City."

In reply Mrs. Menor spoke out in public for the first time and questioned the wisdom of ripping down a perfect old house with a historical background, during a housing shortage.

"In any case I won't sell my property to any one at any price," Mrs. Menor said.

Having gone public the oil company sent its own officials to talk to the elderly widow and they came in a pecking order: chief legal council, vice-president, chief executive officer, and then the presidents himself and raise the company's ante to twice the market value of the property but to no avail.

Mrs. Menor insisted, "My old brick house is something money can not buy. The house embraces a bygone era and many memories I treasure."

The company president realized Mrs. Menor was a difficult nut to crack so he advised the company directors to back off from making additional offers.

For her part Mrs. Menor advised the president that the company could have first option on the house and said, "I have willed it to my son Jun, and when I die you can negotiate with him."

In the meantime the oil company proceeded with construction of the service station minus the restaurant and Mrs. Menor paid dearly for this.

Next to her house the building contractor worked behind a wire fence, and Mrs. Menor's quiet street echoed to the noise of a jackhammer and a bulldozer.

Pile drivers rattled her dishes and dust covered everything inside the house but Mrs. Menor was determined not to sell no matter what the problems meant.

To relatives and friends she said, "Money has no match for a household of memories. That is why I now take sleeping pills to blot out the sound of the drills."

Three months later, the Mayor officially opened the service station and those who came to fill up with gas, watched the elderly Mrs. Menor as she sat on the front porch knit or crochet.

A month after the official opening, Ed decided to see Mrs. Menor if she had changed her mind about the house only to discover that she had died, and the house where she lived, was torn down and buried under tons of parking lot pavement.

Mrs. Menor was a hard nut to crack and so was her 50-year old son, Jun who after inheriting the money from the sale of the house applied for a zoning change to establish a used-car lot next to the service station which was in a semi-residential neighborhood.

The zoning change was opposed by a well organized Community League and the first thing that surprised Ed about the David vs. Goliath battle was that the activists managed to win sometimes. Faced with developers who can afford to pay high-priced lawyers to attend public meetings may be stressful because ordinary people often have to rustle up baby sitters and parking money in order to have their voices heard.

In this instance, the Community League let Jun Menor know in no uncertain terms that neighbors in the area were going to make it difficult for any developer who threatened to eat up their quaint close-knit community with used cars.

Mondaluyong City Council eventually turned down Jun Menor's application for a zoning change and the Mayor said, "To establish a used car lot on the proposed site would be Cultural Vandalism."

The following week, an investor from Toronto, Canada was in search of property to open a Subway outlet.

Ed drove the prospect up and down Metro Manila and when they drove past a cock-fighting arena the Torontonian commented, "Toronto's Air Canaada Place is in better condition, much larger and there are more fist fights inside during NHL games than there are cock fights in your cock-fighting arenas."

While holidaying in the Philippines, the Prince of Wales of England met with Ed to discuss if the prince could purchase land that was his criteria.

"I want something my children will have which I never had," the prince said.

After searching for a day Ed asked the prince, "Can you be more specific?"

"Yes, something similar to India."

Although Ed tried, he could not find such a vast piece of land and suggested that perhaps the entire Philippine islands could be repurchased at the right price.

Other Experiences Ed had as a real estate salesman:

Ed approached an unkempt house and the puzzled owner said, "I didn't send for real estate salesmen."

Ed's reply was, "True, but your neighbor did."

Howls of pain emerged from a bathroom during an Open House Ed held on a Sunday. Those attending found a prospective buyer glued to the toilet seat by a practical joker who had passed through the house earlier, but luckily an ambulance crew managed to pry him from the seat.

A prospect phoned Ed and gave him the requirements for a home on an acreage he wished to buy. "About a hectare in size on a gently rolling fertile land with some of it forested, some suitable for cultivation with a pond or a stream through it. And it must have a view."

Ed listened with patience and when the prospect was finished said, "Sir, we deal with real estate and not fantasies."

The same day Best Realty was holding a salesmen meeting when the personnel manager asked, "How many people do we employ broken down by sex?"

"Sir," Ed replied, "I think there aren't many. Liquor is more a problem with our company.

And Initially Ed knew little about farming. While appraising a property in Cavite Ed found several milk bottles in the barn and came shouting, "Sir, look, I found a cows nest."

The farmer burst out with a roar of laughter and said, "Ed, that's not a cow's nest but three bottles of milk."

Best Realty maintained that sales or lack of therefore, sometimes is the fault of a salesperson. With the right training a real estate salesman can become a super-producer. Sales can also be affected by marketing. Poor marketing skills lead to low sales volume. Face to face marketing skills are secondary importance's remembering that pressure selling relates to lack of prospects. A realtor should never feel that one has to make a sale in order to drive an expensive SUV and even to survive.

Marketing campaigns often underestimate customer attitudes, and overestimate a products appeal. The traditional marketing focuses only on products and benefits from the salesman's point of view.

This arcane form of marketing does not seek to solve or answer immediate and long-term concerns of individuals. The paramount sales environment is one that is created and supported by an active marketing plan.

When marketing is driving the company's overall strategy, present customers are better served and satisfied, new doors open, former customers are reclaimed and sales personnel spend their time doing what they do best—making sales.

One of the secrets of marketing is for a salesperson to nab an award or win a contest which lead to being recognized as a distinguished professional in the industry.

With that premise Mr. Best invited a motivational speaker from the University of Manila who gave seminars for employees of Honda, Pepsi and Visa to give his salesmen a pep talk that would leave competition in the dust.

Professor Dindo Reyes, an expert in time management, used illustrations that Best Realty salesmen would never forget. He stood in front of a group at a seminar and began:

"It's time for a quiz," and set a one gallon, wide-mouth Mason jar on the table in front of him, and brought out a dozen fist sized rocks carefully placing them, one at a time, in the jar. When the jar was filled to the top and no more rocks would fit inside, he asked, "In your opinion is the jar full?"

All the realtors said, "Yes."

Dr. Reyes replied, "Really?" reached under the table and pulled out a bucket of gravel. He dumped some into the jar, shook it, causing pieces to work themselves down into the spaces between the rocks.

Dr. Reyes asked the group one more time, "Is the jar full?"

This time one of the realtors said, "Probably not."

"Good," Dr. Reyes replied, reached under the table and brought a bucket of sand, which he dumped into the jar. The sand went into spaces left between the rocks and the gravel, and one more time asked the salesmen, "Is the jar full?"

"No," all the realtors answered.

Once again Dr. Reyes said, "Good," and took a pitcher of water, poured it until the jar was filled to the brim. He looked at the realtors and asked, "What is the point of this illustration?"

Ed raised his hand and said, "Sir, the point is, no matter how full your schedule is, if you try really hard, you can always fit more things in."

"No," Dr. Reyes said, "That's not the point. The truth this illustration teaches us is: If you don't put the big rocks first, you will never get them in at all. What are the Big Rocks in your life? Your children. Your loved ones. Your education. Your dreams. A worthy cause. Teaching or mentoring others. Doing things you love. Time for yourself. Your health."

And then, Dr. Reyes continued, "Remember to put these Big Rocks in first or you will never let them in at all.

If you add gravel, sand and water in that order, then you will fill your life with little things to worry about that really don't matter, and you will never have the real quality time you need to spend on the big important stuff like the *rocks*.

So, tonight or in the morning, when you are reflecting on this short story, ask yourself this question: What are the big rocks in my life? Then put them into the jar first."

After being a participant in the Dr. Reyes seminar Ed's lackadaisical attitude changed, he entered and won, the Best Realty two-week *Get a Listing Contest.*

Salesmen who got the most listings within a period of two weeks would win as first prize not a holiday in Thailand or Singapore but 100,000 pesos, and an overnight stay at the Coconut Oasis Motel in Angeles City, one of the most active night-time entertainment districts in Asia.

FOUR

Now that Ed had received several commission checks, he decided to buy a transportation method, and when he stopped at the Pinoy Go Auto Used Car Lot, the salesmen convinced him to buy an ostrich, which the lot accepted as a trade-in on a previous sale.

"Riding an ostrich during the high price of gasoline, is much cheaper and more fun than driving a used car," the salesman said and continued, "An ostrich lives up to 50 years and capable of doing sixty kilometers an hour," and continued, "The bird is sturdy, sure-footed and has good traction."

Observing the ostrich from the front, sides and rear Ed said, "Does it really work?"

"It does, and when it comes to personal safety, the ostrich has been known to chase stray chickens and dogs and kick them. This ostrich stops at red lights."

Ed was debating with himself when the salesmen asked, "Ed, do you play golf?"

"I do."

"Then I have more good news. You can use the as an ostrich as a caddy."

"You mean to say that the big bird can tell the difference between 3 and 5 irons?"

"That is still researched, but would you like to try one?"

"I was going to ask if I could."

"Go ahead."

The salesman explained the commands "Gee" and "Haw" Ed then got on top of the ostrich and took off in heavy Manila traffic, when a jeepney pulled up behind him and Ed heard the driver say to his passengers, "Look at that jerk on top of the ostrich."

Ed was back at the used car lot within an hour, where the salesmen asked, "What happened?"

Ed had a look of distrust and said, "The ostrich stopped at a red light alright but when a jeepney pulled up behind me, and I heard the driver say to the passenger, "Look at that jerk on top of the ostrich."

"And?"

"I got off the ostrich to see the jerk."

"And then?"

"The ostrich ran towards the Manila Zoo."

Ed did not buy the ostrich, but was determined to find something cheap that he could ride in or on, and take advantage of the listing contest he had won. This time, Ed decided to buy a horse from farmer Jefferson Rodriguz who initially did not want to sell. Finally he said, "Prince doesn't look good, but if you want him you can have him."

Ed bought the horse, but the following day, became frustrated with it, so he returned the horse and said, "Rodriguez, you sold me a blind horse."

Rodriguez casually replied, "I told you the horse did not look good."

It was a case of Buyer Be Aware, so Ed purchased another horse instead and was on his way to Angeles City to claim his prize.

Halfway to Angeles City, the entertainment capital of the Philippines, Ed and the horse came upon a vicious wind and rain storm along the McArthur Highway which caused chaos.

Even the Aquino International Airport was closed and prompted health warnings by the Manila Health Care and Wellness. The storm was so severe that when it ended, a motorist found Ed's head sticking out of a mudslide.

Seeing Ed's head, the traveler excitedly said, "Wait, I'll get a shovel and dig you out."

"Thank you, but you better get a bulldozer because I'm sitting on top of a horse."

The traveler called in a bulldozer and cat skinner operated it. Ed and the horse survived, and both were on their way to Angeles City again.

As soon as Ed reached the outskirts of Angeles City, he drove up to a Mini-Stop Convenience Store and said to the owner, "I've passed through a severe rain storm and a mudslide several hours ago and my horse is thirsty. Please, give him a bucket of your best water to quench his thirst."

It took 24 bottles to fill the bucket and the horse was so thirsty that he drank it all.

Ed paid the bill and continued riding to the Angeles City, until they reached the Coconut Oasis Motel which isn't to grand or stuffy, where the food in the restaurant is good but not flashy and according to some, sleep is possible only with the double glazed windows are closed firmly because the motel is located on a street which turns into a drag strip near midnight.

Ed made the horse comfortable for the night, and then entered the motel, which recently was purchased by an investor from Switzerland, and management was ho-hum and a linguistic boo-boo sign at the reception desk read:

DEER GUESTS NOTICE

1   It's forbidden to steel towels in this motel. If you are not a person to do such things, please do not read this notice
2   Please keep your valuables at the front desk. If you keep them in your room we are not responsible
3   Please do not P in the swimming pool
4   Visitors are expected to complain at the front desk between 9 and 11 a. m.
5   You are invited to take advantage of the women who are employed to clean your room
6   Yodeling lessons are given daily. See front desk clerk
7   See our dress shop next door where you will find dresses suitable for street walking
8   Cold and Heat. If you want condition in your room, please yourself
9   Today's Special—No Ice Cream
10 We are pleased to announce that management has personally passed all water served here

The receptionist gave Ed a key, and a valet carried his suitcase to the second floor.

As soon as Ed unpacked, and had several cocktails in the bar, and although he could not swim, wondered what it would be like on top of the diving board. After putting on his bathing suit, Ed went to the swimming pool, where several minutes later, he made his blunder when the manager, after seeing Ed, hollered, "Hey, Mr. Ramos, you can't swim in our pool any longer!"

A bit unsteady on his legs, Ed hollered back. "Why, I want to learn how to swim and dive."

"Because I saw you pee in the pool that is why"

"I'm certain other guests had done that," Ed replied.

"Could be but not from the diving board."

Ed went to his room and fell asleep.

At precisely midnight, however, the manager knocked on the door and in a loud voice said, "Mr. Ramos, have you got a woman inside your room?"

"Definitely not," Ed said as he opened the door.

Seeing the door opened, the manager as pre-arranged with Rogelio Best of Best Realty, handed Ed a 100,000 peso check in an envelope, and before leaving said, "Congratulations Mr. Ramos on winning the Best Realty Listing Contest. Enjoy your prize and stay at the Coconut Oasis."

Next day, Ed returned to Mandaluyong City and decided to invest his pesos in purchasing a car, so he returned to the Pinoy Go Auto Used Car Lot and was highly impressed with a relatively new model that a salesman was anxious to sell.

"This like brand new blue Toyota was previously owned by a lady wearing tennis shoes. She drove it only several times.

"You will notice that there are only 3754 kilometers on the odometer. You'll find that this car is a great bargain. It's our special this week," the salesmen said.

With caution, Ed checked the name on the registration certificate and phoned the woman, Angelina Fernandez, and told her what the salesman had said about the vehicle.

"The salesman told the truth," Mrs. Fernandez said and went on, "I'm a 63-year old, and I always wear tennis shoes when I drive.

The 3754 kilometers on the odometer is the correct mileage. I have participated in stock car races and came second once and third twice and would have finished the last race except I blew the engine."

Ed did not buy this particular car, but went to the Queen of the Orient Motors Used Cars lot and during a "Blowout Sale" purchased a 1993, 4 door, burgundy colored Honda with custom wheels and tires and a lush interior of tan leather.

The salesman who sold the car put his am on Ed's shoulder and said. "Ed, if you are easy on the throttle, steady on the gears, roll her over gently and she'll last you for years."

The Honda also featured a bumper sticker that read "Manila: Queen of the Orient." and a horn which when pushed did not go "toot, toot" but made the sound of a rooster crowing.

To fill a hole in his soul, while enjoying a chocolate bar, Ed paid for the car, pulled on the choke and left the used car lot in a cloud of smoke.

Next on Ed's career agenda, was to leave his parents and buy a condominium with 5% down, and a 25 year mortgage in Mondaluyong City. He found one with a kitchen that was a bit small, but Ed had no intention of doing his own cooking.

As soon as Ed moved into his condo he conducted a month-to-month survey to determine why at tines Best Realty sales were not what they were expected to be. Here are the reasons.

January	People had no cash left over after Christmas.
February	Potential customers gone to Singapore, Thailand or Malaysia
March	Everyone preoccupied with Income Taxes
April	Money spent on graduation exercises and during the Easter holidays

May	Summer temperature reaches 38 degrees. Residents change clothes three times a day, shower twice and buy repellant to kill mosquitoes
June	Couples getting married. Expensive weddings
July	Typhoons usually cause mudslides. Roads need repair
August	Shortage of rice. Have to import from Thailand
September	Parents need money for next school semester
October	Barangay elections
November	Clients waiting to see how autumn clearance sales turn out
December	Customers' too busy getting ready for Christmas. Credit card limit reached.

The following day, Ed sold a home to Antonio De Guzman, and sent him flowers for the occasion which read, "Rest in Peace."

De Guzman got annoyed and called Ed to complain. After Ed had informed De Guzman of the obvious mistake and how angry he was, Ed apologetically said, "Sir. I'm really sorry for the mistake, but rather than getting angry you should imagine this: There's a funeral taking place in Edsa today and a man being buried has received flowers with a card saying, "Congratulations on your new home."

When it came to newspaper advertising Ed most of the time did his in the *Inquirer*. One day a prospect was looking for a home to purchase and picked up a page with Ed's listing in it.

The prospect phoned Ed that he had found a termite on the page and wanted to know if the termite meant good or bad luck. Ed replied by saying, "Finding a termite on my advertisement is neither good nor bad.

The termite probably was checking out the ad to see who isn't advertising to sell their home, so that it can go there and lead a life of undisturbed peace."

Another way of creative advertising Ed tried wasn't a ringing success. It seems that Ed sent out too many ringy-dingies in the middle of the night. The call triggered by a sophisticated dialing machine, woke hundreds of Manila residents between 3:00 and 9::00. a. m. to ask sleeping residents, if they would like to list their home or buy a new one.

Following a flood of phone calls to the Best Realty office Ed admitted that he had made a mistake by hitting a.m. instead of p.m. on the automatic dialing machine. Ed admitted too, following the blooper, that Filipino's did not appreciate this form of canvassing. When it comes to waking up, they still preferred the roosters crowing in the morning.

FIVE

A year into his career as a salesman Ed was doing relatively well, well enough to keep body and soul together, however, his parents suggested their charismatic son, his father's pride and mother's love, might be more successful if he were married. Being s religious type his mother reinforced the suggestion by quoting the *Bible*: *Be faithful, multiply, and replenish the earth* and reminded her son how she gave up smoking and contact sports in order to bring him safely into the world.

Reassuring his parents that he now had his own car and a condominium with a mortgage that if one cared to live, just miss a payment, Ed felt he could support a wife and took his parent's challenge seriously to find a true loving mate.

Ed's condo was on the top floor in the middle of the Mandualyong City commercial and residential district where onlookers swell each Friday night on Shaw Boulevard to see drag racers hit a light pole and an area where street people are begging on every block corner.

Ed's domineering mother, however, worried about her son so much that she had to use herbal medicine to cure her ills. It was a time when the family doctor, Danilo Perez, took Ed aside, placed his hand on his shoulder and said, "Ed, a good wife is difficult to find. That is why I never got married," and warned that Ed's mother would die of heart failure should Ed not be married within a year. "You have little time," Dr. Perez warned.

As a close friend to the Ramos family the doc was large in stature, had a kind heart and a teetotaler with a leonine face and a tenor voice. He had little time for patients who had an axe to grind about his prescriptions or people who for any reason wanted to get close to him.

Ed soon discovered the vicissitudes of his fortune and his search for a wife would be full of hope, exultation and disappointments.

To please his parents Ed agreed that marriage was the best and perhaps the only means of increasing his sales but initially discovered that most Filipino women aren't tall, smile even during an economic crises, wear no shoes inside a house and enjoy music, lechon and balut, the jeepney is the most popular means of transportation and marriage fraud is big business when it comes to a Filipina contract worker marrying a Caucasian in Canada.

Ar any rate Ed first met Carmen Bitang who he knew in college but Carmen was a recycling advocate and said, "Ed, I'll never marry again."

Carmen said that husband number 1 was a Philippine Airlines pilot who fell in love with a flight attendant during a layover in New Jersey and never came home.

Husband number 2 was a polygamist and presently serving time in prison and number 3 no longer wanted to be a male and decided to have a sexual realignment.

After many phone calls for a date, Ed finally connected with Penelope Tindugan who Ed thought would be a great catch, but Penelope did not want to latch on to man to fulfill her life nor did she want to change her single status. Penelope told Ed about her experience of a dating service she used to find a beau.

"My first date was a truck driver who hardly could speak Tagalog or English and wanted to crawl into bed 10 minutes after we met," she said.

Experiences such as this had convinced Penelope to remain in single blessedness.

Next, Ed dated Carmel Galdo, a crush who he knew while attending college, and now lived in the same condo complex. But Carmel wasn't looking for a relationship where commitment was the key element although she went out with men occasionally. Carmel, a sweet little thing, wasn't tired sleeping with a vibrator and an electric blanket. A mortgage and a couple of kids weren't on her agenda.

After several more tries for a relationship with women he personally knew, Ed picked up a copy of the *Inquirer* and began reading the personal pages where men and women, and those in between, were hoping to find love, or at least compatibility, through the pages of a newspaper.

Some ads sounded funny, a few descriptive words provided comic relief. Others, however, allowed a glimmer of insight into the lives of females whom loneliness had been excruciatingly painful and took to the newspapers as a last resort.

The *Inquirer* carried several success stories from the Cupids Diary page that advertising in a newspaper for a mate gets results. Ed's quest to find a mate continued. Here are several *Inquirer* success stories in a nutshell.

Felix and Nellie

Moments after Felix read the Cupid Diary page, he met Nellie. A short time later a kicking horse injured Felix's face.

Nellie stood by Frlix during reconstruction surgery when she said, "I do." They are happily married.

Adam and Michelle

The fun-loving couple fell in love in a pea garden after reading Cupid's Diary.

They were married eight months later and can't help but smile each time they pass through the produce section in a store.

Bryan and Ceriza

Bryan was a waiter at a local restaurant when he read the Inquirer. Next day Bryan got a tip of his life time when Ceriza, a customer at one of the tables asked him for a date. Ceriza has since agreed to stand by his side for ever as his wife.

Dean and Cora

Cora didn't speak a word of Tagalog when Dean read the lovelorn page in the Inquirer and found his pen pal in Mindanao. But that did not stop them from falling in love and spending the next 33 years (and counting) together.

Roberto and Vicky

Roberto was a patient at a hospital when he read the Cupid Diary and a cute nurse was attending him. Roberto was about to move to Dubai as a contract worker in a few days. But after just one date with this beautiful nurse they were destined to make their home in Pangasinan.

Richard and Helen

In less than a week, reading the *Inquirer* Richard and Helen met while scuba diving in Mindoro. The couple courted and was married. Twenty-five years later they are living proof that whirlwind romances don't just work in movies.

Roberto and Eileen

Roberto was interviewing high school students for positions as summer research students.

Eileen was the interviewee that captured Roberto's heart. Talk about a teacher's pet. Eileen is still at Roberto's side after 24 years of marriage and four children.

Jun and Krista

Jun was in search of an apartment when he came upon one managed by Krista and advertised in the local newspaper. After six months being a tenant Jun married his landlord.

Now Jun and Krista managed the apartment complex together.

After reading the endorsements and flipping several pages Ed thought, "Perhaps here's a capable housewife."

Dear Prince,

If you have found my glass slipper and a professional, I'm your slim brunette, 23-year old attractive Cinderella Dy. Why don't you phone or write me.

Ed did phone and after meeting Cinderella decided she did not suit his criteria, but maybe it was wishful thinking, the power of suggestion or sheer osmosis Alfa Bryson did, but after several dates she dumped him. In a lengthy letter Alfa wrote:

Dear Ed,

I regret to inform that you have been eliminated from contention as Mrs. Right. You are probably aware the competition for my affection has been exceedingly tough and dozens of well-qualified candidates as yourself also failed to make the cut.

I will, however, keep your name on file should an opening become available. So that you find better success in your future romantic endeavors, please allow me to offer the following reasons why you were disqualified.

Your family name, Ramos, is similar to Remus and therefore objectionable. I can't imagine taking it, hyphening it or subject my children to it, because the legendary twins Romulus and Remus were brought up by a female wolf and were friendly to each other as teenagers, but when they became adults they fought among themselves.

And before Romulus became king of Rome he murdered Remus. In your journey through life I'm afraid, you like the Remus long ago, will have a violent death and as you know funeral expenses are steep these days. And Ed, I do not believe in Joe Harris's Uncle Remus stories that a rabbit is sharper than a fox. Do you?

And then there's the possibility if we did hook up that one could call me an ignoramus meaning that I'm utterly ignorant which I'm not. I know what I want. Also your first name Eduardo, Ed for short, is easy to remember but it is objectionable.

It's not a name I can picture myself yelling out in a fit of passion. And please note, Ed rhymes with lead that is a potential dangerous element. Lead acetate is poisonous, lead oxide is explosive. Two characteristics I have noticed in you. And the family name Ramos sounds so much like Ramses who long ago, the Egyptian Pharaoh, maintained a harem and subsidiary wives who bore him many children.

Your admission that 'You buy condoms by the truckload' indicates that you may be interested in me for something else than my personality. And the phrase 'My mother' has popped up too many times.

Just in case you are interested, the mate I chose is a taciturn man that is handsome, financially successful, a caring listener. He dresses with style, appreciates finer things and an imaginative romantic lover. In addition to the above Angelo has promised that when he gets older he doesn't have a bald head, able to rearrange furniture, remember to put the toilet seat down, shave on weekends and still breathe.

Sincerely,
Alfa

Ed was ticked off. It was as if the sky had fallen and Planet Earth had come to a ruin with a crash. Ed could not imagine being rejected by Alfa or what it would be like if he placed an ad of his own in a newspaper. To find out, he placed one in the *Inquirer* with the heading: *Single Attractive Realtor Looking for a Mate for Companionship and Possible Marriage.*

There were 33 replies within a week, but of these, 23 were husbands who wanted to get rid of their wife, and the remainders were after all they could get.

Faye Remok, for instance, wrote that she was spending sleepless nights waiting for a reply. "Seeing your ad makes me think you might be my Mr. Right. You appear to be a builder, a self-made man, striving to make something out of your life. Ed, I'm not after your money but if you have some extra, that's a bonus and our hearts could be in touch for all eternity."

And Christie Salar wrote enclosing a snapshot of her posing by the front gate where a sign read: *Beware of Dog.* The sign and Christie asking for a photograph of Ed's Honda instead of himself, was the end of finding a mate by mail. Each reply had a discreet message—they were lonely and could not satisfy Ed's high standards.

Following the negatives Ed went for a walk along the Pasig River and met a guru by the name of Ricky Nemeses who approached him and said, "Ed, if you have the money I can find you a homey." And promised Ed that all he needed was a computer and the internet, and could easily find a loving mate. The catch was that Ed would first, have to buy his 5000 peso, software, take training lessons, and when completed with one click of a button hundreds of female resumes would pop up on the computer screen.

The following night, while the moon was at its brightest, Ed wandered on foot and a taxi throughout Metro Manila in search of a mate, first visiting Rizal's statue, then the Philippine Opera Company performance of Mozart's Don Giovanni, and while there, discovered that Nemeses had stopped at Shakey's to enjoy a pizza and minutes later, was arrested at Robinson's Department Store for operating a scam and leaving without paying for an umbrella.

Getting rid of one scam Ed ran into another the following afternoon, when he accidently met 43 year-old, Leslie Sebastian on Shaw Boulevard. The world can at times be weird but she was a really, really weird woman, a librarian in Quezon City, and said she desperately wanted her 23-year-old daughter, Melody, to be married, but first the prospective mate had to join a protest movement, drink a black Sambucca, enjoy a squirrel pie, hold a tarantula in his arms and have a skinny dip with Melody in the Pasig River, and if no skinny dip, then sign a petition to make the game of strip poker an Olympic event.

Ed realized he was expected to say something profound like: "Is Melody good looking?" but after reviewing the list, he frowned, shook his head and politely said, "Good luck." to a prospective mother-in-law.

After 2 long and stressful days, Ed took the next day off after word reached him not about an earthquake, a mudslide or a massive flood but a maritime disaster. The passenger ferry *Donna Pez*, while traveling from Tacloban to Manila, collided with the oil tanker *Vector*. The resulting fire and sinking wasn't as serious as that of the Titanic in 1912 near the Canadian Atlantic coast, but still, left more than 300 dead, which included 4 of his relatives.

Next day, Ed was rejuvenated however, when by a strike of luck he received a creative chain letter from an unknown source who was watching Ed's mate-hunting progress. Unlike most chain letters this one did not cost a penny and read:

> "Just bundle up your last interviewee and send her to the man whose name appears at the top of the list. Then add your name to the bottom of the list and send a copy of this letter to 5 of your friends who are equally having difficulty in finding Mrs. Right.
>
> When your name comes to the top of the list, you will hear from 300 cuties and some are bound to be better suited than those you have dealt with earlier.
>
> Do Not Break This Chain.
> Ed we are counting on you.
>
> Signed—A satisfied mate hunter.

Ed listened to the promulgated wisdom of the other mate hunter, but did not bundle his last interviewee and send her aloft. He, however, connected with a youthful Filipina nanny from Southern Leyte province employed by his employer, Rogelio Best and his family.

Ed found Vanda Banda, sweet, smart and pretty who ate with bare hands, sometimes with a fork and spoon but never used a knife.

Vanda always wanted to share her food with Ed that included fish, rice and lechon (roasted piglet) and anything cooked with coconut milk, but especially her wanton soup, noodles, spring rolls and deep-fried bananas which Ed found delicious.

Ed and Vanda were on the same page until she introduced Ed to Balu*t* (a fertilized duck egg meant to be an aphrodisiac.

Ed could not imagine having a sexual desire that included crunching on a partially formed baby duck swimming in noxious fluid and one had to eat feathers, beak and claws in order to be a macho. When Vanda said, "Look Ed, from Alaska to Dubai where Filipinos migrate to work, balut can be found."

Ed chose not to pursue courting feisty Vanda, so they stopped seeing each other.

The following day, as Ed was on his way to take a listing he drove into a parking lot on Shaw Boulevard and noticed that a pickup truck with a Maltese dog sitting behind the wheel was rolling towards a pedestrian. The person, Katie Vitor, standing there seemed oblivious to the oncoming vehicle, so Ed hit his horn to get her attention. Katie looked up just in time to jump out of the way of the truck's path, and then Ed rushed to Katie's side to see if she was all right.

"I am," Katie assured Ed and continued, "But I hate to think what could have happened to me if that dog hadn't honked."

Ed and Katie began dating but after several days Katie with thoughts flowing in all direction took Ed aside and cautiously said, "Ed, to be loved and remain unhappy is interesting but I doubt that I could be your happy mate."

Katie then handed Ed a list of reasons why it was better for her to choose a dog as a companion rather than a husband:

1   Dogs don't necessarily prefer blonds
2   Dogs sometimes dig the garden
3   In a canine world, boxers are sometimes intelligent
4   Dogs will wait patiently outside a clothes shop

5   Dogs can be taught the meaning of No
6   Dogs can find their way home, even after a really heavy night out
7   A dog is better protection from intruders
8   Puppy love doesn't wear out so quickly with a dog
9   A dog will fetch the morning paper for you
10   A dog gets a new coat each winter
11   You can call a dog a schitzu without offending it
12   Dogs do not attack other dogs because of color
13   Dogs are really good with most children
14   Your dog will never refer you as a 'bitch'
15   A dog is less likely to leave a filthy, stinking mess for one to clean up

It was in an elevator at the New Horizon Hotel next day that Ed hooked up with curvaceous Veronica Itbale who was single with a gentle disposition and financially secure. Ed's object of course was to convince Veronica to be his true love.

And then while dining in the food court Veronica asked, "Well, how much could you love me?" Ed replied, "I'd love you more than I love my condo mortgage."

It was a wasteful remark drawing Veronica to say, "Ed, my heart knows what the wild goose knows and since I'm a sister of the goose it suggests that I should not be fenced in with a husband if I want my heart at rest. I have fallen in love with nature and hope I haven't disappointed you."

Ed was disappointed as Veronica continued, "You see Ed, the more affection I give to nature and the more she gives me in return."

Being an inquisitive salesman Ed said that in wooing nature there probably could be less heart-ache and one can admire the landscape, but he would rather prefer to look at Veronica's brown eyes and pretty face with a full moon or a setting sun for a background.

With that premise Ed did not pursue Veronica as a possible mate and with a resonant voice said, "Veronica, my love is true, but since I have a deadline to meet and time is of the essence, I will not argue with you. Meanwhile I suggest that you attend a Save the Planet workshop."

SIX

Ed Ramos was a survivor and in the search for a bride it seemed he experienced more obstacles than King Arthur's knights had in their search for the Holy Grail. He was prepared to convert to another faith if that would help to find a suitable mate but was startled to discover that Jews, Muslims and Christians had distinct beliefs about dating. The Jewish method was most methodical, Ed thought, in that Jews turn to their faith communities for helping one to find a date and ultimately wife or a husband.

Islam was out of the question. The Muslim approach for dating was straight forward. It was forbidden. Instead Ed found that Muslims rely on a network of friends who supply suitable mates for their children.

Ed found that Christian courtship varied greatly. He next dated Emerita Salvo who was Catholic, but only several times, because he learned that the Catholic Church did not believe in divorce and the use of contraceptives.

Ed felt the churches found by Calvin, Dr. Knox and Wesley were to puritanical and following Luther and Ron Hubbard's Scientology did not appeal to him. Ed found problems with Henry V111 as an Anglican Church honcho. With an aroused conscience Ed then studied the Church of the Flying Spaghetti, Iglesia ni Cristo (Church of Christ) founded by Felix Manalo or El Shadai led by Brother Mike Velarde and Buddhist religions, Bertrand Russell's Celestial Teapot theory about the non-existence of a Supreme Being along, with Reverend Moon's Unification church, and the Church of the Omniscient Google. Ed rejected them too.

As Ed still hadn't found a mate that suited and the odds seemed against him, so he thought, "Maybe I should try the bars?" and as it was getting dark he had not walked further than the nearby Rex hotel that had an ants' nest of ugly rooms and where customers waited for something exciting to happen.

At the bar Ed met down-and outers, some of them fugitives, gang members and criminals and a dainty sinful kind of a cuss named Tapioca Pudding who could be made in a minute. But Tapioca's social life was suddenly destroyed when alcohol brought out the devil in a patron who stabbed her with a hunting knife and more than fifty patrons saw it happen.

At a time when the crime rate in Philippines was rising Ed did not want to be stabbed by a weirdo wielding a knife or even to be hit across the head with a tennis racquet, so he left the bar.

Ed's next possible mate was Scarlet Milo who he had met in the lobby at the Lancaster Hotel. Aside from being friendly, she could do magic. Scarlet entertained friends by performing what Ed thought were slight-of-hand, tricks but, it turned out she could do real magic.

Ed so far avoided females of questionable character, but this time he thought he had hit a jackpot when he and Scarlet suddenly fell in love.

Their life was idyllic until Ed's mother phoned and said, "Ed, you are breaking your mother's heart. You haven't visited your parents in a month and now I hear that you are dating a floozy. When was the last time you had your eyes examined?"

"I'm sorry Mom, but I've been busy listing and selling real estate, doing charity work for Meals on Wheels and dating Scarlet. I assure you Scarlet isn't a floozy and I want you to meet her."

Although Scarlet dreaded the event, she agreed to meet Ed's parents and when she did, for dinner, the family sat at a table and his father said, "Never in my entire life would I have thought that Ed would be embracing such a beauty."

And his mother, while shaking Scarlet's hand, continued, "Oh, you poor dear," hugged her and then said, "Perhaps we can now close our eyes and bow our heads as Ed says grace before we eat."

Ed intoned, "OK mother," and said this prayer:

"Dear God,
Ruba dub, dub
Thank you for the grub.
Some have hunger, but no meat
Some have meat, but can not eat
Bless those who are able
To enjoy the food on this table
Forgive us sinners
And pray that Scarlet and I become winners
Lord, we give you thanks and praise
Bless Scarlet and me throughout the coming days."

The dinner went well. Beside Scarlet's ability to do magi, she was also an excellent conversationalist and had a sense of humor.

After dinner, Ed's mother took him aside and said, "I apologize. Scarlet seems like an ideal mate for you. You must make an effort to marry her."

Ed agreed and true to his word, proposed next night and Scarlet said, "Yes."

Of course, Ed's mother insisted that the couple have a grandiose June wedding at the No Name Universal Church and a reception at the Edsa Shangri-La Manila Hotel. She met Scarlet many times to plan the June wedding.

Ed's mother picked out Scarlet's wedding gown, her bridesmaids and their gowns, rented the ballroom for the reception, hired a band, ordered flowers, made out invitations and did everything that needed to be done to make the wedding perfect.

Scarlet merely had to nod her agreement with Ed's mother choices. Ed hired a limousine while his best man planned a bachelor party at a strip club.

The night before the wedding, Scarlet came to Ed to say she was worried. "You know Ed," she explained, "I have never been inside a church before. I don't know how to behave."

Ed put his arm around her. "Don't worry dear. Simply walk slowly up the aisle. When you reach Reverend Autopan, just follow my lead and do what I do or what the Pastor tells you. There's nothing to worry about."

Finally the great day came. First, Ed and his groomsmen wearing long sleeved barongs that made them utterly handsome and took their places by the altar. Ed's dark hair was slightly ruffled and his eyes full of adoration as he looked towards his bride to be.

The church was filled with Ed and Scarlet relatives, friends and neighbors.

The bride and her entourage arrived carrying a bouquet of miniature orchids. As the organist played *The Wedding March* the flower girl sprinkled petals as Scarlet made her way up the aisle.

Next, came the ring bearer, followed by the bridesmaids in their colorful wedding dresses. In her white gown Scarlet's coiffured hair was partially covered by her veil as she solemnly walked up the aisle. If she was nervous, she did not show it.

Ed's marriage was within his grasp. It inevitably was yanked however, when something unusual happened at the No Name Universal Church as Scarlet passed the last pew. There was a rumbling sound inside like that of an earthquake. The lights went out. Next Scarlet's white dress turned black. Smoke curled out of Scarlet's ears. Before Scarlet reached the altar she burst into flames and disappeared in a horrendous cloud of sulfurous smoke.

That's when a thunderous evil voice called out, "Hold it, Ed! Back off! Let's not get carried away! Scarlet is mine! You shall not have her!"

Everyone in the church started screaming and running about. The scene turned to chaos.

No one was more stunned than Ed as his lady love had magically disappeared in horror and they hadn't even got married.

Ed grieved for three days and he wondered if it was possible to love someone more than once. That thought disappeared when he visited the Mandaluyong City Hall to pay his annual property taxes where he met alderwoman Vilma Herrera who looked good even though she didn't wear make-up. At first glance Ed thought Vilma was a possible mate. As it turned out, however, she was considerably older than Ed and a member of the City Council which was considering initiating a host of bylaw fines, including the use of a radar camera to catch traffic violators in the city.

Ed was against the use of a radar gun as a means of filling the city coffers, and he wondered, why city council didn't vote to repair the streets filled with hundreds of potholes. Ed therefore disassociated himself with Vilma and moved on.

At the Liberty Center Mall in Mandaluyong City, there is a favorite bar with a juke box. A pool table is located to one side of it. Towards the back there are tables and a dance area where on most weekends regulars come for their pick-me up. On Friday and Saturday nights, a local band plays there. On these nights the place as a rule is mobbed.

The smoke was so thick, one could cut it with a knife and the volume of noise made conversation a shouting match.

It was on such a Friday evening that Ed sat at the bar when a most knockout gorgeous Caucasian woman sat on a stool next to him. Her low cocktail dress revealed so deep it was like staring into a bottomless pit. Her waist was narrow, her hip flaring.

Her sculptured face was capped by flaming blonde hair, her full lips were devilish carmine and the mascara on her green catlike eyes seemed to make them glow mysteriously.

Eying this blonde lady carefully, Ed was about to ask the Australian tourist for a date, believing she could be his potential dream mate. He lost Brittney Saxton, however, as soon as her husband returned from the 'Men's' comfort room and sat next to her.

Upon hearing that Ed was having a difficult time in finding a mate, his mother warned, "Son, I'm telling you. Don't marry a White woman. She won't eat bagoong, and then she'll divorce you. Listen to me!" while his father said, "Son, all relationships are a balance of power. Start giving your ideas and dreams a chance. Why don't you try Toastmasters or attend a fiesta? And Sushi bars are a great place to meet females. That's where I met your mother."

Although Ed had no fear of public speaking, he enjoyed dinning in restaurants, so the following evening he darted across the street from his office to the *Deep Sushi Restaurant* where inside the smells of cologne and soy sauce permeated the environment.

The lights were low and single women seemed plenty. In the end however, Ed was piqued not because of the raw fish on the menu or that there was a *No Smoking* sign posted, but because Dahlia Matias, whom he met, was an introvert with low smarts and knew nothing about the Arts and didn't have an opinion on anything.

Always on the go, the following night, Ed was more than usually cautious when he connected with pretty Lina de la Cruz, a full-time actress at the Liberty Center Theatre and could double as a tree. Lina, who was tall, graceful and owned four pet mice which she had taught to sing, Ed accompanied Lina as she took the rodents to a talent agency in downtown Mandaluyong City believing she could make a fortune promoting them instead of acting.

Lana placed a suitcase on the agent's desk, opened it and in seconds the Field Mouse Quartet was positioned on the table. With the snap of Lina's finger the mice began singing like the Beatles.

She snapped her finger again and this time the four mice sang an aria from Die Fledermaus. Lina snapped her finger a third time and the mice sang a medley of Lea Solanga tunes.

"Well," Lina said to Ed and then to the agent, "What do you think?"

"Can't use them," the agent replied.

"What do you mean, you can't use them? What's the matter with the act?"

"To tell you the truth," the agent said, "The mice don't sing that badly but the leader looks quite a bit like yourself."

"What do you mean?"

"The mouse is needs a face lift."

Disappointed with the outcome of the interview, Lina let the mice loose and it was several months later, that Mandaluyong City had the greatest mice attack in its history.

The infestation was so great that the local SPCA let out 100 cats in a single day to deal with the rodents. But wait!

The original Field Mice Quartet was clever and survived. Lina then took the mice to the Kirei Karaoke Bar where they sang a medley of Country and Western karaoke songs and won first prize.

An American talent scout who discovered Alvin and the Chipmunks in 1958 was watching the mice sing and invited Lina and the Four Field Mice Mice to record an album in Nashville, U. S. A. Any romantic inclination that Ed may have had with Lina discontinued.

The following weekend, the Mandaluyong City Chamber of Commerce held its annual Scavenger Hunt promoting tourism.

The challenge was to visit downtown locations while deciphering clues, solving puzzles and answering local and provincial trivia questions.

Ed coupled up with Sarah Benaue, an extravert visitor from Baguio. The couple drove to Parma Spring and Rubber office, along Shaw Boulevard with stops at the Jollibee restaurant, Commonwealth Food office, the Post office and City Hall where Sarah, while holding a clip board said to a security guard, Sir, Ed and I are on a scavenger hunt, and all we still need is 30 grains of rice, a pork chop and a bottle of rum in order to win a prize."

"Wow!" the security guard said, "Who sent you on such a challenging hunt?"

"The Mandaluyong City Chamber of Commerce."

"Sorry but I can't help you."

Although Ed and Sarah did not win a prize, Sarah left Ed a *Girlfriend's Lament* before she left town. It read:

> It was the day of the Scavenger hunt when I
> was in your kitchen;

I was cooking and baking and moaning and
    bitchin'.

I've been in your condo for hours and did not
    stop to rest.

Ed, your bedroom is a disaster, just look at the
    mess.

Take a look at all the people we had to feed.

You expected all the trimmings but not what I
    need.

My feet are blistered. I've got cramps in my
    legs.

I was so nervous that I spilled a bowl full of
    eggs.

Oops, there's a knock on your condo door and
    the telephone is ringing.

At the same time the microwave oven is
    dinging.

Two pies in the oven, desert almost done.

Your duct taped cookbook is soiled and not the
    right one.

Ed, I have all I can stand. I can't be your mate
    any more,

In walks your condo neighbor Rolando who
    spills his rum on the floor.

He weaves and he wobbles, his balance is
    unsteady;

Then he grins as he chuckles, "Sarah, is the
    eggnog ready?"

Rolando looks around with total regret,

And asks, "Sarah, aren't, you through with Ed
    yet?"

As quick as a flash I reach for the kitchen knife;

He loses an earlobe although I wanted his life.

Ronaldo flees from your condo in terror and
    pain.

"My God Woman!" he screams. "Sarah you're
     going insane!"
Now what was I doing, and what is that smell?
It's the pies! They're burned all to hell!
I hate to admit it Ed, when I make a mistake,
But I put them in the oven on Broil instead of
     Bake.
Are there still more discomforts ahead?
Ed, this isn't my life style, I'd rather be dead.
Don't get me wrong. I love Mandaluyong City.
And the scavenger hunt was lot of fun.
But I promise you one thing, if I live till next
     year,
You won't find me pulling my hair out here.
It was Sarah's turn to say, "Ed, I wish you well.
     Best of luck, in your mate hunting."

The following weekend, Ed entered a three-day
September Wack, Wack Golf Course Singles Only
Tournament where in each foursome there were two men
and two women. On the first day Ed was paired up with
Amanda Tangos who he thought he would like to date so
he casually said to her, "Do you believe marriage is like a
lottery?"

As soon as Amanda replied, "No, in a lottery a woman
has a chance."

That did it. Ed did not ask Amanda for a date.

Ed didn't take no for an answer and during the second
day of the tournament was paired off with a foursome that
included Jade Farinas who he thought would make an ideal
mate. After they reached the 13th hole, Jade's ball landed in
a sand trap where after several tries to get it on the fairway,
she picked up her golf club and broke it into two.

Jade then picked up her golf bag, tore it into shreds and finally the golf balls she had left flung them into the woods. Ed could not cope with temperamental females so he did not ask Jade for a date.

On the 2nd day, Ed was paired off with Brandy Dellaporte who was three years older than Jade and still paying off her students' loan and failing to return 20 books to the library.

On the 9th hole, however, Ed and Brandy got into an argument over the definition of the words *hooker* and *tricks* and neither would give way.

Ed decided if he was going to be the bread winner, any possible romantic relationship should end, there in the middle of the golf course.

As taking part in a Singles Only golf tournament did not work Ed decided to have his hairstyle changed. Not anything dramatic, just a tinge above his natural color somewhere between brown and black and streaked in the middle.

But that didn't work, nor the use of a different underarm deodorant, red socks instead of black, a strict fat-free diet, exercising, wearing dark colored glasses or growing a mustache that is when his mother suggested, "Ed, try riding the local transit."

Ed took his mother seriously. To make sure his search did not lose momentum Ed climbed into a bus at the bottom of a barangay hill, hoping a lovely lady would sit by him.

That did not happen, however, because when a gargantuan male sat next to Ed and thirty tourists from Japan sat behind him, the bus became overloaded and climbing the hill was impossible as it unexpectedly stopped when a stray dog was crossing the road. Due to its age the vehicle had to be towed to the city transportation garage for a major repair.

This had been a bad weekend so Ed walked into a tattoo parlor about the possibility of a tattoo injection.

"Women love men with their tattoo on their arm, that's why so many jailbirds get one," the tattooist said, but after Ed was explained the process he felt having a heart tattooed on his chest was going to be painful and one could cause an infection.

Ed was hungry at the time so Ed asked the tattooist where he could find packaged dates to enjoy. The tattooist gave him and odd look and said, "You can try the Yellow Pages under the heading *Escorts.*

Ed wasn't interested in an escort showing up in his condo and that evening his mother called again and said, "Ed, why don't you spend some time at the Mandaluyong Healthcare Resort where unattached females hang out?"

Ed did do so and during the weekend had a conversation with Candy Macalino who was from Samar.

While sitting at a spa table Ed asked the stout lady, "What is the main diet food in Samar?"

"Fish," Candy said.

"I always thought fish was a brain food and do you want to something?"

"What?"

"I'll be candid. To me you appear to be the most beautiful woman I have ever met. Tell me, are you married?"

"I am, happily married."

Ed did not succeed with Candy or with Amatulla Mohammad, a pretty Arabic speaking Filipina, a, la crème de la crème of a lady from Mindanao. During a preliminary conversation Amatulla said, "Ed, I enjoy traveling and have been to Mecca during Ramadan."

"And,"

"And while in the holy city in Saudi Arabia, I filled the requirements of self-restraint, fasted for a month, prayed to God asking Him for steadfastness until I meet Him in heaven."

"You appear to be a hot potato but do you mind if I ask a personal question?"

"Go ahead."

"If you had only one wish, what would it be?"

"I would have the Koran printed in braille because I'm nearly blind."

Ed was surprised but continued, "Another quick question for you. Now tell me the truth, how do you feel about the Muslim part of Mindanao separating from the rest of the Philippines?"

"I'm in favor," Amatulla replied but Ed wasn't, so he suggested this potential mate to do what is happening to the Philippine monkey eating eagle—be an extinct species."

At this point Ed's search for a mate and happiness was in a mess. He had not convinced a single female to be his lifetime mate, only to find out that day by day it got worse and friends of his constantly reminding him daily, "Ed. do not let your mother down."

In order to speed up his search Ed took a 3-day 101 evening course at Arellano University on *Dating and Food* which mainly dealt on how to reach one's heart through the food they ate.

At the university Ed met three stunning wanabe females who wanted to find a mate for themselves, but neither cooked for a male before. The first was Claire Camador. Claire and Ed agreed to a guest-relationship where she would visit his condo on weekends to do his laundry and prepare his meals but there wouldn't be any sex.

Claire was an excellent cook and made the best ice cubes one ever tasted. Her specialty was fried water but one weekend while having breakfast she got fancy with her cooking and screwed up the rice and noodles.

To Claire a balanced meal was one which Ed had a 50-50 chance of surviving. She sliced tomatoes by throwing them through the screen door and one day she had chicken on the menu and Ed was tickled. Claire had forgotten to take off the feathers. Things between Clair and Ed came to a head however, when Ed discovered a crate containing twelve dozen eggs which were left near the kitchen oven and chicks began hatching.

Seeing the chicks pop up one after another Ed said, "Claire, why don't you say something interesting to the chicks?"

Claire got on top of the crate and yelled, "Chickens of the world unite for better egg laying conditions!"

That's when the relationship with Claire ended, and a new one began with Alice 'Big' Laluna, who he also met while taking the dating-food course at the university.

The relationship with Alice, didn't last long, however, because she fell over one of her meatballs and injured her spleen.

Ed called 911 and an ambulance took this possible mate to Emergency at the Unciano General Hospital where she lay in the sun and the heat that month was so intense that she became petrified and spent the rest of her life in isolation

Why was this cook so afflicted? Because according to geologists she was deposited on Planet Earth during the Ice Age.

Ed did not believe that theory. however, but one suggested by a private investigator who said that why Alice 'Big' Laluna was afflicted this way was because she had stolen a blanket at a five-star hotel where she was previously employed.

Today, Alice 'Big' Laluna is an imposing sight and site at the National Museum of the Philippines as a tourist landmark attraction for the entire world to see, if not stolen.

Ed's next weekend relationship was with Honey Demitilo but on a Friday evening when she began her weekend relationship, Ed found Honey depressed so he asked, "What's the matter? "Your cooking and baking are excellent."

"Well, to be truthful," Honey said, "Some of the people I work with are spreading lies that before I met you I had twins."

"Relax," Ed said, "I make it a rule to believe only one-half of what I hear."

Actually Honey was an excellent cook. "Your mango pie was delicious," Ed said.

"Thank you."

"And the half-moon decorations on the crust, how did you make them?"

Ed was surprised when Honey answered, "By using my false teeth."

Honey was known throughout Mandaluong City as an exceptionally creative cook. For example she wrapped spaghetti around meat balls and called them, "Hot yoyos."

She could cook up an order of fish in ten minutes: Fish steak, fish croquettes, fish salad and fish soup. Once a year those who ate her fish meals got the urge to jump into Manila Bay and spawn.

Since Ed couldn't swim, he let Honey loose, and thus his weekend relationships with the 3 lovely lady cooks ended. But another began when Ed was taking photos of the Shaw Boulevard tall buildings and met Leslie Jamin.

After several dates however, Ed discovered that Leslie had converted from the Satanist to the Luciﬁarian cult which enabled her to have her predictictons come true.

She predicted that the real estate market would soon crash and the interesting part was that she had already won a furnished luxury home in Tarlac City, a motorcycle in San Fernando and a two-week, expenses paid, stay at the luxurious Peacock Garden Hotel in Bohol.

The real clincher came when Leslie predicted Lotto numbers and actually won two in a row, becoming wealthy. Not wealthy as billionaires Henry Sy, Lucio Tan or Enrique Razon, but still got mentioned in *Forbes Business News* thus abandoning Ed to live in Hawaii.

Because of a real estate transaction, Ed didn't have time to search for a mate the next two days but on the 3rd, returned to Shaw Boulevard, to take more pictures of buildings that might be repossessed or for sale and met Cassandra Lutgo where they became fast friends. Ed thought Cassandra was the best thing since sliced bread was invented.

She was no troll under a bridge but had one trait that Ed did not appreciate—she had a perpetual smile on her face and was a daughter of a witch.

Ed and Cassandra, however, updated each other on their lives—the sales Ed had made and Cassandra her involvement with Unidentified Flying Objects.

The following afternoon while in Rizal Park, an unidentified triangular-shaped UFO with rows of bright orange colored lights flashing, landed in the park, abducted Cassandra and left just as fast as it had landed.

Ed described the three alien creatures as humanoid and three to four feet tall. They had dark brown, hairless skin, big triangular heads with three short 'horns' on top, and huge red eyes that were vertically oval.

According to Ed the most extraordinary encounter was witnessed by security guards and wondered why the Philippine government hadn't started a special investigation to make certain that they weren't terrorists and no nuclear weapons were inside the object.

Meanwhile a science and technology professor at the University of the City of Manila, Benjamin Ocampo, when he heard about the UFO landing said, "The evidence that Planet Earth is being visited by extraterrestrial civilization is now extensive both in scope and detail. In totality, it comprises a body of evidence which at the very least supports the general assessment that extraterrestrial life has been detected in Manila and that a vigorous program of research and serious diplomatic initiative is warranted."

Once thought the preserve of cranks, weirdoes and eccentrics this Manila UFO phenomenon soon caught the attention not only of mainstream University of Manila academia but also Philippine's leading ufologist, Eva Benito who was a good candidate to become Ed's bride. While driving to Laguna City they came upon a perfect crop circle in a rice field.

To Ed and Eva the sound of music being linked to crop circles was most intriguing and Eva wanted to stop and do research.

Ed parked his car and as soon as the couple entered the circle to encode the design, a magic-like thing happened—there was an electric charge which stopped their wrist watches from ticking.

The crop circle, thirty meters in diameter and the City of Cebu logo inside, was an artistic accomplishment to say the least.

Ed remained open-minded that the circle may have been created by aliens from another planet. He was skeptical at Eva's theory that during the night the Cebu Tourist Bureau created the circle to spite the city of Manila and attracts more tourists for itself.

Ed's dating Eva was cut short after she said, "Ed, I don't take anything at face value, either when presented by academics or the ill-informed media.

The rice circle phenomenon has inspired me to the point that I want to take time off chasing unidentified flying objects in order to do my own crop circle investigation."

That cut Ed and Eva's relationship short.

While renewing his library card at the Nimoy Aquino Library and Learning Center Ed met journalist Sheila Grace Napalan, who he found intelligent and fascinating.

Sheila Grace, a single parent, had just published a controversial 300 page novel *Manila Place* featuring sex, violence, hypocrisy, decadence, bribery, traffic jams, hostage-taking and corruption in Metro Manila.

Sheila Grace had completed her novel based on what she had seen every day and centered on the fortune of a single-parent woman.

Sheila described the city of 14-million as a petty, a mean spirited city with industries booming in which, alcoholism, drugs, stabbings, mental illness, hostage-taking, pick-pocketing and sexual passion seethe behind a façade of old-fashioned propriety.

In a conversation with Ed, Sheila Grace said that she had experienced hostility during book signings and on talk shows although the function of her novel wasn't to educate but to entertain. Censors' however, thought differently. The scandalous novel was banned in several cities declaring it was *indecent* and the Manila Parent Teacher Association as *a complete debasement of taste.*

A sign in front of the Cebu Library read: This library does not carry the novel entitled *Manila Place*. If you want it go to Manila.

The Manila library did stock her novel but there were no plaques or statues to be found in Sheila Grace's honor.

The setting of *Manila Place* may have seemed like a new and alien world but in some ways it was as old as the Philippines gaining independence from the Spaniards in 1898. Ed thought the novel was a bit trashy but that didn't exclude his interest in the subject matter. Still he didn't start a relationship with Sheila because she wanted first-hand experience in the Muslim insurgency in Mindanao province. As soon as Ed dropped her off at the airport, Sheila made a sign of the cross before taking her flight, and while in Mindanao walking with the Abu Sayaf insurgents, disappeared for ever.

Ed was on the run and next met Jane Payne who was plain and appeared in pain. The good-looking nurse was employed by the Department of Health public relations department. The department had just passed an ordinance that Filipino wild geese living in the region, particularly in Mandaluyong City, had worn out their welcome.

As a member of the *Coalition to Prevent Destructions of Urban Geese*, Ed asked Jane, "But why the ordinance?"

"Because urban geese peck up lawns and golf courses, and in the process cover them with blobs of doo-doo which is a health hazard."

Jane said that the City of Manila officially tried scaring the geese by chasing them in golf carts, and by blasting a starter gun placed at strategic locations and, "City Council was going to recommend to the local restaurants to include cooked geese 'specials' on their menu.

The Mayor's exasperation was echoed by many who lived in Manila so the Health Department sent out a bulletin recommending the following ways for the public to reduce the number of Philippine geese in the city.

1   Shaking goose eggs or coating them with vegetable oil so eggs don't hatch.
2   Rounding up the adult geese and shipping them to Cebu.
3   Using inflatable plastic dogs and dead geese decoys, especially on the Pasig River and nearby rice fields.
4   Use swans, imported from Canada, an even bigger bully that kicks out the geese.
5   Giving the male geese vasectomies. Although Ed did not manage to date Jane because she was already engaged to someone else, he learned from her that:
6   Filipino geese relieve themselves more often than animals, every three minutes, if they eat only grass.
7   The life span is eight to ten years but some geese have been known to live into their thirties.
8   While Filipino geese are refuted to have a mate for a lifetime, some geese do divorce.
9   Filipino geese do not lay eggs until they are several years old. After that they lay an average of five or six a year and when grown up can cause planes to crash.
10 In Vancouver, Canada wild geese are such a problem the town's health commissioner says he would like to kill 5000 of them.

It was a week later that Ed hooked up with Roxana Baldovino, who initially made his day but only for 15 minutes, because Ed discovered that the lovely lady was a militant ecological activist of the Save the Philippine Forest protesters.

And instead of dating Ed, Roxana led a demonstration at Ocean Park to wipe out the use of toilet paper. The group was demanding a complete world-wide ban on the use of toilet tissue. An angry throng of about 50 nature lovers vehemently rallied against the human slaughter of millions upon millions of beautiful, pure innocent trees annually used to make the ubiquitous tissue rolls. The irate throng then stunned curious onlookers by collectively dropping their pants and defecating en mass on the lush green lawn. They then proceeded to wipe themselves with whatever Mother Nature had kindly provided nearby with fallen banana and mango leaves, moss, bamboo chips, bird feathers and squirrel tails and even coattails of passed out winos.

The following evening, after taking a late listing in Laguna, Ed was on his way home listening to the radio and had about a 100 kilometers to go, when he stopped at a tourist rest area to stretch his legs and two giant monkey eating eagles chased Ed up a cocoanut tree.

There were no monkeys in the car nor did Ed look like one, but the hungry eagles, perhaps thought that Ed looked like one, so they shook and shook the tree and nothing happened. Suddenly the two eagles disappeared and minutes later, returned with flock of the protected species who took turns shaking the tree. Ed was petrified and his rosy face turned white as he clung for his life.

Minutes later, while the eagles became frustrated, they attacked, Ed's car, first his front tires and then the grill, when a stranger passing through, saw the predicament Ed was in, stopped his vehicle, took out his revolver and fired at the eagles, frightening the birds away. Luckily Ed wasn't hurt. The stranger later, was identified by police as a fugitive, who had just committed a gun robbery in Laguna City and had a warrant for his arrest.

As soon as Ed reached his condo, feeling faint and exhausted, he turned on the lights, sat down to relax, picked up a copy of *Romantic Poems*, a newspaper had published while holding a competition with the most romantic *first* line, but the least romantic *second*.

Ed felt the two line poems were a reflection of his search thus far for an ever-loving mate.

And read out loud.

Love may be beautiful, love may be blissed.
But I only slept with you because I was pissed.

I thought I could love no other	I love your smile, face and your eyes
Until, that is, I met your brother	Darn it, you are good at telling lies.
Of loving beauty you float with grace.	Darling, my beautiful possible wife
If only you could hide your face.	Marrying you would screw up my life
Kind, intelligent, loving and hot.	I see your face when I'm dreaming.
This describes everything you are not.	That's why I always wake up screaming.
I want to feel your sweet embrace,	What inspired this amorous rhyme?
But not before you have surgery to your face.	Two parts vodka, one part lime.

If you love me, let me know
If you don't, please let me go

SEVEN

By now, Ed's world of finding a suitable mate was crumbling. His failures however, would not stop him. Ed was determined more than ever and would stop at nothing in his quest to find a suitable mate, excluding murder of course. This young man when he attended the Philippine Opera Company production of Mozart's *Don Giovanni* met the leading lovely lady, Florida Godoy; he met his match and more of a challenge than expected. As Ed wanted to be a successful realtor, Florinda equally wanted to eventually be a leading operatic star at the Met in New York or Milan's jewel, La Scala. As one must plow before he/she harvests Ed and Florinda's dating process did not continue after several dinners at the Lancaster Hotel Restaurant because for Florinda, marriage was not a priority.

Ed's search for a bride was daunting and since his deadline was fast approaching, he kept searching, and the following week, when the annual Mandaluyong Fiesta took place and mating was prevalent, Ed thought he was in the driver's seat and shed his business suit

and dressed in casual clothing, which consisted of blue jeans and a Hawaiian shirt.

Since Ed's latest dates were a disaster, he thought, "This time I'm going to lasso me a mate tonight," and waited in line where the fiesta was held.

It is said that a strange phenomenon occurs during Fiesta celebrations. It is cock-fighting, enjoying fine food and socializing. It's also a week of disco dancing and carioca singing, a mating season for some counterfeit folks who two-step from bar to bar and Ed for his part was ready for the attack.

Once inside the community park, Ed met Dusty Penobello, who initially Ed thought was an evangelical porno star, but turned out to be a rap singer from Baguio, who was upbeat, positive and in a playful mood. The evening began with Ed and Dusty doing a two-step, a foxtrot and a polka where on several occasions Dusty got dropped to the floor after being spun around and around, colliding with other couples.

In between dances, like other prospects, Dusty had her love story. Her boyfriend had been killed when during a rain storm; his motorcycle went out of control and hit an on-coming jeepney. And as hours pressed on Dusty got pie-eyed and wanted to drink Ed under the table.

It was after midnight that Ed finally lost his patience and said, "Dusty you are either flaky or careless, maybe both. Although I love dancing, a lifetime with you isn't my idea of being compatible. And do you want to know something else?"

"What?" Dusty slurred

"I'll have to see a chiropractor in the morning to put my back in order."

The following morning, while at the Chiropractor Institute of the Philippines, Dr, Ben whose actual name is Ben Adorable, an American-trained chiropractor, who has been practicing in the Philippines for more than a decade, was examining Ed's back and listening to radio station DZMM at the same time.

Ed was surprised when the station management phoned Ed and announced that in a recent survey the station had taken, he was voted the most popular bachelor in Mandaluyong City.

The station also offered Ed a prize to take part in a Love-At-First-Sight charity contest. Ed and a chosen mate were given an opportunity for an all-expense paid honeymoon trip with free staying at the Fairmont Singapore Hotel and golfing for a week at the Marina Bay Golf Course.

The single female contestants between eighteen and thirty were screened by the station staff until there were only three finalists left that Ed did not know and had the privilege of interviewing each with the possibility of one becoming his bride.

It was a love-at-first sight event and after Ed's photo appeared in the *Inquirer* newspaper hundreds single female candidates from all walks of life, each seeking happiness, and paid five thousand pesos and hollered, "Pick me! Pick me for the opportunity of becoming Ed's bride!"

Of the three finalists Ed first interviewed Rita Benito but she wasn't as pretty as Bonita Villamor and Bonita wasn't as pretty as Margarita Anne Aquino who was gorgeous and whose surname was hyphenated Berry-Strawberry. Margarita Anne had the greatest potential of becoming Margarita Anne Berry-Strawberry-Ramos.

Like Jack Horner, Ed and Margarita Anne sat in a corner and were in high spirits. They kept talking and laughing what it would be like to go golfing in Singapore. No person on earth, even Ed's mother, could prevent Ed from getting married until a press conference was about to be called to announce their engagement when Ed's hopes of Margarita Anne becoming his bride was dashed.

Word dribbled out that Margarita Anne was married and worked at the Huff attorney office.

Hearing that Ed had failed to have Margarita Anne as a bride his mother anxiously phoned and said, "Ed, listen, start facing your problem head on. We can't wait for a miracle to take place. What sort of a man are you who can easily find houses to sell but can't find a mate? How will you face death when it comes without procreating a son or daughter? It's unthinkable that you remain single for the rest of your life. Do you know what I'm saying?'

"Yes, mother."

"So to start giving our dream a chance let's attend a church service together next Sunday and I'll put 10.000 pesos in the collection basket and our prayers may be answered."

"Good idea, Mom," Ed affectingly said, "I believe when things go astray my guardian angel will come to show the way."

Ed believed in prayer, saints, miracles, angels and reincarnation but not in unidentified objects. The following Sunday Ed accompanied his parents to the No Name Universal Church where Pastor Benito Atupan, a 50 year old, balding bachelor, whose lenses in his glasses were quite thick, and spent half of his life spreading the message of God's work.

A sign on the front church door read:

> Pastor: Benioto Atupan VNP
> The NO NAME UNIVERSAL CHURCH
>   (Franchise Available)—One Week Training
>   Held in Quezon City Next Week
> Confessions between 5:00 pm and 6:00 p.m.
>   each Saturday
> Confess 3 sins and the 4th is free

Have your Visa, Master Charge or American Express ready

Every full-moon there's a blockbuster deal. Confess all your sins and you have one-year to pay with no interest charge

All Individual Sins Kept Strictly Confidential

Free I. Q. and a stress test upon request

The Sunday Church Bulletin read:

Parishioners, don't let worry kill you—let the church help.

Thursday night—Potluck Supper—prayer and medication will follow.

Next Sunday a Special Collection will be taken to defray the cost of the new rectory carpet. Parishioners wishing to do something on the carpet please come forward and do so.

If bored at the service. Give your soul a shake and please turn off your cell phones.

This evening at 7:00 there will be hymn singing in the park across from the church. Bring a blanket and come prepared to sin.

On Wednesday night, the liturgy committee will meet. Mrs. Sadili will sing, "Put me into my little bed," accompanied by the pastor.

Thursday at 7:00 p.m. there will be a meeting of the Little Mothers Club. All ladies wishing to become Little Mothers will meet with the pastor in his study.

The Itty, Bitty, Ditty Committee of the Women's Auxiliary is holding a bean supper at 6:00 p. m. Friday in the church hall. Music will follow.

Near the front door entrance, there's a Community Bulletin Board for parishioners to place short classified ads. On this particular Sunday, the following classifieds appeared:

> Selling hopia—Polland hopia and Ho-land hopia
>
> For sale—Filipino rice grown in Thailand
>
> For sale, Filipino flag—1000 pesos—pole included
>
> Free kittens—ready to eat
>
> Reminder—On Monday police begin to run down Shaw Boulevard Jaywalkers
>
> Antique stripper to display wares at the Gonzalez Antique Store—All day Tuesday
>
> For sale—Chinese pastry baked by Mr. Ho Poo Dung
>
> Notice—Angry with city council not recycling?—See the pastor

On Monday, Road Construction in Pioneer area—expect delays

> The New Veggie Restaurant—Everyone on the premises is a vegetarian except the dog
>
> Asphalt Assessment Company—Let us fill your cracks
>
> City Hair Parlor—Dye now
>
> Ace Exterminating—We kill bugs. Walk-in's Welcome
>
> Lost—small neutered poodle—Like one of the family
>
> Auto Pinoy Used Car Lot—Why go elsewhere to be cheated? Come here first
>
> For Sale—Modular sofa. Only 5000 pesos— ideal for rest and foreplay

As a member of the parish pulled lustily at the bell-rope, parishioners from all walks of life entered the church wearing their Sunday best clothing. The women however, including Misty Park, a friend of the Reverend's friend, because of the Sabbath sunshine appeared prettier than on week days.

As one entered the church the ushers asked, "Do you want a smoking or non-smoking pew?"

One should know more about the franchised No Name Universal Church in Manaluyong City which serves up spiritual nourishment and friendship in a modern age by an executive committee. Not like some other churches. Worship is celebrated each Sunday morning at 10:30 followed by chatting with one another like: How are you? That's a nice dress you are wearing. Nice to see you, Have you heard? Isn't the weather grand?

It allows women as ministers and self and same sex marriages. The Church believes there is only one God, in its own marriage vows, and parishioners can enjoy games of Mahjong in the rectory basement as soon as the service is over.

It's a rule that a member should tithe ten percent of his/her income and if after losing at a casino or following a drinking bout and in a gloomy frame of mind one, should be rehabilitated.

No murder, adultery or drugs. In order to save the world one must recycle and have his/her lawn cut at least once a week, and for their happiness, grow their own vegetables and keep a flock of back yard chickens. Members shouldn't wear garments with animal fur in them. The Church places a dollar value on human life in that women should receive equal pay to men

And each third Sunday of the month a Pet Service is held when parishioners can bring their dog or cat and pat other dogs and cats, provided it is on a leach and accompanied with a pooper scooper.

Instead of a communion wafer, each dog is given a bone and the cats, a Kitty cookie.

The service itself is a special gathering, fashion show and a circus all rolled into one. There are four types of church goers. Their pecking order can be gleaned from their choice of pews with respect to the distance to the altar. The aged, devout and handicapped worshipers like to occupy the front seats. Volunteers are ushers and assist in the offertory and collection.

While attending a service, the humble folk come early to ensure themselves pews in the back rows. Shy, they favour this part of the church as not to be seen, yet able to see everybody and everything in front of them.

For people who arrive just in time or late, there are rows of empty pews in the middle of the church waiting to be filled, and then it's hard not to miss the clickety-click clatter of their heels on the tiled floor with children in tow.

Regardless if all the pews are taken or not, there are always people who prefer standing by the fringes. They drift near the entrances and outside within hearing distance from strategically located sound speakers.

They are referred to as "outstanding" members of the church. They compromise the fourth group in the short list. As the largest group, they consist of many interesting characters. Among these are the "drop bys". They come in late and leave ahead of everyone else.

It seems they hardly have time to hear the entire service but show up just the same, if only to fulfill his/her duty Few venture to kneel at the pew, bow their heads in silent prayer, genuflect and depart quietly.

Occasionally, one can find their direct opposite—They are there before the service begins and remain in the church long after everyone has left. More often than not, they are there for a special reason, to light a candle or Devine intervention.

They kneel in one corner, deep in prayer and oblivious the Bible being read. Still others in this fourth group are sweethearts and barkadas. To them the church is an assembly area to congregate and date. They opt to stand by the entrances, no matter what, where it is easier to spot a possible mate or a friend as soon as they enter or leave.

There was a time when rubber shoes, miniskirts, moang jeans and sleeveless attire would raise eyebrows if worn to a service Of late, however, new fashion trends and a relaxing of standards have emboldened man to hear Pastor Atupan preach while wearing strapped leather sandals, high heel shoes, walking and cycling shorts, midriff blouses, miniskirtz and hot pants.

Teenagers have been greatly infected by this fashion revolution at the No Name Universal Church. Before advent of the karaoke, singing in the church was the only permissible excuse for performing in the public. Everyone now sings in the church lustily and with spirited gusto. During Christmas and Easter they sing with hands clapping and feet tapping. Trouble is everyone likes to sing either one octave higher or lower. Thank goodness there is no rapping yet doing the *Lord's Prayer,* although there are combo drums to complement the church organ.

The No Name Universal Church in Mandaluyong City is new in history and the home of birds: sparrows and maya are popular.

They nest in the rafters, crevices and nooks above. Their cheerful chirping as they hop and flutter over the chandeliers heighten, rather than diminish, the solemnity of the service as the birds may on occasion, drop dung on one's head or shoulder.

Pastor Atupan's homily that Sunday was going to be about the seven colors in a rainbow.

The Pastor, however, when he entered the pulpit, dressed in his finest vestments, delivered a sermon for 5 minutes, half the usual length of his regular sermons.

He paused and then in a melancholy voice said, "One must remember, the Ark was built by amateurs, the Titanic by professionals. No matter what the storm, when you are with God, there's always a rainbow waiting."

And then said, Dear parishioners, I regret to inform you that my dog, which is fond of eating paper, ate that portion of my sermon which I'm unable to give this morning."

Ed enjoyed the cheerful hymns that were sung instead and afterward the organ that pealed forth as parishioners filed out where at the front door Ed shook hands with the Revered Autupan and cautiously said, "Pastor, if that dog which you mentioned has pups, I sure would like to get one for my mother."

Minutes later, the Pastor introduced Ed to Misty Alcoran who had a cosmic secret that brought all the promises of the Law of Attraction. Misty had sparkling eyes, was rather slim and short in stature and compared to a monkey was gorgeous looking.

After the couple had a chit-chat Misty agreed to be Ed's date at a forthcoming Halloween masked party.

When Halloween night arrived, Ed and Misty were scheduled to attend a swanky charity masked party at the Ocean Park Hotel. Ed had purchased new costumes for each, but on the night of the party, Misty claimed she had a terrible headache and said, "Ed, you better go to the party alone."

Ed protested vehemently, but Misty argued and said she was going to take some aspirin and rest. "There's no need of your good times being spoiled by not going," she said.

Ed finally relented, took his costume and went to the party alone. Misty on the other hand after sleeping soundly for an hour, awakened without pain, and as it was still early, decided to go to the party also. In as much as Misty did not know the costume Ed was wearing she thought she would have some fun watching Ed's demeanor, and how he acted at a time when Misty wasn't with him.

Misty, who never quite got over her childish habit of talking to her self, said, "I best join the party," and thought, she spotted Ed cavorting on the dance floor, dancing with every female he could, planting a kiss here and there. Eventually Misty a seductive babe herself, sidled up to Ed, and there were more kisses and hugs exchanged.

Just before unmasking at midnight, Misty slipped away, went to Ed's condo, put her

costume away and wondered what kind of an explanation Ed would make for his behavior.

Misty was still reading the *Science of Kissing* magazine in the living room, when Ed came home and with perfunctory solitude she asked, "Well, what kind of a time did you have, dear?"

"You know, I didn't have a good time because you weren't with me."

"Did you dance?"

"I never danced even one dance."

"How come?"

"Because when I got to the party, I met other real estate salesmen. We went into a den and played poker all evening. But I'll tell you something."

"What?"

"The guy I loaned my costume said he had a fabulous time."

Since Ed could not trust Misty their relationship discontinued.

There is no winter snow in the Philippines at Christmas time, except at several shopping malls, and very few pine trees.

Filipinos are proud to proclaim the Christmas celebrations fiesta to be the longest and merriest in the world. It is time for family, for sharing, for giving and time for food, fun and friendship.

By placing the extra pesos in the church collection basket, may have brought results because, it was during the month of December, that there was a silver lining as Ed discovered Norma Salazar who prior to Christmas Eve, both celebrated the holiday like children listening to the latest Christmas hits on the radio Magic 89.9 which included: *Grandma Was Run Over by Rudolf the Reindeer, Our Turkey Died of Fright On Christmas Eve* and *A Flying Caribao is Pulling Santa's Sleigh This Christmas Eve.*

Ed bought a tree at Robinson's Department Store and Norma helped him decorate it. Then they as a couple placed their presents at the foot of the tree gift wrapped with multi colored paper and ribbons.

On Christmas Eve, Ed and Norma attended a midnight service at the No Name Universal Church and listened to Pastor Atupan tell an ancient story of Emperor Augustus's personal decree on how the world became taxed.

Norma still had not paid her income tax for that year. Feeling alarmed she returned to her apartment to fill out a Revenue Philippines form. Ed didn't see Norma again until the following Easter holidays.

On Boxing Day, Ed didn't shop for block buster discount blow-out specials but continued his quest to find a bride thinking that he was cursed. Since there weren't many real estate sales made during this period Ed decided to go to the Oriental Mindoro Porto Galiera and take swimming lessons

In denial Ed learned that it wasn't a curse but a romantic twist of fate when he met a local socialite Esther Canalas and they became intimately involved, Ed learning how to swim and Esther how to dive.

After making several dives Esther had her head split open and wouldn't be able to dive for at least another year, if at all.

When an ambulance arrived and took Esther to Emergency at the local hospital a waiting doctor said, "We'll have to take Esther for an x-ray."

The x-ray showed that Esther had split her head open and wasn't able to dive for at least another year, if at all.

Since Ed was struggling and had a deadline to meet, his relationship with Esther discontinued, but a new one began with the beautiful nurse that was taking care of her. Her name is Gloria Caberera.

Gloria had every shade of brown in her sparkling eyes and a curvaceous body. She graduated from the University of the Philippines Manila.

In a days' time that Ed had known Gloria, he was swinging from chandeliers and each Friday brought her a bouquet of flowers, and eventually asked if she wanted to meet his parents.

Gloria said, 'Why not?" and then asked, "Are your parents rich?"

"They aren't, but my uncle Saint Anthony, is. His income from stocks and bonds along with his regular and old age pensions is the talk of the town and many widows want to change their name to his."

Neighbors called Anthony 'Saint Anthony' because his name was Anthony and also, perhaps because he had many traits of Anthony of Padua who was canonized in 1232 by Pope Gregory 1X at Spoleto, Italy.

This Anthony at one time was a janitor at the Rainbow Theological Seminary in Cavite. He was, despite his 65 years, a gifted speaker and sympathized with the plight of the poor people, urging them to come before City Council to protest that they were in need of employment, better shelter, food and clothing, so his name "Saint Anthony" had become kind of a proverb.

As soon as Gloria and Ed arrived at his parents' home Ed introduced Gloria to them and then Saint Anthony who shook her hand and said, "I'm delighted to meet you."

Gloria acknowledged with "And I'm delighted to meet you too, sir."

Then Saint Anthony said, "I hear that Ed wants to marry you. Is that true?"

Gloria looked at Ed, his parents and then Uncle Saint Anthony.

Second later she said, "Look, this is embarrassing. Please get me out of here."

Ed had never known to have bad luck, and if he had, he had forgotten it, until he watched his uncle take Gloria by her arm and walked out the door. A moment later he heard the roar of a Mercedes Benz.

A week later, Ed received a message from his uncle that read:

"Gloria and I are on a European Honeymoon."

Ed lamented, "The only reason Gloria married you instead of me isn't because she loves you, but because she thinks you are rich."

A week later, Ed received an email. This one from Gloria and read:

"Your uncle Anthony died today. I'm waiting for instructions where to bury him."

With shaking hands, Ed called to notify members of Uncle Anthony's immediate family of his death.

Ed then hooked up with Carina Miguel who was enjoying a holiday as a foreign contract worker in Edmonton, Canada. While dating, Carina said the English language in Canada was difficult and showed him a list where a word spelled the same but had a different meaning.

"It's a bit confusing as Filipino and Canadian English isn't equal," Carina said while handing Ed a partial list.

1   The bandage was <u>wound</u> around the <u>wound</u>
2   The farm was used to <u>produce, produce</u>
3   When dumpster was full management had to <u>refuse</u> the <u>refuse</u>
4   We must <u>polish</u> the <u>Polish</u> furniture
5   He could <u>lead</u> if he could get the <u>lead</u> out
6   The soldier decided to <u>desert</u> the <u>desert</u>
7   Since there was no time like the <u>present</u>, he thought it was time to <u>present</u> the <u>present</u>
8   A <u>bass</u> was painted on the <u>bass</u> drum
9   When shot at the <u>dove</u> it <u>dove</u> into the bushes
10   I did not <u>object</u> to the <u>object</u>
11   The insurance policy was <u>invalid</u> for the <u>invalid</u>
12   There was a <u>row</u> among the oarsmen about how to <u>row</u>
13   They were too <u>close</u> to the door to <u>close</u> it
14   The buck <u>does</u> funny things when the <u>does</u> are present
15   A seamstress and a <u>sewer</u> fell into the <u>sewer</u> line
16   To help with planting, the farmer thought his <u>sow</u> to <u>sow</u>
17   The <u>wind</u> was too strong to <u>wind</u> the sail
18   Upon hearing the <u>tear</u> I shed a <u>tear</u>
19   I had to <u>subject</u> the <u>subject</u> to series of tests

20   One had to <u>live</u> in order to be <u>live</u>

<u>And in the alphabet, the letter 'C' like in the word 'Ice'</u>
<u>and also like a 'K' in 'Coca Cola'.</u>

After reading the list, Ed agreed that for a foreigner
the English vocabulary can be difficult and dated Carina
only occasionally because after a month holiday she had to
return to her employer in Canada and while texting, "LOL"
(Lots of Love) on her cellular to Ed, she fell into a manhole
in the Millwood subdivision in Edmonton and like the
historical *Lost City* hasn't been heard or seen since.

Ed said, "Gung Hat Fat Cho!" (Happy New Year) soon
after Carina disappeared and celebrated the Chinese New
Year with Sandy Chua who was a dancer he had met before
and large crowd gathered at Manila's Intramurus Main
Street. They watched as a large dragon swayed back and
forth chasing a red rooster. Following the dragon there
were people playing drums and gons, and lion dancers with
paper lion heads on sticks.

As the parade proceeded, store and business owners
came outside to give the dancers money. As Ed had already
spent most of his he gave Sandy a one-pound roll of
bologna instead.

Chinese New Year's Day is celebrated as a family affair,
a time for friends, reunion and thanksgiving.

After the parade and fireworks ended, Sandy and Ed
went to Sandy's home where they sat around a stove and
ate a fortune cookie, cracked jokes and, Sandy being a bit
hungry, ate the entire bologna roll and soon had a bloated
stomach.

Not feeling well, she called her mother.

Seeing the daughter's stomach was larger than usual, her mother thought Sandy was pregnant and with her hands clenched into fists indignantly screamed, "What's the matter with you? God have mercy daughter, look the shape you are in! How could you be so blind and disgrace our family?"

Sandy was taken by the arm and sent to her bedroom.

Ed thought he had learned a lesson. When one is full of baloney its best he/she keep quiet.

Since Ed still had not found a suitable mate, this concerned his parents, especially his mother, who suggested that Ed go to the Community Food Bank and there would be lineup of poor and destitute men and women seeking food hampers and clothes to wear.

"Surely in the line-up you'll notice a mate potential," his mother said.

Ed never experienced hunger or pain and did as told. He had not known anyone in the two block long lineup and was lucky when on a stormy day it began getting dark at 6:00 p.m. he caught the attention of a stunningly beautiful Anita Curzon.

Anita wore a wrinkled blue dress under a red jacket and looked graceful and innocent, not at all like some of the other girls who worked the nearby streets and intersections.

It was Ed's destiny to have dinner with Anita the following day at a nearby Chowking restaurant. Anita wore the same wrinkled dress when they met a day before. Up close she was even more captivating than when he saw her earlier. Anita had the most beautiful eyes he had ever seen. Her cascading black hair flowed onto her shoulders.

She wore no makeup, was shy, pensive and reserved and barely said a word all that night but seemed to know that she was a special person on a special occasion and possibly Ed's bride. Anita did not eat much however, and that night asked for her food to be bagged to go so that she could share it with her mother.

Over the next several evenings, Anita and Ed met again, and on one occasion Anita was full of surprises and asked for Ed's picture.

"Sorry but I didn't bring any," Ed said but if you wish we'll go shopping tomorrow afternoon and I'll have one taken."

"That would be kind of you."

When Ed and Anita went shopping Anita took him to the Salvation Army Thrift Store to purchase subsidized clothing. It was a store favored by the poor and homeless.

Ed gave Anita his photograph and wanted to buy her something more uplifting. At Robinson's, he purchased a designer dress whose price was six thousand pesos.

When they left, Anita was all smiles, overjoyed with the fancy shopping bag in her hand.

In parting Anita shook hands and said, "Thank you Ed for your picture and a wonderful present. I'll be wearing it tomorrow night when we meet again."

But the following night, Anita stood Ed up and when they met the following night he asked the reason.

Anita replied, "Because yesterday my mother took the dress back to Robinson's Department Store to get the money instead."

A tear ran down Anita's cheek. She paused silently for several seconds and then said. "My mother said I could not have the dress because we didn't have enough food to eat."

Ed said that the dress was no big deal and Anita had no reason to be upset.

"I'll buy you another dress."

As Ed was about the sweep Anita off her feet, she held back, and after pensive pause while wiping her tears replied, "Thanks a lot. I can't live with that but I shall never forget your offer. I first must work myself through the endurable poverty my mother and I are in, and then we can meet again."

Ed was bewildered. As it turned out Ed and Anita did not meet again but during another rainy evening, Ed believed Pastor Atupan could spiritually support him in reaching his passionate dream to find a life-long loving mate.

EIGHT

Pastor Atupan and Ed met in Ed's condo Saturday evening and after discussing heaven, earth, the recession and Ed's search, which was floundering, they played baraha the Ukyabit-Baybayin card game while enjoying several bottles of beer. During the conversation the pastor said he was nervous about a homily he was preparing for Sunday's service.

"Relax," Ed said, "It may help if you take some beer home with you. After a bottle or two everything should go smoothly. Here, take a dozen home with you."

On Sunday morning, Ed went to the No Name Universal Church and Reverend Atupan felt great. He was able to talk up a storm using Ed's suggestion. However, upon completion of the service and returning to the rectory, Reverend Atupan found this note from Ed:

> Dear Reverend Atupan, my friend,
> Even clergy can have off days.
> I said a bottle or two of beer, not a dozen.
> There are Ten Commandments not twelve.
> There are twelve disciples, not ten.
> We do not refer to the cross as, "The Big T."
> The recommended grace before a meal is not necessarily, "Rub-a-dub-dub, thanks for the grub. Just say, "Pa, ta."
> We do not refer to our savior Jesus Christ and his apostles as, "J. C. and the boys."

When David slew Goliath, he did not use a
machine gun, it was a slingshot."
The Father, the Son and the Holy Spirit are not
referred to as "Big Daddy, Junior
and Spook."
It's always the Virgin Mary, never Mary with a
cherry
Next Wednesday there will be taffy pulling
contest at the No Name Universal Church
and not a Peter-pulling contest at Saint
Taffy's.
Last but not least, the title of the Book is The
Holy Bible and not, "Our Sexy Savior's
Saucy Story."

Next day, Ed dealt with who he thought was a tramp. This
occurred in front of Ed's condo where a female identified
herself as Natasha Raler and said she was blind and asked,
"Any recyclable beer, wine or pop bottles or cans, sir?"

"Do I look like some one who drinks liquor so early in
the morning?" Ed replied.

"I also collect vinegar bottles but perhaps you could
spare some change for a cup of coffee?"

Ed handed the simpleton several peso coins and in the
process one fell to the ground. Natasha picked it up which
prompted Ed to say. "My dear lady, but you aren't blind."

"I know sir," Natasha replied, "I'm working for my
brother who is, and enjoying his holidays in America

After a short flirtation conversation Ed felt that he and
Natasha absolutely nothing in common therefore it would
be a pointless exercise to date her. Natasha, however, did
have some advice for Ed when she said, "Mr. Ramos, I have
a retirement plan."

"Oh, tell me more."

"Well, Mr. Ramos, if one had purchased of *Nortel* stock in American dollars, one year ago, it would now be worth $49.00.

With *Evron* you would have had $16.50 left of the original $1000.

With *WorldCom*, you would have had less than $5.00 left.

If you purchased $1000.00 of *Philippine Airlines* stock you would have had $49.00 left.

But if you had purchased $1000 of wine one year ago, drank all the wine, then turned in the bottles for a recycling refund you, would have had $214.00.

Based on this knowledge, the best current advice is to drink heavily and recycle."

On Valentine's Day, Ed was invited to an office party where he met Blossom Lemon, who was in the real jewel category, and gave her a heart-shaped box of chocolates but she suggested a bouquet of flowers instead. The following day Ed offered to take Blossom to go shopping at the SM Megamall but she preferred the Star Mall. When Ed offered to take her to see the movie *Ang Aswang* she wanted to see *Patria Amor* instead.

The bottom line was that Ed found Blossom similar to the weather changes, "On one day there is sunshine, next a rain storm and on the third, a typhoon, Blossom's moods are like, sudden climate changes. It's something I can't contend with, if I want to be a successful real estate salesman."

The following weekend, after Ed said, 'Good-bye' to Blossom it was, 'Move over Diane Padilla', who was beautiful but haughty, conceited and had a fiery temper. After dating Diane for a week Ed discovered she was a long time member of the Scientology faith established in 1950 by science fiction writer L. Ron Hubbard. Scientology opposes medical exams for new born.

And according to the tenants of faith known as *Dianetics*, words, even loving ones, spoken during the birth and other painful times are recorded by the 'reactive mind' are subconscious. Those memories, adherents feel, can eventually trigger problems for mother and child.

Ed, a real estate conversationist, couldn't make such a promise and suggested to Diane

Suggested, "Promise me that the next time you and I discuss Scientology and you get angry, take a deep breath and count 100 before you speak."

Hearing the suggestion, Diane slugged Ed over the head with a Ouija board. By the time she counted 75, Ed had the happiness of seeing Diane pick up her backpack, jump into a waiting taxi and drive out of sight.

At home Ed had planted a rose earlier and watered it faithfully. Before it blossomed he carefully examined it and saw the bud that would soon bloom.

Noticing thorns upon the stem Ed thought, "How can a beautiful flower come from a plant burdened with so many sharp thorns?"

Because of his busy schedule in dealing with real estate matters and searching for a mate at the same time Ed neglected to water the rose, and just before it was ready to bloom, it died.

The following day, Ed phoned Earth Garden, local gardening and plant specialists, wondering why the plant had died.

An expert replied, "Look Ed, it's the same with people. Within every soul there's a rose.

The God-like qualities planted in us at birth, grow amid the thorns of our faults. Many look at ourselves and see only the thorns, the defects. We despair, thinking that nothing good can come from us.

We neglect to water the good within us, and eventually it dies.

We never realize our potential. Some people do not see the rose within themselves; someone else must show it to them.

One of the greatest gifts a person can possess is to be able to reach past the thorns of another, and find the rose within them. Why don't you ask Pastor Atupan, and see in which direction your career is heading?"

On Monday, Ed and Pastor Atupan, an expert in many theological subjects, sat at a table in his rectory and Ed asked the question: "Reverend, my real estate career is okay but my search for a mate still isn't. In your candid opinion, despite my success and failure, can you tell me where in my life am I heading?"

Clergyman Atupan, as Ed's spiritual counselor, felt he couldn't help and suggested that as an oncoming realtor he should contact the Filipino Saint Lorenzo Ruiz in heaven.

Ed, like many Filipinos, did know who Saint Lorenzo Ruiz was, so he Googled, and under *Wikipedia*, the free encyclopedia, found that San Lorenzo Ruiz de Manila is the first Filipino saint venerated in the Roman Catholic Church. He was martyred during persecution of Japanese Christians under the Tokugawa Shogunte in the 17th century for declining to leave Japan and renounce his beliefs.

Lorenzo Ruiz was born in Binondo, Manila, of a Chinese father and a Tagalog mother.

Because of his penmanship he became a member of the Cofradio del santissimo Rosario. He married and had two sons and a daughter with Rosario, a native. In 1636, while working as a clerk at the Binondo Church, Ruiz was falsely accused of killing a Spaniard.

Due to the allegation Ruiz sought asylum on board a ship with three other Dominican priests, a Japanese priest and a leper layman. Ruiz and his companions left for Okinawa, Japan on June 10, 1663 with the aid of the Dominican fathers.

On September 27, 1637, Ruiz and his companions were taken to the Nishizaka Hill, where they were tortured by being hung upside down in a pit. The method was extremely painful.

Though the victim is bound, one hand is always left free so that the victim may be able to signal recantation of beliefs. In such a case, they would be freed. Ruiz refused to renounce his Christian faith and died from blood loss and suffocation. His body was cremated and ashes were thrown into the sea.

Appearing on Ed's computer screen, Saint Ruiz began by saying, "Ed, I have been watching you down below and it has come to my attention that you now sell taller buildings and have a shorter temper, travel on wide freeways, but have a narrower viewpoint; you spend more, but have less, you buy more but what you buy enjoy less.

You sell bigger houses with smaller families; more conveniences but less time. You have more 'Best Seller' awards but less sense; more knowledge, but less judgment. Best Sellers Realty employs more salesmen but it has more problems.

I notice too that you haven't learned how to swim yet and drink too much, spend too recklessly, laugh too little, drive too fast, get angry too quickly, stay up too late, get up too tired, read too little, watch TV too much and pray too seldom.

It appears to me that you talk too much, love too seldom, and hate too often. You've learned how to make a comfortable living, but not a comfortable life. You have added years to life, not life to years.

"Ed, from now on you'll have to change your ways.

Those on Planet Earth have been all the way to the moon and back but you seem to have trouble crossing the hallway to meet your new condo neighbors. Outer space has been conquered but you haven't conquered your inner space. You've done large things but you haven't done better things and still can't swim.

At the suggestion of one girlfriend you've cleaned up the kitchen in your condominium but polluted your soul by being naughty with several of your potential mates. Scientists have split the atom but you haven't your prejudice. You write more deals but earn less. And you plan more but accomplish less. How come?

"Ed, I realize you are looking for an everlasting mate and learned to rush but not to wait. You have a higher income but lower morals.

These are the days of two incomes and more SUV's but more divorces; of fancier houses but broken homes. Especially in Manila there are a lot of stabbings and gun-related gangs.

These are the days of quick trips, disposable diapers, throw away morality, one-night stands, overweight bodies and pills that do everything from cure, to quiet and to kill. And Ed, you are asking where are you heading?

Well, let me tell you, if your mother dies before you find a wife she can not be replaced and I warn you, you will feel the loss for the rest of your life."

After a short pause Saint Ruiz continued, "You were not made to last for ever, and God wants you to be in Heaven with Him. This is your dress rehearsal. God wants you to practice on earth what you will do forever in eternity.

Life is a series of problems as you are in one now. You are reasonably happy on earth, but that should not be your goal in life. Your goal should be to grow in character to become more Christlike."

With that premise in mind Ed checked his "check list", read his weekly horoscope and then hooked up with Norma Salazar who he had met at Christmas, the second time. As Easter approached, Ed and Norma celebrated the holiday as if it was Christmas holiday time. Ed had a lot of unpacking to do, unpack the plastic Christmas tree and decorate it with Easter lights which were multi colored and shaped like Easter eggs.

Pussy willows and oh-so-adorable bunnies were used to decorate the tree. Mind you many of the bunnies were made of plastic imported from China where labor making such things was cheep, much cheaper than in the Philippines.

While decorating the tree Ed and Norma sat by candlelight and listened to the radio and the latest releases that included *Rocking, Rolling with a Bunny, Mummy Forgot to Put Yeast in the Hot Cross Buns* and the *Last Easter Karaoke*.

When Easter Day arrived, the first thing Ed and Norma did was to attend a sunrise church service and listen to Pastor Atupan tell an ancient story about a Superior who died on a cross for those living on Planet Earth.

Although one could not see the sun in the horizon because of fog and pollution, it was a celebration of a feast of child born on Christmas day who grew into adulthood and died on a Friday and rose from the dead on a Sunday.

Then Ed and Norma exchanged Easter presents. Norma received sweater with a bouquet of red tulips and a card that read: "Norma, you can be my mate frisky as a filly."

Ed did not receive a gift or flowers as Norma turned in her friendship ring and handed Ed a card which read: "Ed, you have been naughty since I began dating you and here's the scoop. The balcony which you used to climb into my room has been removed and I have changed the lock to my front door apartment. All you get for Easter this year is my farewell and a caribao poop because I'm pregnant."

Ed was taken aback and nearly peed his pants. As a child he never lied and wasn't going to this time, and as he shift one foot to the other, sighed, and blushingly said, "Norma, I'm not guilty. I've seem other men climb your balcony to enter your room and have a duplicate key just like the one you gave me. So you are pregnant but please do not blame me because unknown to you and my parents before I arrived in the Philippines I had a vasectomy."

If you really want to hear about it, the first thing you probably want to ask is why did I have the surgery? If you want to know the truth, I was still living in Edmonton, Canada and seventeen. It began after I attended a hard rage party where there was excessive drinking, taking pills, flirting, holding hands, necking, and later I had hooked up sexually with a young lady, if you know what I mean.

Later still, while having a pizza at Shakey's I met Dr. Tom Chua, a friend of a friend, a nice old guy, and he said that he had heard about my escapade and promised to keep a secret while suggesting at the same time for me to stop being wild, angry and wasting my life. The doc suggested that in order to change direction in my life that I should have the surgery."

"And," Norma said

And, I'm very happy to have done it and it's funny, because I always assumed that I would have some twinge of regret every now and then but I haven't.

And the doc promised not to tell my parents because if he did, they each would have a heart attack. Thank you for a wonderful past and our life most go on."

There are approximately 165,000 Amish that live in the United States and another 1500 in Canada. No one knows how many live in the Philippines but while listing a cafe in Laguna province Ed got the attention of pretty Hanna Hershberger riding a camel.

Initially Ed thought Hanna possibly could be an ideal mate but when during a lengthy conversation asked Hanna for a date, she apologized and said to him, "My rule of day to day living prohibits to date anyone who doesn't belong to our church. It also prohibits or limits the use of power-line electricity, telephone, and automobiles, as well as regulations on clothing we wear. And there is more, members of the church may not buy insurance or accept government assistance such as Social Security. The Amish church seeks to maintain a degree of separation from the non-Amish world. There is generally a heavy emphasis on church and family."

Then Ed said, "One more thing. Do the Amish enjoy drinking Coke or Sprite?"

Her answer was, "Neither. Camel milk is our favorite drink."

Ed loved his Coke and Sprite and believed he could not date Hanna with what she had said, and in the event he did marry her, he most likely would be excommunicated from the Amish church, because he enjoyed his car, television, cell phone, and internet and eating at fast food restaurants, so the search continued.

After taking a listing in Lapu Lapu City, Ed was on his way home, with less than 30 kilometers to go, when he stopped to relieve himself, and met an angry caribao that chased him up a banana tree. The caribao shook and shook the tree, but nothing happened. Suddenly the caribao disappeared, and in minutes, returned with another caribao, and they took turns shaking the tree, but still nothing happened. Ed was petrified until a local farmer, claimed the cariboa were lost and his. Fortunately Ed wasn't harmed by the king of the Philippine animal world, and when he returned to his condo, feeling faint and exhausted he sat down to by a window to relax, picked up a copy of *Confucius Says*, book of universal and timely quotes, and read:

Joe Remesz

1   Passionate kiss like spiders web. Soon leads to undoing fly
2   Man who run in front of a car, get tired
3   Man who run behind car, get exhausted
4   Man who fly plane upside down, have crack up
5   Man who scratches ass, should not bite fingernails
6   It takes many nails to build a crib, but one screw to fix it
7   Foolish man give wife a piano, wise man gives wife an organ
8   Man who fight with wife all day, get no piece at night
9   Wife who put husband in doghouse. Soon find him in cathouse
10 Everything has beauty. But not everyone sees it

NINE

Moody and frustrated, but not angry, Ed felt that he was stuck and about to give up hope in his search for a mate, until he met Rachael Bitang at the SM Supermall. Rachael who was the daughter of a Revenue Philippines tax collector who had been dead several years and the mother, hoped to find a husband for her daughter. They had moderate means and were an honorable, gentle, quiet couple.

Rachael was weighted with diamonds and Ed believed she was a perfect type of the virtuous women who men dream of one day intrusting their happiness.

Her simple beauty had the modesty, charm and an imperceptible smile which constantly hovered reflection of a pure, honest and lovely soul. Ed thought he could not find a better wife.

Ed was unspeakably happy kissing and hugging Rachael, but then in the second week, she stole his heart and credit card when she charged up all sorts of jewelry and gems, and while smilingly one day said, "Look Ed, are they not lovely?"

On receiving a bill with 18% interest to pay, Ed was beside himself. He was astonished and now in considerable debt, wished time for reflection.

The theft caused Ed much sorrow. He thought once, twice and even thrice while overcome with fatigue. Ed then called police and Rachael was charged with theft of over fifty thousand pesos. After Ed paid his account, he received a bill stating that he still owed 0.00 pesos. He ignored it and threw the notice away.

A month later, Ed received another bill and threw that one away too. The following month the credit card company sent him a nasty note stating they were going to cancel his credit card if he didn't send 0.00 pesos by return mail. Ed called the credit card company and talked with an officer who said it was a computer problem and he would take care of it.

The following month, Ed decided it was about time he tried out the troublesome credit card, figuring that if there were purchases on his account, it would put an end to the ridiculous predicament. However, in the first store that he produced his credit card in payment for his purchases he found that the credit card had been cancelled.

Ed then called the credit card company who apologized for the computer error once again and an officer said he would take care of it but the following day he got a bill for 0.00 stating that the payment was now due.

Assuming that having spoken to the credit card company, only the previous day, the latest bill was another mistake, so he ignored it, trusting the company would be as good as their word and sort the problem out. The following day, however, he got a bill for 0.00 stating that he had ten days to pay his account or the company would have to take steps to recover his debt.

Finally Ed gave in and thought he would play the company at its own game and mailed it a check for 0.00 pesos. The computer duly processed the account and returned a statement to Ed that he now owed the credit card company nothing. A week later Ed's bank called him asking what he was doing writing a check for P0.00? After a lengthy explanation the bank replied that the P0.00 cheque had caused their processing software to fail.

The bank now could not process ANY check from ANY of its customers that day, because the check for 0.00 pesos was causing the computer to crash.

The following month Ed received a letter from the credit card company claiming that his check had bounced and that he now owned it P0.00 and unless he sent a check by return mail it would take steps to recover the debt.

As far as Ed knows the credit company is still trying.

Ed was in his office, when he received a phone call from Domingo Cane who lived on a rice farm in Laguna and said, "Ed, will you please come and appraise our farm. I shall be delighted if you will."

Ed accepted the invitation with a promise that a Cane daughter would hold the measuring tape for him. And also that in reality he was inexperienced is marketing farms and ranches,

An hour later, Ed set off in his Honda to the backwoods where the farm was situated.

On his way to evaluate the farm, Ed found a bridge over a stream washed away due to a torrential rain storm in the area.

Ed noticed a farmer nearby watching ducks swimming back and forth so he asked the farmer, "How deep is the stream? Do you think I can drive through with my car?"

"I believe you can," the farmer replied, and Ed began driving through it, however, the car sank in the middle and he barely escaped with his life.

"What do you mean telling me I could cross the stream? The stream is at least 2 meters deep," Ed said.

The farmer scratched his head. "Funny," he said. "It only reaches to the middle of the ducks."

The farmer eventually got his tractor and pulled Ed's car out of the stream and after sparkplugs were died, he arrived at the Cane farm and noticed that Mr. and Mrs. Cane were blest with a large family which included a bare footed daughter named Linda a senior student at the De La Salle Araneta University in Metro Manila.

Linda was no more than 20 with dark shoulder length hair, brown eyes, and earrings that looked like rain drops. She wore blue deans and blue blouse.

Linda assisted Ed in holding the tape at one end as he measured the house and then the barn, While inside the barn, Ed found 3 bottles of milk, became excited and said, "Hey, Linda, look, I have found a cow's nest."

Linda burst out with laughter and while shaking her head said, 'That isn't a cow's nest, but 3 bottles of milk. For a realtor you seem to know little about farming."

Embarrassed, Ed apologized and said, "You are correct with that assessment but I'm willing to learn. My real estate experience thus far has been limited to marketing commercial and residential properties."

Ed enjoyed dealing with rural properties had he been given the chance so a week later he sold his condo at a profit and purchased an acreage with a cabin on it along the Pasig River where one could go swimming or fishing and where the neighborhood birds wished Ed happiness and eventually to be as wealthy as Henry Sy or Luciano Tan.

The two bedroom cabin on the acreage was made out concrete blocks, had a bay-window a cellar, a large front lawn and space for a garden in the back yard. The disorderly furniture it contained was more than he bargained for so he donated to the Salvation Army and purchased a new set.

At the same time Ed had the cabin interior painted an eggshell white.

Next, as a hobby, Ed decided to make home-brewed beer and from the Cane family purchased a Jersey cow with a star on her forehead and a curl at the end of her tail. The cow had large brown eyes, which, were crossed and not the least gentle. The eyes had a gleam in them, and when Molly became excited, she became quite wild. Ed also purchased 2 chickens.

"Aside from selling real estate, I'll do some farming and brew homemade beer," Ed said to his parents, which they approved.

Ed dug a hole in the back yard and buried the chickens, like one buries seed potatoes. In the morning E discovered that the chickens were dead.

The following day, Ed purchased 2 more chickens, but this time planted them upside down. In the morning, Ed discovered that these chickens died also, so he wrote a letter to the Philippine Department of Agriculture enquiring how to operate a chicken ranch. Within a week Ed received a reply, In part the letter read: "Please send us a soil sample."

As soon as Ed sent the sample and Linda's parents weren't home, Linda who was on a break while studying at the De La Salle Araneta University, told Ed all there is to know about raising chickens including the tragic things that happen to them, in order not to become a Kentucky fried chicken. Linda said it's the rooster that crow in the morning, but it's the hens that lays the eggs out which come other chicks which who eat quantities of grain, often get a disease, picked up by a hawk, and even while crossing the road, get run over by the wheels of a motor vehicle.

Then Linda added, "Chickens grow faster and lay more eggs while being played music, and it doesn't stop there. With music playing the background the chickens are less capricious, less agitated and do less feather pecking."

"Cool." Ed said and then asked, "If one is to take a survey among the chickens, which type of music do you suggest they prefer?"

"From experience, I find chickens show up with a cluck for Country and Western music and a squawk for rock n roll, classical or jazz."

Linda showed Ed how to do the Chicken Dance, and then said, "Ed, here are some pumpkin seeds you may wish to plant in your garden."

Before Ed returned to his cabin, he had with him, besides the pumpkin seeds, 10 hens and rooster named Mario. As Ed was setting up the stereo system that played Country and Western music, he decided to enjoy his home brewed beer, and poured several bottles into a jug and placed it on the lawn beside him.

Since it was a hot and humid day, the chickens led by rooster Mario, felt they were thirsty too, and while Ed had his back to them, one after another they put their beaks into the jug, swallowing the beer, thinking it was herbal water. Minutes later, the chickens became emotionally intoxicated and there was a cock-a-doodle here and a cluck everywhere. The hens then flew on to a fence and Mario onto the cabin roof and each fowl cock-a-doodled louder than before.

Half an hour later, they flew back onto the grass where Ed joined them, and together they did the Chicken Dance.

From that day onward, thanks to Linda, the outlook for chicken raising and Ed brewing beer, looked promising. Ed could eventually enjoy pumpkin pie alamode and a glass of milk for lunch, bacon and eggs for breakfast and paint the eggs in multi-colors during Easter. Eventually, Mario could compete at the annual Rooster Crowing Contest during a fiesta.

Should Ed be successful in growing a large pumpkin, the gourd would be entered in the annual Philippine Big Pumpkin Contest held in Manila.

Each evening after a busy day at the office, it was time for Ed o feed the chickens and milk the cow that was tied to a stake in the middle of the acreage, but the rope was so long that that Molly soon began scarring the chickens and invading the lawn. This had a strange effect on the animal. Every time Ed tried to shorten the rope, the cow jabbed him with her horn. When the rope was finally shortened, Molly wouldn't stand still and appeared angry and cross eyed. Every time Ed came close to her hind legs, Molly swished her tail and kicked him. But Molly had to be milked. If she wasn't, she might get milk fever and even die.

On an evening, after Molly had sent the milk pail flying, Linda was summoned and gave Ed instructions on how to properly milk the cow. Soon milking her became relatively easy as the cow kept chewing her cud, but one day, Ed made a pot of coffee, the cream ruined its flavor, as the cow began giving sour milk. This time Ed called a vet to see what the trouble was. The vet informed Ed that the reason Molly was producing sour milk was because her eyes were crossed and asked Ed to find a 3 foot hose, and that he would arrive at the acreage within an hour. As soon as the vet arrived he put the hose into the cow from behind and started blowing,
After 5 minutes the cow's eyes were straitened and cured, and the vet walked away with a 5000 peso fee. The milk was pure, but a week later, the cow became cross-eyed again and produced sour milk.
This time Ed didn't want to lose another 5000 peso fee, so he decided to do the doctoring himself.

After blowing for an hour, Molly's eyes remained cross-eyed. Ed realized he was doing something wrong, so he picked up a phone and called Linda to help, and asked her to blow while he watched Molly's eyes. As soon as Linda arrived, she removed the hose from the rear and turned it around and which time Ed said, "Linda, what are you doing?"

Linda's response was, "Ed, you don't expect me to put the same end of the hose in my mouth that you had in yours. Do you?"

Fortunately Molly was cured and again produced excelled milk and cream and Linda returned to her university to continue with her agriculture husbandry lessons.

Referring to Linda, Ed said, "Ah nabigo! I wonder who is kissing her now."

The following day Ed hooked up with Lodi Labastida, and after his work day was done, helped her filling out coupons found in shopping malls, newspapers and magazine and those conducted on the radio and television.

In a short while Lovelita had over 500 entries for various contests and although she had sore lips from licking envelopes, she won hundreds of cans of veggies, pasta, cheese, sacks of rice and dried mango which began to pile up in her apartment.

"What am I going to do what all that food? I have no room to breathe. It's a shame to have all this food to go to waste," Lovelita said anxiously.

"Why don't you compact them into pill form and then you'll have all the space you need," Ed suggested.

"An excellent idea," Lovelita said and with Ed's help took the cans and packages into the kitchen where Lovelita ran the contents through a meat grinder and then a food processor.

Next Lovelita laid out the concoction on a table and with a rolling pin, rolled out the ingredients thin. A cookie cutter was used to have the concentrated food made into pill form. This done, the pills were put into the stove oven to dehydrate.

Once out of the oven, each pill contained enough energy for an entire day, was placed into a refrigerator as Lovelita said, "There, no more food that will be wasted. It's in pill form now and all that is needed is a bit of water to sustain life."

Lovelita even looked forward to market the pill as a new concept in the fast food industry but it had its drawbacks compared to a pizza or even the Big Mac.

In the morning, while alone and enjoying the new discovery for breakfast, Lovelita was impressed with the pill's small size, containing a pound of concentrated nourishment but the pill she was enjoying, soon got lodged in her throat causing Lovelita to cough and choke.

Lovelita slapped herself across her back but it had little effect. Seeing a glass of water beside her Lovelita swallowed a mouthful but this was fatal. The water caused the pill to expand in her stomach and minutes later there was a huge explosion.

You may have heard of the Zamboanga Airport blast? Well, this explosion wasn't quite that large but fragments of her body were found on a nearby rice farm, eventually making the plants a luscious green in color.

It is sad to think that Lovelita, this pretty, vivacious, young woman who would possibly become Ed's bride, instead became a fertilizer.

Men are supposed to be hunters, the aggressors in the dating world so Ed swiftly got back on track, and met Trisha Agon from Davao City, at the Health Center/ who wasn't divorced, overweight or exposed her cleavage.

Joe Remesz

She was very beautiful as she walked about the resort and the nearby Pasig River.

Trisha appeared self-confident, but Ed wasn't certain this charming and heart free, young lady was a 'good for now' of a woman with wife potential.

To find out, Ed invited Trisha for a moonlight walk along the Pasig River. The crickets and frogs serenaded them and there was a breeze that had a lesson to teach, the tides a story to tell and the moon and stars sing a song of glory that Ed couldn't put into words.

Every woman wants to look alluring. In beauty, as in everything else, there is no level playing field but Trisha had God-given good looks that deserved Ed's attention as she maximized her natural assets.

Ed enjoyed Trisha's company immensely, but his father didn't like her and said, "Son, love has a tendency for one to be blind. With Trisha you have stumbled on someone who I believe is clear off the radar screen."

Even though Ed did not have his father's consent, before he would propose marriage or even buy matching face towels and tooth brushes or share the same umbrella, there were areas of exchange much deeper than a casual conversation. At this point, Trisha appeared confused and finally said, "Ed, before we talk about caterers and flower arrangements let's wait a bit longer."

"How long?" Ed asked.

"At least another year."

Ed wasn't prepared to wait that long and sadly said, "It's now or never. I can't wait that long. One year from now will be too late."

The conversation then took on a new twist when Ed asked, "Why so long?"

"Because I don't know your flaws and you don't know mine. One never knows when a prince may turn into a toad and vice versa."

Stunned, gone was a romance that was divine when Ed threw up his hands, took a deep breath and then groaned; "Ugh, very well. There is aa proverb that says, One can lead a horse to water but one can not make it to drink. I'll continue my search and eventually will find another."

Did Ed regret the time he had spent with Tara? Ed never doubted that he loved her despite her heritage, but feared he had wasted precious time courting her.

Recovering from a broken heart, Ed resigned himself that a marriage with Trisha wasn't forthcoming, so the search for a bride continued. Ed wanted to get married but at the same time would settle for nothing less than perfection and his parents' happiness.

Whatever the circumstances, even if one has bad breath and teeth, the end of a love affair can be painful so at the suggestion of a former classmate, Louis Esma, Ed went to the Greenbelt Cinema to relieve his agony and take in the Pinoy movie *Dugo Bayan*. Ed sat in an empty seat next to Eugenia Tobias, a LadyBoy beauty pageant winner with caressing brown eyes.

Several days in succession Ed and Eugenia lunched at Eugenia parents' home and while playing cards and drinking tea, talked for hours, where at one point their conversation dealt with family life and love and she said with a grave face, "Ed, now you know my attitude towards family life and my view as to the sanctity of marriage. I have a moral code which I follow. Look, I like you but as an unmarried woman I won't live with you. Let's just be friends."

Ed cleared his throat and heaved a sigh. For several seconds there was silence which was broken when Ed continued," Just friends, why?"

Eugenia was devout and religious, and her conviction would not allow her to, "Live in sin."

Despite making no end of promises, Ed did not know what to think or theory to adopt, so he softly drawled, "Very well. That's how the cookie crumbles. A fair exchange is no robbery."

For reasons unfathomable it's still a mystery why Eugenia did not want to live with this handsome, intelligent real estate salesman, at a time when it was a common practice that when marriage was forsaken or annulled, many couples in the Philippines lived common-law.

Ed's next date was also a mystery This one on par with why Emilo Aguinaldo did not sign the 1898 Declaration of the Independence from Spain or how San Miguel beer can be kept cool without the use of ice.

Ed's next date was an enchanting humming bird with the name, Salome Orapa, who he had met at a Chowking restaurant.

Salome originally came from the province of Mindanao where the monster *aswang* is the most feared supernatural creatures on the islands. They can enter the body of a person and through this person they inflict harm on those they dislike. Ed had no idea why anyone would dislike the petit Salome when upon short notice she returned to the island to be at her parent's 50th wedding anniversary.

Most common aswang are the female variety that appear as an ugly old woman with long, unkempt hair, blood-shot eyes, and long finger nails, and a long thread-like black tongue.

But the most striking trait of this creature is her ability as a self-segmenter, is to discard her lower body from the shoulders down, from hips down and also down from her knees. She has holes in her armpits which contain oil.

This gives her power of flight. Seldom does she ride on a broomstick or a carpet. Being of enormous power, an aswang can transform herself into any shape, even inanimate objects. She preys on children, pregnant women and ill people.

Once she has overpowered a victim, she takes a bundle of sticks, talahib grass, and rice or banana stalks, and transforms these into a replica of her victim.

This replica is sent home while she takes the real person back with her. Upon reaching her home, the replica becomes sick and dies. The victim is then eaten. She is particularly fond of the liver.

Ed then was on the run to find another one. Not an aswang, but a mate, and sought advice from contemporary lovelorn writer, Miss Nehring, who ran a syndicated column in a Manila newspaper. Since Miss Nehring seemed to know everything about mating, Ed gave his best shot and wrote:

> Dear Miss Nehring,
>
> My mother is suspicious why I can't find a life-time partner is because I'm running around and wasting time.
>
> For instance, last night she asked if it was Gina Dalida, a mail sorter at the post office, Cherry Tia, the cashier at the Jollibee Restaurant or Carol Valenzuela, a server at the Ocean Park Hotel restaurant. What should I do?

Miss Nehring answered:

Dear Ed,

Cheer up. You may not be fooling around with
the women you mentioned, but you certainly
gave your mother three good reasons to keep
an eye on you.

Why don't you consult with a matchmaker?

Since Ed had a frustrating time finding a mate he took
Miss Nehring's advice and made arrangements to meet a
traditional matchmaker whose profession was making a
comeback.

The following evening, Ed met the elderly, garrulous,
toothless widow Elizabeth Salvadore, who wasn't pretty,
short in stature with wrinkles on her cheeks roughened by
hardship which she endured during her life. To avoid the
danger of high blood pressure Mrs. Salvadore sprinkled flax
on her cereal and to save money, lived in a small meager
bamboo nipa hut. It was the most God-forsaken looking
hut found in the neighborhood. Children playing nearby
called the place, "The Old Lady's Freak House."

Mrs. Salvadore was happy living in the hut and
wouldn't live anywhere else. As far

as Ed was concerned, a consultation didn't cost a peso.

Supporting herself on crutches, Mrs. Salvadore at
four score and three, however, was a wise woman who
understood courtship rituals and when she was active in
matchmaking interviewed more than 200 singles about
dating choices. One may truly say Jessa Salvadore in her
hey-day, was the Manila's anthropologist of dating.

Mrs. Salvadore helped Ed overcome his initial nervousness
by handing him a cup of herbal tea, and he to her, his resume.

After going over the resume Mrs. Salvadore in a hoarse voice said, "Ed, you appear to be an intelligent young man, which gals should go for but first, let me evaluate several and I will call you."

Since all is not gold that glitters, and beauty is but skin deep," Ed said, "Let's try."

That evening Ed went to his cabin and waited for a phone call, which did come as he was having a shower.

He picked up the receiver after the sixth ring and on the other end Mrs. Salvadore said, "Ed, I have found your first date that is willing to meet with you. Vivian Dy is a high profile lady your age, an intelligent doll who reads books, has no life trauma or emotional roller coasting. Can I give Vivian your phone number? You won't be disappointed."

Within an hour the phone rang again. It was Vivian, the high-profile cupid Mrs. Salvadore talked about. Following a brief conversation Ed and Vivian agreed to meet in the lobby of the Legend Vilas Hotel where following an exchange of pleasant greetings, the couple entered the bar, sat at a table, where Ed asked, "Vivian, which would you like to drink, vodka or gin?"

"My favorite is rum and coke."

When the cocktails arrived, Vivian accidentally spilled hers and apologized.

"That's all right. No problem. I'll order another, Hey waiter!" Ed hollered.

After the initial nervousness subsided a three-piece combo began playing and up-tempo tune. Ed and Vivian took to the dance floor and like ballroom dancers their footwork went forward and back, back and forward, dipping and flowing.

Following several more rounds of cocktails and dances, Vivian began thrashing her previous dates, made self-deprecating comments about her waistline that made Ed embarrassed.

Following still more exploratory conversation, Vivian beamed with delight and came right out and said, "I have already applied for maternity leave. Ed, are you ready?"

"To leave? Any time."

"Not to leave home."

"Then what?"

"To get married."

Ed wasn't prepared for an instant marriage or to walk up an aisle towards the altar without his parents present. Ed thought Toyota would be the first to invent a solar powered car but did not believe he wanted to connect with his first prospect who was a major disappointment.

Ed left Vivian behind and his next date didn't turn out much better when he met Pepe Amara, a substitute librarian that was an intellectual without intellect, met Ed in the Mandaluyong City Public Library to read about the state of the real estate market in Metro Manila.

Both were the same age, but Ed soon found out that Pepe spent nights sleeping in a nearby cemetery, because she couldn't afford public housing.

Pepe wasn't scavenging dumpsters or buying her clothing from the Salvation Army Thrift Store, but then when she said she was a widow, Ed wasn't interested.

"But only recently as my husband died in a fatal motorcycle accident on the Strong Republic Nautical Highway," Pepe said.

"Marrying a widow hasn't entered my mind," Ed replied.

"That's because you have no experience living with one. A widow, especially if she is young and healthy as I am, can make a lovely bride."

Ed felt there was a stigma attached when a young man marries a widow, especially if one was already five months pregnant, as Pepe was.

In the 2nd round, Hanna gave Ed the names of three other women: Love Moreno, Patience Abella and Prudence Lanita. With romantic names like that, Ed thought one of them had a strong possibility of becoming a permanent mate, and again it did not happen.

First, Ed dated Love who had bad breath and teeth and they wouldn't be compatible as a married couple, because Love also snored when asleep and when awake there was hostility and dislike for each other. It wasn't a relationship that Ed wanted, so he sidestepped making an invitation, as one would have been a recipe for a disaster.

Then, Ed dated Patience. Ed as a real estate salesmen had the capacity for waiting. He had the ability to enhance waiting or delay without becoming annoyed and upset, or to persevere calmly when faced with difficulty.

Patience, however, was totally opposite to Ed's demeanor. When Ed took her to see a movie or when she went to the bank, Patience was impatient waiting in a long lineup.

Often she would go to sales in department stores and buy things, because of the discount coupons, and even though she did not need the article. In searching for a mate, one thing on Ed's agenda list was not to get involved with shopaholic and an impatient woman.

Finally, upon Mrs. Salvadore's recommendation, Ed dated Prudence, who was flirty, always chewed gum and thought she knew everything. Prudence appeared to have a good sense in managing practical matters, but since she was a weather forecaster for a local television station, her forecasts were always topsy-turvy.

Ed realized in a flash that in a world of unpredictable weather, there would be a wall between him and Prudence and felt she would not help him increase his sales.

The following evening, at a time when Ed was absorbed in real estate matters and enjoying a beer that he felt embarrassed when during darkness an intruder with wings unexpectedly entered his cabin. Puzzled by the home invasion, Ed asked the stranger, "And who might you be?" and was told, "I'm your guardian angel Saint Michael."

Skeptical, Ed said, "And how did you get here and what is it you want from me? All I have in the fridge is a loaf of bread and several bottles of beer to drink."

"I'm doing a heavenly Analysis of your searches for an everlasting mate. At any rate while I think of it, in heaven there is no beer so I'll accept a bottle to quench my thirst while I'm here."

Handing a bottle Ed continued, "And once you are finished drinking it I'll call police that you leave."

"I wouldn't do that if you want me to help you find an ever lasting loving wife," the guardian angel imperturbably replied, at the same time touching Ed on the forehead with his wing.

Thinking that the angel could be a combative alcoholic Ed could not endure the intrusion, even from an angel. However, a friendly conversation followed and with considerate kindness of the angel, Ed was mollified which led him to ask, "How did you find Mandaluyong City? Las Vegas with its bright lights but Metro Manila, is the size of a pinhead on the on the planet Earth map?"

"Good question. To show the way I followed a star like the one that led the wise men bringing gold, incense and myrrh to baby Jesus in Bethlehem."

Ed was dismayed and about to ask another question, "And ..."

"And with the help of the full moon and a back wind I flapped my wings and in no time I was above the clouds and a short time later, I leaped into your condominium balcony.

Mind you, initially it was a bit difficult to find because of the air pollution in Metro Manila which is harming the Planet Earth environment."

At this point, the angel apologized for the intrusion and minutes later, said, "Ed, my time with you is limited as the Angel Department in heaven is extremely busy and I have other calls to make."

The angel bowed his head, flapped his wings, and after shaking hands with Ed, on departure, like the time General Douglas MacArthur when Japan occupied the Philippines during World War11, in a gentle and soft voice said, "May God bless you. I shall return.

Since Ed was pacified, he closed the door by which the angel entered, drew the blinds in the bedroom and then said to himself, "Please God help the angel," and went to sleep and slumber tranquility till morning.

A day passed, and then another, and still another and the process of finding a suitable mate remained at a slow pace. It seemed that all Ed's effort and the days allotted to him were fading. But Ed wasn't a quitter and stopped at the *National Book Store* on Pioneer Street where book shelves were filled about astrology, numerology, unidentified flying objects and Hollywood celebrities who were divorcing or undergoing rehabilitation treatment. Ed usually didn't get too excited about the articles until he scanned and purchased Dr. Phil's *Strategy* which said pets make good companions and walking a dog could stave off depression.

As soon as Ed finished reading the book he got excited and rushed to the SPCA bringing home a German shepherd dog named Spot whose coat suggested fleas and squalor.

Spot put his tail between his legs and howled all night and during the day ran around sniffing and licking all kinds of stuff on the ground.

Spot was a hard working dog however, and the article also said that if trained a dog could sniff out marijuana, cancerous tumors, bedbugs and cockroaches and possibly a mate.

In hopes of finding out Ed took Spot for a walk and struck up smiles and conversations with other pet owners but still failed to find a partner because Dominic began eating his own feces thus frightening females away. Aside from being a hard working dog Spot was also clever and used Ed to meet other female dogs.

Although Ed was disappointed he rewarded the dog for his effort with a bone which the pooch chewed voraciously but then disappeared.

Smart, tough and stubborn Ed then rescued a stray cat in the back ally, had an identification chip put in her ear, and soon Kitty became his favorite playmate, but Kitty needed a bath so Ed thoroughly cleaned the toiled bowl in the bathroom, added some soap and put the cat inside, closed the lid and flushed three times.

This provided a "power wash and a rinse" which Ed found quite effective. When he lifted the lid, the cat jumped out and Ed dried her with a towel.

Following her bath, Kitty did not barf, but several days later, became a pee stain carpet decorator. Kitty liked to sit on Ed's lap and jump onto his bed and lay at his feet. For his part Ed showed her where she could catch mice.

Kitty soon got into heat and kept making weird 'Meow. Meow' sounds which neighbors found annoying.

The feline had never been fixed, and one night as Ed opened the door, and watched a pack of dogs chasing her. That night Kitty got lost, but a week later, was found by a pet lover in Quezon City.

The following night, at about 3:00 in the morning, Ed was awakened by a strange noise that he had not heard before coming from the kitchen. He reached, blindly groping for the light switch, found it, and discovered that he had cockroaches in his kitchen and that a cockroach is one of the most common creatures capable of inspiring fear instead of love. Ed was horrified when he saw dozens of roaches which slinking across the kitchen floor and the males began to fly. They could also swim. When several; climbed up his leg, that is when Ed called Vira Pest Control in Makati City for help.

Not many women become pest exterminators, but one that did, her name was Edna Dagohoy.

Edna wore heavy clothing, wrap-around glasses, a safety orange vest and a respirator. Using a small hand-pumped can she strutted from room to room, corner to corner, and sprayed with a product that sounded like another Schwarzenegger movie, *Killmaster 11*.

Then after Edna had sprayed the baseboards, cupboards and under the kitchen sink she marked areas where the cockroaches were likely to pass with a poisonous putty-like substance painted green.

As Edna was cockroach hunting, more ran out of the kitchen sink, but Edna gave them a spray and instantly they were dead.

"I was told that pet cockroaches, especially the albino ones, should be treated with respect and a little compassion," Ed said

"Could be, but on the other hand, cockroaches are notorious harbingers of filth and disease. They leave droppings on their ways that resemble fragments of pencil lead."

"You are right," Ed said, "There is nothing worse than when I found my bedside dresser drawer sprinkled with these. And the infestation I have noticed is also accompanied by an odor which what shall I say is kind of roachy."

"And, Ed," Edna continued, "Remember when you pour grease down the drain, you're feeding the roaches so don't let that happen again."

Although Ed did not ask Edna for a date, because she was already married, she gave him a tip to list a home in the Shangri-La Place subdivision.

TEN

That same evening, Ed drove to the Shangri-La Place subdivision where Edna's friend, Gillian Itabale, lived and upon approaching her home saw a sign on the lawn that read: "For Sale by Owner. Best Deal in Town." and underneath, "Only 100.000 pesos."

Ed thought the price was a misprint, but he called on Gillian just the same. Gillian, who appeared a bit distressed, showed him the 5000 square foot home which had a panoramic view of Metro Manila and the Pasig River that flowed through it.

While showing the swimming pool and the tennis court Gillian said, "You are the second person to show interest in my home."

Ed said the house and the landscaping was the most beautiful he had seen in Shangri-La Place, but leery about the one hundred-thousand peso price, when most homes in the area sold far above five-million.

"What's the catch?" Ed asked.

Gillian assured Ed that the mortgage and taxes were paid, "And there are no liens against it."

Ed was still leery about the price.

"Well, I'll be truthful," Gillian said, "Last week I got a call from my husband who informed me that he's leaving me for his secretary.

He then told me that I could have everything we owned as long as he could have his half-share from the sale of the house. I agreed and asked if I could sell it quickly as I can while he and his lovey-dovey are spending their time in the America"

Then Ed said, "I live in a cabin and enjoy suburban living. If that is the case I'll buy your home and pay you the real market value."

Gillian's response was, "Ed, you are a bit late. The man ahead of you did. We are just waiting to have it conveyed."

"Congratulations! Then can I at least take you out for dinner?"

"Thank you for the invitation, but the gentleman who bought the house, I already accepted his."

Ed was disappointed and the following evening, while relaxing in his cabin, thinking about his failure, Ed's father phoned and reminded his son by saying, "Look, your deadline is fast approaching and your mother's health is deteriorating. Here's a tip. Why you don't you erase the boundary between your dream and reality and try bungee jumping? I hear by the grapevine many young women have taken up the latest phenomena."

"Don't," his mother argued, "Bungee jumping can be dangerous. Why don't you go to the Equestrian Center, and while riding horses you may possibly meet a mate and fall in love."

Not to displease his parents Ed did both.

At this time bridges were beginning to replace telephone towers as a favored spot to practice jumping, Ed traveled to the Agar-Agar Bridge in Southern Leyte to brave the jump thirty stories down from a ninety-meter high bridge which straddled between two mountains and traverses along the Mahaplag-Sogod section of the Tacloban-Lioan highway. There were female jumpers and Ed had a fall of his life time. The jump however, gave Ed an adrenaline rush that only a near-death experience can provide.

Ed wasn't prepared to die so on his next day off, he headed to the Laguna Equestrian Center where he hoped to meet singles who were as horse-loving as he was.

Ed chatted with Yvonne Jasnico, who he thought was 'all-right' and got the latest equestrian news. He watched Yvonne make a practice run on Prince, a four-year-old quarter horse she was training for barrel racing.

Yvonne was an accomplished rider who competed since she was a child but as she and her horse rounded the third barrel, the animal slipped and fell. As Prince struggled to get up Yvonne's foot became trapped in the stirrup.

Startled, the gelding broke across the arena at a run, bucking and kicking. Everything seemed to move in slow motion as those present rushed into the arena to trap the horse. Suddenly, the horse kicked out, his hoof catching Yvonne in the middle of her back. The blow knocked her boot from the stirrup and Yvonne lay unconscious with blood streaming from beneath the helmet secured on her head.

Minutes passed an ambulance arrived. Following the trip to the Makati Medical Center it's a psychological mystery why Yvonne used abusive language and became combative in the trauma room. Ed felt let down and did not see Yvonne again.

Ed did not sleep that night and during next, when he came home as he felt tired and weary and needed time to unwind from the strains and stresses he had suffered. Frustrated, he drank a glass of warm milk, tossed and turned, and fell asleep.

When Ed woke up in the morning rain was tapping against his window, a torrential rain storm was taking place, so instead of going to work he sat on his bed thinking what a traditional wedding could be like and who to invite. Should the wedding be a grand event or a small gathering with close friends and family?

What the brides wedding dress would be like? The color of the bridesmaid's dresses and of courses where the reception would take place and how much liquor to buy. Who would do the catering and type of refreshments to serve? There was no doubt in Ed's mind that Pastor Atupan could perform the ceremony, although he wondered how much to tip him and who was going to pay for the wedding expenses.

Then after thinking about his marriage, love and expenses Ed had a creative idea. At the appropriate time he would not depend on his o his bride's parents but sell ads to corporate sponsors to pay for the wedding expenses.

Still, Ed wasn't feeling well so during a pause in the storm went to a 'No Appointment Necessary' clinic where following a physical the doctor on duty, Dr. Eric Espinosa, diagnosed Ed's condition as CRAFT disease.

"Craft disease?" What is it?" Ed asked, "I haven't heard of the disease. What are the symptoms?"

"The symptom is that you can't remember a friggin thing. It's the first stage of dementia."

Ed wasn't the type of person who accepted jokes, so he went to similar clinic on the next street for a second opinion, and a doctor on duty there, Henry Yutuc, following a physical examination twitched the ends of his mustache and said, "Sir, my diagnosis is that you have a slight case of what is commonly know as Furniture Disease."

Again, Ed asked for the symptoms and was told, "Seems that your chest keeps falling into your drawers."

"This is no laughing matter," Ed thought. He was concerned about the state of his health and made a swift exit to see his regular family doctor, Danilio Perez.

Once another physical examination was completed the doc sat next to Ed and confidentially said," Ed my friend, your other diagnoses is wrong. There is really nothing wrong with you that *Viagra* can't help."

Dr. Perez wrote a prescription, which Ed held in his hand, and then purchased the sex enhancement pills at the nearest drugstore.

Ed was excited thinking his down-feeling would disappear and hastily drove to his parent's home where upon showing the pills to his mother she got angry.

"At your age? You should be ashamed of yourself," she complained, and flung the prescription bottle out the door which landed in a neighbor's back yard. There, the chickens, believing the tablets were a food supplement, swallowed them one after another and the following day, began laying hard boiled eggs.

By now, Ed was tired of searching for someone that he could love, lean on, do his laundry and cook. He even had thoughts of remaining a bachelor for rest of his life until his condo neighbor in # 27, Antonio Nopalin, visited him and said, "Hey, Ed, why don't you go Farmer's Plaza Mall where all sorts of beautiful women shop and congregate?"

Ed listened eagerly and in the end said, "An excellent idea my friend!" And while jumping to his feet, a picture of Chris Aquino fell off the living room wall facing him, and shattered.

Ed then said, said, to his neighbor, "I'm tired of kissing any more toads. Maybe you are right that I've been searching in the wrong places."

To find out, on the following evening after work, Ed drove to the SM Mall of Asia where he found a directory, and then went to the Galaxy Amusement Park where he met up with Rosa Catabato who rejuvenated him as they laughed and screamed as they rode the indoor triple load roller coaster.

"I have heard this mall is a magical place," Ed thought and then invited Rosa to ride a mechanical bull.

Ed rode first and when it was Rosa's turn she climbed the animal and circled her hands over her head.

As Rosa rode the mechanical bull, he went wild beneath her, bucking her off before she knew her ride had begun. Poor Rosa had injured her spleen and like when Michelangelo lost his paint brush, hasn't been seen or heard from since.

The following day a co-worker at Best Realty, Ace Gaston, ran up to him and said, "Ed, why don't you take a holiday? I've been to Borocay City and it's a resort where girls in bikinis stroll the sandy beaches."

Ed who was in a good mood went straight to *Everything Under the Sun* booking agency, and after the clerk flew over a keyboard while humming a Christian Bautista tune, said "An agenda for your holiday in Boracay is completed."

Ed took the first flight available to Boracay City and during the 1st day of his vacation,

while picking up sea shells on a sandy beach, met Courtney Rosario, but she turned out to be a Creep so Ed thought, "I'll pass."

On the 2nd day of his vacation, Ed hooked up with curvaceous Louisa Gullez.

He tasted Louisa's lips. No one had ever kissed him like this before. Not Trisha, Paulette, Alfa, not any of the predecessors. Louisa's kisses ignited deep into Ed's body shooting fireworks through every nerve ending.

Ed couldn't get enough of Louisa and thought he was in Heaven. As Ed looked into her eyes and about to make a marriage proposal an unusual thing for Boracay happened. As the seagulls shrieked a violent typhoon approached with thunder, lightning and whitecaps began rolling. Ed got frightened and as he could not swim, a possible marriage proposal ended quickly as Ed picked up his belongings and headed home.

On arrival back in Mandaluyong City Ed used creative showmanship by putting on his Halloween costume, had a sandwich board spray painted that read: *Looking for Companionship—Possible Marriage*, with a phone number underneath and paraded back and forth in front of City Hall. Some critics called the innovative method of advertising, 'Crazy', 'Undignified' and 'Desperate' while other women in front of City Hall cheered Ed on.

As soon as the one-hour parade was over Ed interviewed fourteen ladies who were married and had left their husbands because they were abused in one way or another.

There were several singles too which included Begonia Orapa who was the most unlikely possible mate Ed had met, and thought should have been arrested for Terminal Ugliness.

Begonia was short and dumpy with one leg shorter than the other and the left foot had six toes.

Seeing Begonia, Ed almost passed out but had enough energy left to say, "I'll see you tomorrow."

But tomorrow never came and Ed felt Begonia's mother should have thrown her daughter away and kept the stork.

Ed was disappointed, but then came Cynthia Torbella, an athlete who excited Ed's senses. Cynthia was his height, had a small waist, very large brown eyes and auburn hair.

Her earrings where shaped like miniature basketballs and they sparkled as they dangled from her ear lobes to her chin. Cynthia wore a blue and red dress and had a same color as the Philippine flag and had basketball by her side. Ed and Cynthia hit it off and dated that evening.

Each enjoyed each others company and both liked the same things but Cynthia's topics of conversation seemed to be more important than Ed's.

After Ed and Cynthia met on the City Hall steps, the couple played a game of Hide and Seek, and then enjoyed delicious Western food at the Liberty Center. While enjoying the dinner and the panoramic view, Ed and Cynthia exchanged smiles, and aside from talking about basketball and trivial things, they compared notes about the Philippine Basketball League and which team would win the seasonal championship.

Ed thought it would be Ascof Lagundi Natural Cough Busters and Cynthia the Cobra Energy Drink Iron Men.

An argument erupted which team had the better club and neither would give in at a time, when Cynthia had to leave and join her ladies basketball team for a practice before heading to the Asia Games.

This was one example of frustration and another took place when Ed made contact with the most saintly, retired, and most trusted American CBS newscaster/journalist icon in America, Walter Cronkite, in New York. Ed felt that since Cronkite helped many Americans during the Viet Nam war he could possibly could perform a miracle and help him find a mate. Cronkite, as he was busy, suggested that Ed contact Canadian hockey icon commentator Don Cherry for advice.

After this frustrating date, another took place when Ed placed a phone call to Toronto, Canada and discussed his search with Don Cherry of *Coach's Corner* during Hockey Night in Canada television fame. Since the legendary Cherry gave public tips about playing hockey and had a successful marriage, Ed figured the high-profile personality could also coach him in mate hunting.

Ed wasn't disappointed when Cherry advised, "Ed, set your goal, be your own cheer leader, never cross check or take a slap-shot at a female and never change a winning lineup."

And advised, "Do not be afraid to take your next prospective bride fishing during a weekend getaway."

Ed took Cherry's advice seriously and met Nora Fazloon in a lineup at a Jollibee fast food restaurant. Nora was pretty and shaped like a Coca Cola bottle. After several dates Ed and the potential bride agreed to go fishing.

Without knowing why, they found themselves at Caliraya Lake, Laguna and the town of Lumban, the embroidery capital of the Philippines.

Of course if one lives in Manila, Cebu or Davao one may be tempted to call the Lumban town site as the largest cemetery in Laguna with shining lights.

But there are occasions that make the town come alive, especially during the tourist season and when property owners receive their annual tax notices each spring, at election time and the annual Fiesta.

Although there are no tall buildings in Lumban city, many wealthy and elite tourists flock there in order to catch the 'big' one. Ed and Nora registered at the Fishing Hole Motel.

Although it is said that birds do it, bees do it, even educated fleas do it, not that Ed couldn't try doing it, nothing happened between Ed and Nora because the motel had a strict policy that required tourists of separate gender to sleep in separate beds.

And the beds had to be a minimum of two feet apart when a couple rented a room for only a week. At the same time it was illegal to make love on the floor between the beds.

It was a beautiful sunny day in Laguna and as soon as the two anglers registered they threw their lines into the lake where there were many fish, but the one Nora hooked, was a Titanic, that defies imagination.

The Largemouth Black Bass was so huge that instead of Nora pulling it out to shore; it pulled Nora into the lake. A struggle ensued, and eventually Nora and the fish drifted into the Caliraya River, where there was a bridge across a road, and Nora caught a corner of the bridge by the seat of her pants. While the fish swam on its merry way Nora stayed suspended in the air until Ed rescued her an hour later and freed her from her misery.

On the 2nd day, Ed and Nora went fishing again.

And when they launched their boat, more fish were caught, but then, when a mosquito bit Nora on her forehead, she gave it a whack with her hand and in process lost her balance and fell into the lake.

Seeing Nora struggling those on the shore hollered, "Fish her out! Fish her out! Fish her out!"

But Ed still didn't know how to swim or dive. Nora did, but going through an unforgettable experience to stay alive, she didn't want to fish again, nor did she want to be Ed's mate.

The trip with Nora wasn't the only time that Ed a traumatic experience during his search for a mate A week later he had met Sunday and Monday Paler, twins born 11 minutes apart before and after midnight on a Sunday and a Monday, at the Mandaluyong City Medical Center, on Boni Avenue.

They each weighed five pounds but Sunday was longer and remained taller as she grew.

Sunday and Monday were best of friends and always even as adults stuck together. They dressed in opposite colors of the same outfit, and insisted their hair be pinned exactly the same way and both were employed as cashiers at the Shell gas station in Manila.

Often the twins had arguments of course, but that did not matter, what did was Ed thought both were beautiful women and one could possibly be a mate as they had now reached twenty two years of age.

On a typical Manila Friday evening Sunday got into her car, picked Monday up from work and were planning to go to Hyatt Hotel and Casino for a night of fun and dancing.

While driving, Sunday was making a left hand turn when a pickup truck driven by a young man, T-bared the car. The young man allegedly had stolen the vehicle and had been drinking.

Sunday and Monday were rushed by ambulance to the Mandaluyong Medical Center where both, like during their birth, tragically died eleven minutes apart due to injuries received.

For the next week, Ed was in a state of grief and perplexity. Fearing further rejections he had thoughts of living with a robot instead a female.

A robot would not hurt his feelings nor argue like some housewives do, when his mother phoned and said, "Ed, my health is progressively getting worse. Today I had my blood pressure taken and a x-ray shows my heart is deteriorating and the blood pressure increasing. My heart now beats much faster than usual and it may soon explode." After pausing several seconds, continued: "Look, Bill Gates at Microsoft has come up with Window XP software for the personal computer that is selling like hot cakes. A computer dating service has just opened on Shaw Boulevard. Why don't you go there for assistance?"

Ed accepted the suggestion as he was intrigued how this latest Microsoft Window software could add spice to his social life. One thousand pesos to open an account didn't seem expensive for three printouts. Ed was curious about the criteria the dating service used to match people.

Ed wanted to find out for instance, how this man/ woman scheme worked so he polished his conversation skills and arranged an interview with *Personal Dating Service* where he filled out a detailed evaluation form that included sections on general experience, religion, attitude towards sex, personal interests, a description of himself, a section on reaction situations and several questions which weren't applicable to him.

With questions as thorough as these it seemed impossible not meet the ideal mate but it didn't work out that way. Ed dated three different dates from the computer printout, none of them he knew.

First there was Ayla Obar who was a monster from *Star Wars*, Bamby Frias from *Disneyland* who advised Ed against reading the book *Hitoni Tanaka* alleging that Philippine women as a rule do not have large breasts and the book was full of unpleasant subjects. And then there was Judy Anajao from *An Encounter of a Different Kind* who said her birthday was February 2nd. Well, she did look a bit like a groundhog, but then when she had an asthma attack their conversation discontinued.

Each woman was an emotional basket case and at this point in his search for a mate, Ed didn't know if he should remain single and enjoy freedom or get married and possibly be a prisoner.

Ed, however, ordered three more printouts and again didn't know any of the women. In the end he hoped it would remain that way. The six printouts generally were unintelligent, uninteresting and above all, did not enjoy classical music or current events.

Catherine Motel who apparently fell from the sky and became an island was bubbly and big-chested that when Ed went jogging with her, there were seismic vibrations that could be felt a kilometer distant.

The 2nd, Laurie Jane Gonzales, Ed could not put his heart on the line because Laurie Jane was a pain for sore eyes and had so much plastic surgery done that her face looked like the Chocolate Hills in Bohol.

The third, Melanie Montalba, reminded Ed of a tarsier monkey and in Ed's opinion although she had large brown eyes and was beautiful, ambitions and restless. She was also cold, paranoid and neurotic.

On a scale of 1 to 10 most of the dates rated fewer than 4 and collectively Ed felt their

I Q didn't add up to the minimum wage paid in the Philippines at the time.

The day after Ed's date with Melanie, he stopped at a bank, the post office and then picked up a parcel at the Mandaluyong Bus Depot where he met Lizzy Torio, who had purchased bus fare to Pangasinan City.

They did not date, however, because Ed discovered that like, Lizzy Borden in Massachusetts, this good looking Lizzy, had taken a hatchet and gave her mother 40 whacks, and then when this was done, she gave her father another 41.

Minutes later, the mystery why Lizzy committed a homicide reached its climax, when this beautiful woman was charged with slaying her parents. According to police, the murders weren't done for pleasure or spite but because this Lizzy wasn't very bright.

Ed then hooked up with Tiffany Joson, a gorgeous single and a bit older than Ed, who tended to talk to herself and had a sense of humour. Tiffany took care not to resort to insults and teasing. Her quirks, faults and habits, however, at times could be annoying, and her actions were always environment friendly. During each date Ed and Tiffany would attend comedy movies and enjoyed watching *Wowa Wee* on television.

However, her comic vision survived particularly during shorter and rainy days. As Tiffany was dedicated to help the poor by volunteering as a coordinator at the Inn Roads Housing Co-operative, Ed because of selling real estate and had a deadline to meet, and Tiffany because of her commitment to volunteer poverty work, and attending a How to be a Comic workshop, dated only for a short while but remained friends.

ELEVEN

Several days later, associate realtor Rajiv Sandhu took Ed aside and said, "Friends are an integral part of everybody's life. Look, facing a relationship is a challenge. You are still single, alone, have a deadline to meet so stop struggling and flip-flopping by saying yes or no. I have advice for you which will expedite the process to find a mate. I ordered a mail order bride from India although my marriage failed, yours may not."

Rajiv then handed Ed an International Mail Order Bride catalogue with photos of beautiful women who were disenchanted with the Indian dating scene.

The idea of mail order brides was around since the early settlers, would write back to their homeland for a bride and the term "Mail-Order-Brides" was born. But before Ed would order a potential bride and receive one in the mail, he nosed about and found why Rajiv's marriage had failed.

Pratibha was a beautiful twenty three-year-old university student when she met Rajiv, a handsome, successful Philippine businessman. They met in Bombay. Love however, did not conquer all. At first Pratibha and Rajiv were happy in their married life, but a year later, Rajiv began abusing her. One night he physically abused her at the time she was breast feeding the couple's infant daughter. Pratibha wound up in the Medical City General Hospital emergency room with her face bruised and swollen and a human bite mark on her hand.

Once released from the hospital, Pratibha escaped to a woman's shelter, then got a radical and sued the International Mail Order agency for not screening Rajiv properly.

Ed thought that he might encounter a language barrier and with a mail order bride and also it was a time that Ed's credit card was reaching its limit so he was against the idea.

As before, one failure to meet the appropriate mate led to another. It wasn't because lack of effort however, as Ed did everything possible in a fast paced environment that his parents told him to do. But no matter how hard he worked or how much effort he put in, none seemed to work so his mother suggested, "Ed, you need to brush up on your interviewing skills."

A day later, while shopping at the Shang-Rila Edsa Mall, Ed had a conversation with Merna Encino, but since he was focused on learning how to swim that day, he put dating her on the back-burner. Ed knew however, it was time to burn another bridge, so between praying and crying, the following evening, phoned Merna that at first tried her hand at being a Casino Filipino, but ended up as a merchandiser at Robinson's Department Store and she excitedly replied, "Hey good looking, what's cooking? I'm free and ready to go steady but don't tell your mother."

Ed and Merna, whose forehead was level with his chin, became quick friends which eventually could turn to love, but before Ed would move on, he called his mother to share the good news and arranged for the couple to have dinner with his parents so they could meet his possible fiancé.

To Ed, Merna was stunningly beautiful with sparkling brown eyes with an octopus chasing a star fish tattoo on her arm and a ring in her nose. Strange and stranger, still Merna was wearing a loose strapless red mini dress with green high heels shoes.

Her red hair was done porcupine style. Merna liked to dance, mainly hip-hop and also enjoyed singing the latest rap songs. Her fingernails were long and painted red. Her fragrance was that of a papaya in bloom.

After the sumptuous dinner was eaten, Ed took his mother aside and in their privacy anxiously asked, "Well, Mom, what you think of Merna as your prospective daughter in-law?"

Merna was exactly the sort Ed's mother objected to and coldly replied," Not a snowball's chance in hell. She's a queer one. I can't stand her."

And the following day when Ed introduced Merna to his employer, Rogelio Best, replied, "Ed, if you marry Merna, you'll have to find yourself a new employer."

Since there would be unhappiness between Ed's mother and Merna to be his wife, it was a case of a deaf man talking to a blind woman, so Ed disposed Merna and hooked up with socialite Ivy Ortiz, who with her aging mother, which he didn't particularly like, accompanied the couple on a short vacation to the Middle East to visit their relatives. During the vacation while visiting Jerusalem Ivy's mother unexpectedly died.

Coming out of one crises Ed headed for another when with a death certificate in hand he went to the Philippine Consulate Office to help Ivy make arrangements to send the body back home for burial.

After hearing of the death of Ed's possible mother-in-law, the Consul said to Ed, "My friend, to bring the body back to Manila for burial is very expensive and could cost as much as $10,000, American."

The Consul continued by saying, "In most cases the person responsible for the remains normally buries the body here. This would only cost $5,000."

Ed thought for a moment and then said, "I don't care how much it will cost to send the remains back to Manila. That's what Ivy wants to do."

After hearing about the death in more detail, the Consul said, "Ed, you must have loved your future mother-in-law very much."

"It's not that," Ed said, feeling uncomfortable. "You see, I know of a case many, many years ago of a person that was buried in Jerusalem, and on the third day He was resurrected. Consequently, I don't want to take that chance with my prospective mother-in-law."

When Ed and Ivy returned to Manila the dynamics of the couple was shaky. Humiliated by Ed's attitude toward her mother, Ed and Ivy broke up,

As the trip from Jerusalem to Manila was exhausting and Ed still suffering from jetlag, he slept what he felt was a day and a night but in reality it was only 30 minutes by his watch when Dr. Perez phoned and said in a voice that was soft and tired, "Ed. I have some bad and some good news that you should know. Which do you want to hear first?"

"The bad news."

"The bad news is that your mother has just died."

"Oy, no and I haven't met my deadline. What happens now? What is the good news?"

"The good news is that the doctors at the Dr. R. Potenciano Medical Health Center used

a laser and hypnosis and brought her back to life."

"Wow, really, thank God mother has been revitalized?"

"And in fairly good health but keep on searching because she may have a relapse."

Ed felt hapless and tired at 11:00 that night so in order to energize his sad feeling, Ed stopped at a popular pub where karaoke was taking place and met Pinky Layola. The pub was jammed that night and there was a rowdy crowd.

The DJ gave Pinky a huge build up as she was determined that she could let her hair down.

Pinky decided to sing *Like a Virgin* and dedicated her singing to Ed. Shortly after she began singing she never heard so many boos in her entire life. Although she was a bit intoxicated that did not bother her and continued singing facing Ed, who seemed to be the only one in the pub with a sober face.

Eventually customers began throwing things at the stage, and when the host himself encouraged the crowd to boo even louder, Pinky felt that her role as a singer was done.

When she handed the host the microphone, there was a cheer so loud that the patrons from a rage house party next door came running in and saw Pinky trip and fall on her face. Pinky was taken to a nearby hospital to take care of her broken nose and Ed vowed to never connect with a potential mate who was drunk at the time and tried singing a karaoke tune.

The following afternoon while sitting on a bench at the Nike Recreational Park studying the *Bible* Ed observed a young lady that interested him highly. It was a warm day and she was hot and sweet, dressed in a seductive manner. On her head she had a straw hat profusely decorated with flowers, which was the fashion in those days. No one could look at her face and think she wasn't exceedingly beautiful as if she wasn't made by a man and a woman but a committee. So deeply did the young lady move Ed that he wanted to cling to her skirt and follow her to heaven. But after such a flawed thought, Ed decided to run to his cabin and on the door step hit upon a courage's idea.

Ed had just spent time studying the *Bible* in excruciating detail and noticed that Shakespeare had more quotes than the *Bible*, but in the book, *Leviticus*, warned Christians not marry their sister, aunt, mother, mother-in-law, daughter or even their granddaughter (should they be tempted). But nowhere in the *Bible* was there a rule against marrying oneself.

Of course the *Bible* also neglects to forbid anyone from marrying grandmothers, a budgie bird, or a pet fish.

Although his parents were against self-marriages Ed pondered night and a day as his feelings were split between the devil and the deep sea.

On one hand Ed felt like King Henry V111 of England who wanted to unmake his marriage so his next wife would give him a son and on the other hand, like Saint Thomas More, the king's chancellor at the time who said, "No way your majesty."

That's when Pastor Atupan stepped in and said, "Ed, you have a right to be happy. Marriage is a gift from God. It's OK to marry yourself? Let's begin."

At the no Name Universal church, and no one else inside, Pastor Atupan recited the marriage vows, by saying, "Ed Ramos, will you promise yourself as a husband also to be your own wife, to live as one in marriage? Will you love and comfort yourself, obey and honor yourself in sickness and in health and be faithful and honor yourself as long as you shall live?"

"I do," Ed said.

Ed had reasons for marrying himself when he did. Ever since he knew the concept of wedlock, he longed for a partner he could trust and could tell his deepest secrets without his parents knowing them.

Altogether Ed thought his marriage was a success for most part. He rarely argued with himself. In a few times that he did, he always won. And as far as sex went, well, it was whatever he made of it.

After two weeks of solitary married life Ed's sales weren't going that well, so he decided to split from himself, but Pastor Atupan said he couldn't just file for a divorce or an annulment on a moment's notice, he had to have legitimate justification.

As the pastor explained, Ed couldn't get a divorce because one isn't allowed in the Philippines, only an annulment, and even then, if he had been living apart from his spouse for at least a year, which would be difficult without major surgery, or if his spouse had been treated with cruelty.

Ed wasn't particularly willing to beat himself up or lounge around in prison, so he could annul himself. That left one option—adultery.

Ed got legal advice from one of the leading Manila attorneys, Antonio Huff, who was so caught up in his work that he didn't have time to publish his dream book titled *Making an Annulment Work in Five Easy Steps.*

It was a common saying in Manila that if one got into the rough to consult with topnotch Huff who had twenty 25 years' experience on annulment matters and advised Ed that he did not necessarily have to have sex with someone in order to get an annulment.

Upon that advice, Ed removed his wedding ring and since the annulment was an amicable one, he annulled himself.

Ed went away from Huff's office, whistling, but the following day he felt differently, as his yearning for a female companion returned. Ed still dreamed of the woman who would become his mate so he used his laptop to begin his search again.

He got on the internet and clicked on the website *Find a Mate* chatting room.

Ed first chatted with candidates in Baguio and Vigan and then Rita Corpus from Davao.

Things went fine until Rita had her photo on *Facebook.* Most of Rita's activities centered eating tuna sandwiches, watching television, video games and texting on the cellular phone.

Rita admitted that at age 23 she had an eating disorder and weighed 345 pounds. Not that Ed didn't like obese woman but research showed that obese women die 10 years earlier than one isn't, and an extreme diet wouldn't make one live longer. If that was true and Rita was 50 and Ed 60 it meant by that time Ed most likely would be a diabetic and search for another mate would be difficult, because of rising cost of living making a new search expensive, so he gave up on Rita.

The following day, Ed connected with Angelfish (whose real name was Nina Bandigan), and employed by the Dubai Electric Company.

Angelfish seemed like a genuine single after she bought herself a cellular phone so they could text each other.

Ed and Angelfish never ran out of things to say to each other. They got to meet in person after Angelfish jetted from Dubai and Ed picked her up at the Nimoy Aquino International Airport. As they drove throughout the city there was lot of loving and kissing as she twirled Ed's hair in her fingers.

This continued during dinner that night at the romantic Bruce Lim's Chef Table Restaurant. Ed was pleasantly surprised with Angelfish's appearance and demeanor where they giggled as if they were already married.

"Angelfish has a huge soul and when she laughs the sun comes out," Ed thought.

On the third day however, Ed scolded his potential bride for wasting a roll of colored wrapping paper imported from China. (Everything seemed to be imported from either China or India at the time).

Ed became infuriated when Angelfish tried to decorate a box to give him as a birthday present. Never-the-less Angelfish brought the gift to Ed and said, "This is for you Ed, Happy Birthday."

Ed was embarrassed by his earlier overreaction but his anger flared again when he found the box was empty. Ed yelled at Angelfish, "Don't you know when you give someone a present, there is supposed to be something inside?"

Angelfish looked at Ed pensively and said, "Ed, it's not empty at all. I blew kisses into the box. They are for you, my love."

Ed was crushed. He put his arms around Angelfish and asked for forgiveness. Only during the same day Angelfish received word from her supervisor that she was promoted and to start working in Abu Dhabi.

Ed kept that gold colored box by his bedside however, and when ever he was discouraged, he would take out an imaginary kiss and remember the love Angelfish gave him.

Ed was hurt before and beginning to feel that he would never find the appropriate mate, until he met with psychic Madame Espinosa, a romance specialist who recently published a book entitled *One Step to Finding a Mate and Lead a Contented Life*.

Her success in finding someone special was well documented using a combination of instinct personality, astrology, profiling and science.

While fingering her programmed *Blackberry* Madame Epinosa continued, "Alas, there's someone out there for everybody. In fact there are a lot of someone's out there. It has nothing to do with going to bars, cooking contests, rock climbing, and shopping, fishing or playing golf together.

The problem is that too often people search for their—life-long partner through clubs, organization and suggestions by their parents not suited to their personalities, culture, lifestyle and they seldom make the grade because of mistakes they make.

Ed, this is a reason why so many blind dates arranged by well-intentioned friends and family, tend to bomb, and why so many seemingly perfect marriages end up abruptly in a annulment."

"What kind of mistakes?"

"Well, let's take males for example. It's a fact males talk too much about past dates and themselves and they try too hard to impress attractive females especially if they wear clothing that is red in color. Dating must show a big heart and not a Big Apple."

"How about women?" Ed asked.

"Women mentally march every man they date up the aisle, they tend to burst into tears, dress inappropriately and trash their ex-boyfriends or husbands."

Madame Espinosa next, pulled out from her desk drawer a sheet of paper and said, "For now, here are names of two women: Desire Akuna and Jocelyn Mandac, which I have short listed. Why don't you date one of them and see how you make out."

These were heady times for Ed and to keep the search racing on, said, "Let's do that,"

His first date was with Desire Tempo who suffered from: What if? You know, Whatever and How are you?

When Desire asked Ed, "How are you?" he sighed and replied, "I have been asked that

question, even by my parents, a hundred times and I say, "Fine, thank you, but to be honest I'm not always fine. Do you really want to know how I feel when you ask 'How are you'? Or are you trying to be polite? The next time we are on a date and you ask, "How are you?" I'm going to say "I'm fine, I'm fine. There's nothing wrong with me, I'm as healthy as I can be."

But Ed did not date Desire again, because she sprung a surprise and got lost in the Palanan Wilderness Rainforest.

There are many ways of sending messages. Some are delivered by phone, some through email, Facebook, Twitter, YouTube and Skype. Some are sent as smoke signals; some are made to look like tiny paper airplanes with a written message and sent afloat or slipped inside a bottle and sent to sea hoping someone will find the message.

After watching Erlinda Prado's body language and listening to her love-gone-wrong talk, Ed noticed that this young lady was communicating with the spirit of the former Philippine president, Disdado Macapagal.

Although Ed believed that McDonald's would be the first to open a franchise on the moon, he did not think one should séance publicly with the dead, and discuss the president's 1997 plane crash.

So Ed blinked and was gone. Then, while at Pleasant Hills Park, met and dated Jocelyn Pasha and had a game of sipa with her. During the game which requires speed, agility and ball control, Jocelyn had neither and said that she was trying to find a man willing to become an instant father for her three year old son, Mike.

Ed didn't want a relationship where he would have to take care of one's baggage or a woman who was a member of the *Alien Gospel* sect that had taboos about almost everything including the avoidance of eating red meat but beans instead.

Ed felt that to eat only beans and no *Spam*, one had to fart which would disturb his concentration and keep clients away so the couple split and there was no romance with Jocelyn.

By now Ed was nearly a year older, a little smarter and prayed more often so when things were going wrong as most of the time they did, and the road Ed was trudging was uphill, funds were getting low and debts getting higher Ed took on as his personal motto: "Everything comes to him who waits."

But his mother anxiously said, "Son, you have a deadline to meet and must not wait any longer."

Upon his mother's suggestion Ed made an appointment with a little known medium; Nana De Jesus, who lived in a wooden house with a bay-window and a gravel lawn in the southern part of Mandaluyong and his mother said knew almost everything. "She can tell a horses age by looking at its teeth, the age of a tree by the circles inside and the weather but the sunset the evening before. She can also help those with a hearing problem by putting bees wax in their ears and lose weight by drinking coffee made with African beans and use rhubarb in the event of being constipated. Nana is phenomenal. She's a walking encyclopedia."

Neighbors however, called her, "The Quack doctor with magic power."

On the night that Ed met Mrs. De Jesus, she was still up and energetic with an intuitive sense of knowing how frustrated Ed had been.

Because Mrs. De Jesus loved to inspire people in order to fulfill their dreams she placed her hands on both sides of Ed's head and whispered several sentences. She then asked Ed to take her hand and pray with her in saying the, "Lord's Prayer."

This done, Mrs. De Jesus in a soft but still audible voice said, "Ed, congratulations, may God bless you. Tomorrow your guardian angel will deliver your ever-loving mate to the steps of Mandaluyong City Hall at approximately 12 15 so go home and rest."

Ed stamped his feet with joy and excitedly said, "Just a moment! That I did not expect. Sometimes I'm scared stiff. Other times I feel overwhelmed, and before I go, I must thank you for the part you played."

TWELVE

Although the wait for the day he would meet his wife had been a torment for Ed, the June afternoon following the appointment with Mrs. De Jesus, there wasn't a cloud in the sky and no wind disturbed the fresh warmth of a summer day. The flowers within the Mandaluyong City Maysilo Circle were blossoming profusely as Guardian Angel Michael, flew over the city before landing in front of City Hall.

After landing and hundreds of onlookers, including friends and relatives watching, the angel presented Linda Cane to Ed Ramos and the couple embraced each other. It was true love at first sight. To this point in time Ed had met many great women, but none as great as Linda Cane.

Turning to guardian angel Michael, Ed genuflected and said, "Thank you my dearest angel. I was delivered what I prayed for into the arms I was made for. Dearest angel I went through a one-year struggle but now feel blessed and oh so lucky. Oh mirror, mirror on the wall I have found my true love after all."

Then addressing his true love Ed continued, "Linda Cane, there were many invited but you are the only one chosen. With love that is true you are worth waiting for. I now caress you and want to press you to my heart."

Within an hour, angel Michael returned to heaven and Linda. Ed and his parents to Linda's parents' rice farm to enjoy a goat dinner, discuss how to survive economic crises, finalize wedding arrangements, and make certain that this wasn't going to be a shotgun marriage.

Following a short courtship, Ed found that he and Linda had the same astrophysical sign. Ed found Linda attractive, kind, honest, computer literate and her imagination fertile.

Both enjoyed reading newspapers and watching television about the recent Philippine disasters and calamities which included earthquakes, mud slides and floods, hijacking and the upcoming Philippine election. Above anything else, Linda liked Ed's personality and Ed, hers.

On the minus side, Linda at times appeared insecure. That insecurity eventually disappeared after she invited Ed and his parents to a farm barbecue which was a great success because that evening there was a happy event after Ed said, "Linda, you are adorable," and Linda responded with, "And so are you Ed. I think you are sweet. I feel as if I had known you for a long time. It's great the way you make me feel."

Ed's heart began to flutter as he got on his knees and taking Linda by her arm, asked her to close her eyes and after saying, "No peeking", continued, "Linda, will you marry me?"

Gorgeous Linda unhesitatingly replied, "Yes, oh dear Ed, I kept your calling card close to my heart and soul. I thought you'd never ask. You are patient and loving.

'I don't think I could ask for anything more. I would be delighted to be Mrs. Ramos for the rest of my life and longer. I'm a victim of your charms and letting the world know that I'm yours forever."

Ed had gone through enough storms of his own and if he lived 1000 years, he couldn't have found a more perfect mate.

At last satisfied his expectations had been met and as triumph had been reached over adversity, he slipped an engagement ring on Linda's finger and finally convinced his parents that he could find a bride within 1 year.

Minutes later as it began to rain Linda and Ed were inside the barn, among the hay, flies buzzing, mosquitoes biting, hens clucking, ducks quacking dogs barking and roosters crowing agreed to a traditional Christian marriage.

This done, Linda and Ed promised to love each other until they had to have false teeth and announced their wedding date as the following August 15th.

As soon as Linda changed her status from being a country single girl to Ed's fiancé, Ed never had been happier now that he had found a loving life-long mate which met his expectations. Ed's parents and those who knew Ed were relieved. Ed and Linda were happy too as parents' from both sides promised to help with the wedding arrangements.

Ed then said to everyone who cared to listen, "A dream is worth believing when it's deep within your heart. Even when no one believes, one must do his/her part and never, ever quit. Believe the dream you have, and do your best to make your dream come true.

You're always closest to your dream when you believe in you."

THIRTEEN

No event—not Pope John Paul 11 visit to Manila, the Beatles' first Philippine concert or Manny Pacquiao's winning a boxing match in Las Vegas,—was more exciting than Ed and Linda's wedding, especially the hoops they had to go through including parental consent and pre-marital counseling. By now the couple had paid for their wedding by selling advertising space at the ceremony and reception. Everything from the wedding rings to the reception at the New Horizon Hotel was donated after Ed and Linda got 24 companies to sponsor the nuptials in exchange of having corporate names appear on the invitations to the thank you cards.

The Philippine *Star* newspaper ran a photo of the couple sitting among their corporate sponsored wedding "gifts" in its Sunday edition. Linda however, drew the line by not having advertising banners draped across the No name Universal church aisle but not at the reception. Her perfume came from *Joans Perfumes*. Coffee was provided gratis by *Starbucks*. Advertisers had their names appear in bold print on the invitation and thank-you cards and napkins at the dinner table.

Ed woke at dawn and at 9:00 he and his best man, Adam Calunsag along with Linda's brother, Norman, went to pick up their barong that had been booked 3 weeks earlier but no one had placed the order. The only thing *Formalwear Rental Shop* could come up with was a rental suit and there were no shoes to match. The expected temperature in Manila was forecast to be 31C degrees.

As Ed left the store he placed the bag containing the suit on top of his Honda and drove away. The bag, besides containing the suit also contained Ed's wallet which contained money to pay for the use of the bridle suite, the reception and all his credit and identification cards. Realizing his loss Ed drove back to the store but couldn't find the bag so he called police and *Visa*.

Linda's day was far from her best day. Like women her age she couldn't decide if her toenails should be red or green. And at the *His and Her Salon* Linda's bridesmaids turned shades of white and blue and then after having breakfast at the Oriental Noodle House, Linda herself asked the waitress, "Where is the washroom?"

Linda's day was far from her best day. Like most women her age she dreamed of a fairy tale wedding surrounded by those near and dear to her. She imagined the reception would be the best night of her life and pictured dancing with Ed and all her friends. The reality was different.

As the marriage hours were approaching the comedy of errors continued. Linda had difficulty wakening before she and the bridesmaids had to leave for the church.

Meanwhile at Ed's cabin, Ed, the best man and Linda's brother, were enjoying a glass of beer and decorating the car with crepe paper and flowers.

As the tree men were decorating police called and said they had found the lost bag. It was 1:00 p. m. and the wedding was to begin at 3:00.

Police asked Ed to pick up the bag and wallet before 2:00.

Fortunately Ed picked up the bag and wallet on time but on his way back 95% of the flowers decorating the car had blown away by a gust of wind. Then on his way to the church his Honda had a flat tire. The rim was rusted so badly that the tire couldn't be taken off.

Ed ended up leaving the car where it was while he and the best man rushed to the nearest service station to purchase a can of rust remover. When Ed returned to the car there was a traffic violation ticket with a note attached on the windshield which read, "Hope your wedding ceremony goes better than your car."

It didn't.

As the No Name Universal Church bells were ringing and the birds singing their loudest. The wedding ceremony was an hour late, not because of Ed's doing, but because bumble bees were out in full force that day and Linda had several stuck in her veil and her mother had difficulty to dig them out.

Then while entering the church with her father, Linda was wearing a white dress and veil and carrying a bouquet of flowers. At the same time the organist was playing and the Gospel Choir singing the traditional, *Here Comes the Bride.* All of a sudden Linda tripped and fell. When she picked herself up and continued walking down the aisle someone pushed the organist aside and began playing, *"The Lady is a Tramp."*

Linda was still in the arms of her father who as he was handing his daughter to the restless Ed, Linda paused, kissed her father and then whispered, "Dad, we do not want underwear for Christmas this year. Just give us your credit card."

Those near the front pews responded with ripples of laughter and even the pastor smiled broadly.

Next, as the bride and groom walked forward Ed stepped on her train snapping the elastic. Once the elastic was retrieved Ed and Linda walked together until they reached the altar where they realized Pastor Atupan wasn't marrying them but a novice substitute female minister from Cebu City, Reverend Wendy De Leon.

Pastor Atupan was allegedly taken ill after a noodle at the Oriental Noodle House had stuck in his larynx and the doctor attending him said, "You must not preach for at least another week."

The truth however, is that Pastor Atupan picked up his fortune cookie with a warning, "You will be in danger if you marry a pair of cousins. Say nothing."

The marriage ceremony was going on without a glitch until blessing of the ring and the substitute minister waved her hand and the elastic in Linda's veil gave way flying a meter behind her. The minister then covered the microphone in front of her with her hand and to the bride and groom said softly, "That was a powerful blessing, wasn't it?"

When the minister came to the part, "If anyone has reason why these two people should not marry, speak up now or forever hold your peace," a boy about 5 years of age, ran up the aisle yelling, "Daddy, Daddy, I'm here!"

The joke, planned by the best man, aroused the crowd that it took 5 minutes before the Gospel Choir sang *Bringing in the Sheaves* and the ceremony continued.

When it was time for vow-taking the minister said, "A circle is the symbol of the sun and the earth and the universe, of wholeness and perfection, and peace and love. It is worn on the third finger because of an ancient Greek belief that a vein from that finger goes directly to the heart.

"These rings mark the beginning of a long journey together. Wear them proudly, for they are symbols which speak of the love that you have for each other."

The wedding vows are the words how much the bride and groom love each other. To express exactly how Ed and Linda felt their creative juices were flowing when they wrote their own vows earlier for the joyous occasion.

Turning towards Ed the minister continued, "And do you Ed Ramos, promise that when you go shopping at Asia Pacific Mall that you will not get lost?"

"I do."

"And do you Candy Cane promise that when you are out publicly with Ed you will not eat garlic, onions or sardines and not forget to brush your teeth?"

"I do but my name isn't Candy, its Linda."

Ed and Linda beamed after the minister married the couple by saying, "Linda Cane, Ed Ramos's peach and Ed Ramos, Linda Cane's plum, I now pronounce you a fruit salad."

The substitute minister did not use the conventional, 'For better or worse until death do us part', because it wasn't fashionable in parts of the Philippines to be married for a life time—4 years the most and then an annulment. And there was a movement throughout the Philippines to have same-sex marriages accepted as an individual's right.

Later in the ceremony as the minister was about to preach about bonds and unity Ed and Linda could not light the unity candle because the wick hadn't been straightened out. After a full minute of holding their candles over the unity one with no results, the minister pulled out a pocket knife from her pocket and dug the wick out to everyone's relief.

But due to the smell from the perfumed burning wax and there was no air conditioning in the church, Ed's mother began swaying back and forth and then passed out.

After the ceremony of vow-taking and signing the register, the organist played and the Gospel Choir sang as part of the recessional ceremony, the Realtor's hymn *I Got a Mansion Just over the Hilltop.* Ed and Linda then emerged arm-in arm in front of the church to the delight of the wedding guests and other onlookers, who blew soap bubbles at the bride and groom.

Why soap bubbles instead of rice? Because according to Linda who knew something about agriculture, there was a shortage of rice for dinner plates in Asia.

At the reception, a banner across listed names of businesses which sponsored the wedding and included: Best Realty. Philippine Airline, Coca Cola, Budget Rent a Car, New Horizon Hotel, Hewlett Packard Philippines, Commonwealth Food Inc.

United Laboratories, Puma Spring and Rubber Industries, Forum Robinson's, Jollibee, Market Place Mall, Mrs. Field's Bakery, San Miguel Beer, Alta Moda Furniture Inc., Fareast Bamboo, Starbucks, Wellhead O & G Insurance, Filipino Travel Center and Saint Claire Funeral Homes.

The bride and groom were happy, but could have been happier, if the best man had not been involved in a fist fight in the parking lot with Linda's brother and also the caterer had not forgotten to deliver the bottled Coke and Sprite. Ed was almost in a screaming mood as 150 guests wanted to put a little mix with their liquor

Another reason Ed was tearing his hair out was because the guest book suddenly disappeared and someone prematurely released 12 pigeons inside the hotel ballroom and no fireworks were available for that night. Also the band, *Rock Tunes Five*, was late in arriving because heavy traffic the musicians were late in arriving.

And then when the instruments were in place, the master of ceremonies asked the band leader that the tunes; *Roll Me Over In The Clover, Hokey Pokey, Goodnight Moon, Good Night Stars, Good Night Broken-down Cars, We're All Liberals and The Bank Foreclosed My Home Yesterday* not be played.

When the Coke and Sprite arrived, the bar opened for the night and the reception began with the groom and bride receiving good wishes and hand shakes from those invited who were mostly realtors from the Best Realty where Ed worked, and the neighbors and friends of the Cane and Ramos families.

The reception progressed smoothly with Reverend Wendy De Leon saying grace. The main menu consisted of sliced pork marinated in garlic and pancit, palabok and of course all the Starbuck's coffee one wanted to drink. The meal went well until a bone got stuck in the bride's throat. A guest of the two families, Dr Perez, removed the bone without much of a commotion.

This was followed by burst of laughter and cheers as the guests banged their cutlery against their plates suggesting that the bride and groom should stand up and kiss.

And when they did, each time it wasn't just a peck on the cheek but a passionate tongue-lashing which made the bride's toes curl with happiness. In between each stand/kiss/sit the master of ceremonies read a list of congratulatory telegrams.

One was from Manila's Chief of Police that read: "Ed, I'm sorry you had trouble with your tire. Just a reminder, that your guests at the reception remain sober."

Another read: "As soon as your honeymoon is over, just a reminder that you can get a good deal on your furniture. Nothing down, and two years to pay. Congratulations Linda and Ed.—Alta Moda Furniture.

Then there was a congratulatory message that read: Ed and Linda, congratulations on reaching an important step in your life. Remember however, both of you have neglected to file your SSS tax return. Signed—Revenue Philippines.

Another congratulatory telegram read: "Sorry I'm unable to attend your wedding reception. At this moment I'm campaigning for a possible election at a time when global warming, political corruption, Abusayaf insurgence in Mindanaoa and the high price

for gasoline have become major issues. To say the least, the next session of parliament appears to be stormy. Hope you and Linda have a little son. President Gloria Macapagal Arroyo.

Then it was the MC's turn to propose a champagne toast to the bride and groom but when he pried the bottle cork open, it flew upward bouncing off the ceiling and ending in the bridesmaid's bowl of soup. He then he continued, "I now propose a toast to the bride's throat. Don't you think Dr. Perez did an excellent job in removing a bone from it?"

Some laughed, some smiled, while others booed believing meat getting stuck in one's throat was a reflection on *Spam* imported from America.

The MC apologized and then quoted Montaign, an essayist who lived in the 14th century and at one time said, 'Marriage is like a bird cage: It seems that birds outside are desperate to get in and those inside desperate to get out'.

At any rate may both of you have a long and happy life. And please remember eighty percent of married men in the Philippines often cheat on their wives."

"How about the remaining twenty percent?" one of the guests hollered.

"The rest cheat as contract workers abroad."

Those present laughed uproariously."

As soon as the MC toasted the bride and groom, the best man proposed one whose punch line was, "Marriage is an institution but who wants to live in one?"

And then Linda's father who discarded has farm clothing and was dressed his Sunday best, took over and said, "My experience is that a successful man is one who makes more money than his wife can spend, but a successful woman is one who can find such a man. I think Linda did."

This done, Ed's father said, "Like in the soft drink industry love is a matter of chemistry. Linda, make sure Ed doesn't treat you like toxic waste."

Then Ed stood up and in his poetic toast said:

"Linda, here's a toast to you and me,

In our lifetime I hope we never disagree'

But if, perchance, we ever do,

Then here's to me and, and the heck with you."

The guests burst out with laughter and when the laughter died down Ed continued:

"Linda, I did not mean that, what I meant was, may our married life be long and happy,

The cares and sorrows few;

And the friends around us remain faithful and true.

I now propose a toast to my beautiful wife, Linda, my pride and joy."

By the time toasting concluded and the photographer, a practical joker, had taken pictures of the wedding party, and then unknown to Linda and Ed, he secretly collected keys from members of the guests.

Then when the MC spoke again he said, "Ladies and gentlemen, Linda realizes that that Ed has had many girlfriends before she became his bride.

I understand that there were: Alfa, Eugenia, Lisa, Trisha and many more until he met Linda. Well, Linda at this time would greatly appreciate if any of them are here tonight and have keys to his condo returned."

On a cue from the photographer for all female key participants to bring their keys forward to the head table, ten women showed up, five disguised being pregnant and two as grandmas. One used a cane and the other a walker.

Guests and friends oh, how they laughed at that moment and when the laughter died down each person went to the bar to have another drink.

Linda then enlivened the party a bit more by believing Ed had the finest voice in Manila and exclaimed, "Ed, do sing us something!"

Ed got up, smiled and turning to his bride tried to think of something suitable for the occasion, something with seriousness from the past and began to sing, *Hallelujah*.

The band drum banged, the fiddle growled, the saxophone blared and then Linda herself and the guests joined in singing the chorus.

The loud blend of voices and music, like a hurricane, shook the ballroom inside, and outside in the parking lot, a variety of Philippine birds, animals, and fish, some dangerously close to being extinct, joined in the celebration of their own wishing Ed and Linda happiness every minute of their life.

To begin, all the animals, birds and fish in Manila signed a promissory treaty that there would be no hate or jealousy and neither animal nor bird or fish would be harmed even if one was tempted. Then the monkeys sent out invitation cards with kind regards and suggested the guests be dressed in their fashion best. When this was done, the much loved elephant, as the master of ceremonies, said to the group to be at ease. But a poodle named Doodle said, "I'm unable to be at ease because I'm always chasing fleas."

"Hold it!" interrupted the elephant, "There will be no tears tonight! Just love, fun and laughter!"

An eagle said," Well, our Philippine forests are being destroyed so the invitations should have been void."

The egret agreed, "We should protect eagles, white squirrels and tarsier monkey's as they are without a measure our treasure."

A baboon emailed a message from Saskatoon that he couldn't attend because he had an appointment to ride in a hot air balloon. And the horse was absent too, because he had a hoarse throat.

Hearing the news, the parrot began to swear "O dear, don't cuss", cried out the octopus.

A crab came to the reception in a cab and played *Basang Basa Sa Ulan* with a fork and spoon while on his horn a unicorn played the tune *Pagdating ng Panahon*.

All the nocturnal creatures in Manila City: owls, bats, rats, night hawks, frogs, and even birds that have no wings but can fly at night, participated in the celebration.

As the rooster scratched and crowed, the hen did a chicken dance. The elephant then said, "Attention please. All the guests are now ready to dine and cheer. At the bar we have Coke and Sprite and lots tuba wine but no rum or beer."

"Oh dear," said a deer. "I fear I can't hear because I have something in my ear. Did the elephant say, *"Ikaw Ang Lahat Sa Akin?"*

The goat, after having several sips of Sprite, explained to the deer what the elephant had said, and then sang a song about a chimpanzee that had a bad knee while watching the caribao fights in Iloilo. The song was titled *Umatak Ang Ulan.*

A dolphin then sang *Be My Love* and another about seeing a school of mermaids' during a Manila Bay sunset.

Next, the king of beasts, the lion, said to the elephant, "Excuse me while I enjoy a glass of tuba wine."

"That must be fine," said the porcupine and with a shout, said to a trout, "Did you notice how Leo smacked his lips?"

"I'd smack mine too," said the kangaroo, "If the crocodile wasn't sitting next to the gnu."

This was the time that the elephant bowed reverently and said, "Listen, dear animals, fish and birds to what I have to say. The king of the animal world must have his way and now its time to eat and dance. First on the menu the birds have prepared a delicious bird nest soup and then we can enjoy malatang, other stuff, and a dish of fish."

To which an ostrich replied, "Excuse me but first before I eat I have to go to the bathroom."

As the ostrich did his thing, the cariboa proposed a toast to the bride and groom.

As soon as this was done, and tables cleared, the elephant continued, "Listen everyone, let's rejoice. It's karaoke time, time to sing and dance."

To which a whale answered, "Dear Mrs. Elephant at this moment I cannot dance because I lost my tail, while the raccoon picked up a broom and danced alone while singing the tune "*Congratulations to the bride and groom.*"

As soon as the peacock and a gnu heard the news, each put on their dancing shoes and became a pair on a tear as they danced the popular bamboo *Tinklink* dance.

Next, the bat, a bit fat and wearing a straw hat while resting on a mat, along with the fox put on their dancing socks and with the Flying Lemur joining them, danced the vibrant dance of the Cordilera Mountains. When completed, the elephant urged other animals, fish and birds to have a banana and not to stand around and gossip but to pair-up and dance and sing some more.

"Hi, Hi," said a magpie. "Ho, Ho." said a crow, and "Hi, Diddle, Diddle." said a seagull, who was in the middle, and continued, "This isn't a riddle and although we have no fiddle, we can sing a little, and joined a frog siting on a log and a sparrow on an arrow, and together, as a group, sang the romantic *Everyone Should Love Someone Some Time.*

You may not believe this, but the alpaca named Joe paired up with squirrel named Flo and were on the go. So was a monkey eating eagle with his cousin, named Tarsier. Also dancing were the dwarf buffalo with a black faced spoonbill, a rat with a cat, a sow with a cow, and a duck, who after saying, "Quack, Quack," danced with a lizard, a rabbit with a brown booby, a giraffe with a hippopotamus and a cockatoo with a turtle. The turtle couldn't dance or sing well, because the day before he accidently swallowed a plastic bottle but the other animals, fish and birds began dancing and by leaping, jumping, flying and stumbling.

That's when the pigeon flew onto a table, and still able, paired up with an ass, sitting on the grass and then each couple danced some more.

Despite the slight commotion there was a lot of emotion as everyone danced the fox-trot, waltz, polka, cha-cha and the twist, until midnight, a time when the elephant blew her trunk which awakened a dozing skunk, and after yawning, said. "I'm reluctant to say this, but there is a note on the post from an owl and a sheep that it's midnight and since everyone is exhausted, it's time to go home and sleep."

Meanwhile, inside the ballroom, as Linda and Ed were singing Ed blew his nose with the sound of a trombone and amid the general emotion and commotion, not to be outdone Linda's brother turned the reception topsy-turvy when he tried to show the bride and groom that he could dance.

He leaped on one of the tables snapping his fingers above his head and did strange fancy steps which aroused Linda's father who was slightly intoxicated by now, shout at him but Linda's brother continued dancing. Linda's' father then cried out in a voice like thunder, "Hey! We are tired of your acrobatic tricks!" and tried to expostulate him.

Linda's brother was finally ejected but not before he had another black eye. But then Maria the maid of honor who was a small person with a very short nose jumped onto the same table and sang songs which were rather risqué.

Maria was a little role of fat with very short legs and active as a squirrel. Between each verse she stopped singing in order to have a mouthful of nuts which were in the centerpiece at the head table. But then when she did several wheel carts, she too was taken away.

A half-hour later Linda and Ed planted themselves in front of a wall.

Linda then turned her back to a group of unmarried women and flung her bouquet towards them.

Unfortunately the trajectory of the bouquet was such that it landed on top a chandelier and there were no ladders available to retrieve it so instead those present chanted, "Throw your bra! throw your bra!"

Next from under Linda's dress Ed pulled out a garter. He turned his back towards a group of marriageable men and flung it towards them.

There was a scramble to retrieve the garter but unfortunately Ed's best man, got trampled in the rush and resuscitation had to be given.

By the time he recovered the wedding cake collapsed from the weight of the candles and there were no pieces available for the guests to taste.

As soon as the tables were cleared the party went on until 1:30 a. m. with rockin' and rollin', two-stepping and waltzing. Ed and Linda danced the *Minute Waltz* in 30 seconds.

Why only 30 seconds? Because Linda's right shoe heel came off and the maid of honor, Maria, forgot to include *Krazy Glue* in the bride's emergency tote bag that included just-in-case items: pain reliever, tissue and smelling salts.

The ceremony officially came to a close when bride and groom finally took to the floor and the band played, *"The Last Dance."*

As soon as the reception ended and the band had left, Ed and Linda realized their parents hadn't made arrangements to clean the ballroom which had to be cleaned because it was reserved for a Sunday school classes later in the morning. By the time Ed and Linda arrived at their bridal suite it was 4:00 a.m. And when they entered, couldn't believe their eyes—windows were left open and the bridle suite was filled with mosquitoes.

As Ed and Linda couldn't find anyone in management to rectify the problem nor could they get another room so they crawled into bed and covered themselves with a feathered quilt and slept until noon.

Queen Victoria of England who married her cousin Prince Albert, their marriage and love for each other lasted through turbulent political years. In the morning when the Manila public read a newspaper account of Ed and Linda's wedding, they were in shock to learn that Ed and Linda kept a secret that they were cousins also, and that Ed like. the Queen, was developing a keen interest in Philippine politics.

For those planning to get married Ed and Linda have two pieces of advice. First about marriage—don't get angry when you are faced with sleeping under a feathered quilt as a feather may get stuck in your ear. The second advice is about the wedding itself. When it comes to planning one, don't rely on relatives. Maybe you can arrange to have your reception at McDonald's. After all you can order a beef Big Mac and all those party hats. Ed and Linda had no difficulty in adjusting to their new life until now and and their marriage began to blossom. They seldom argued and when they did, it was over trivial things that amused them after like, who had forgotten to set the alarm clock at night.

FOURTEEN

Boracay Island has everything, including sand for the children, sun for the family, and sharks for the mother-in-law.

Its surprising the obstacles Ed and Linda had to overcome in order to enjoy their honeymoon. In order to reach Boracay from Metro Manila the two-lane Strong Republic Nautical Highway is an integral segment of a vehicle/ferry route with connections available in the city of Iloilo for onward destinations

The honeymoon trip began at Mandaluyong City with a "Just Married" sign hanging from the rear bumper of the Honda. Ed began driving with the thought of spending time in Boracay and other islands including Cebu and Siquijor, the home of Linda's bridesmaid, Maria, who lives in a squatter village.

Frustrated by the slow traffic in front of him Ed pushed the pedal to the floor dodging in and out among slower vehicles which included buses, jeepenys and large transport trucks. Ed seemed convinced that the highway actually had three lanes with an imaginary third lane in the middle for passing, both directions at the same time in a hair-raising game of chicken.

Along the way Ed was stopped by a cop for running a red light. The cop asked Ed for his driver's license. Ed removed his sun glasses and wanted to argue with the cop about how fast he was going. "I' certain I wasn't going 140 kilometers in a 100 zone I didn't see any radar."

"Sir, we didn't catch you in a radar trap. We spotted and timed you by helicopter patrol," the cop replied and gave Ed a traffic violation ticket.

A short distance further Ed almost hit a flock of chickens crossing the highway when he was rear-ended by another motorist. Ed's bumper was damaged only slightly, so both continued on their way without exchanging addresses.

When Ed reached the port of Batangas, he boarded a ferry and when it reached Calapan, Mindoro, they stopped at Eddies Place in the Puerto Galera restaurant for lunch. Just as the food was placed in front of them, three rough-looking, long-haired, tattooed, motorcycle drivers, pulled off their helmets and seeing Ed's car, ripped off the JUST MARRIED sign. Then they went inside the restaurant, harassed the bride and groom, grabbed their food and divided it among themselves.

Ed and Linda did not say a word. They got up quietly, paid their bill, turned up the radio and continued their journey towards Boracay. After they had driven away, a member of the motorcycle gang said to the owner of the restaurant, Donavan Alboro, "He sure isn't much of a man, is he?"

"I guess not and not much of a driver also," Alboro replied.

"What do you mean?' the motorcyclist asked

"He just ran over 3 motorcycles as he backed his car in the parking lot."

Examining the damaged motorcycles, a second gang member became angry and said, "Mark my word; we will get even with him."

After leaving Calapan, a patrolman stopped Ed near Pinamalayan still in Mindoro. Ed didn't think he was speeding so he asked the patrolman, "What's wrong?"

"You are driving without a rear signal light, sir."

Ed got out of the car and opened the trunk. Suddenly he went to pieces. "Oh, oh!" he cried out. "How in the world could this happen?"

"Calm down," the officer said. "Driving without a rear signal light isn't that serious of an offence."

"Rear signal light? I don't care about the signal light. What about our luggage? We forgot my wife's suitcases in Mandaluyong City."

After Ed was given another violation ticket and since he didn't like driving at night and tired after driving all the way from Metro Manila, he tried to register at several hotels in Roxas City, a medium size city and a center of copra and aquaculture production, only to find all rooms had been taken because it was the height of the tourist season. Ed and Linda were having the same experience at the Bela Norte Beach Club Hotel.

"I'm sorry," the night clerk apologized. We don't have a room left in this place. Every room has been booked in advance. I'm terribly sorry, sir, that we can not accommodate you."

Knowing something about the service industry Ed said, "I know for example, that you always hold back a room or two for emergencies. Do you mean to tell me that if the President came here tonight you wouldn't find a room for her?"

"I guess you are right," the night clerk apologized. "We strain a point and would find something for the president."

"Fine, then give us the room because I know that the President Macapagal-Arroyo won't be here tonight. I have firsthand information that she is in Manila getting ready for the next election."

The night clerk gave Ed and Linda a room and after they registered and were alone, Ed picked up Linda and carried her through the threshold at the same time saying, "At last, my darling."

"At last, what?"

"At last we are really one."

"Yes, dear," Linda said, "But from the practical point of view it would be advisable to order dinner for two."

Ed got on the phone and ordered a bucket of sea food delivered to their room.

That night, when it was time to go to sleep, Linda got tired of looking at the view so she wandered into the bedroom and crawled into bed. Ed stood by a window to enjoy the setting sun and fish jumping in nearby Baybay Lake.

"Dear," Linda called, "Why don't you come to bed?"

"Because."

"Because, what?"

"Because my mother told me that if I ever got married this would be the most wonderful night of the year and I'm not going to miss it."

Linda had gone over the honeymoon scene a hundred times in her mind. Ed would carry her over the threshold and murmur sweat endearments. His lips would find hers and they would move to the bedroom. It is true that when Ed and Linda registered he carried Linda over the threshold but after gazing at the multi-colored setting sun and jumping fish, the love-making for Linda was finished before it began. Ed had fallen asleep and Linda lay in bed wondering, what next?

The following morning, Ed and Linda entered the Hacienda Hotel Restaurant for breakfast and sat on a stool. At the counter, to be helpful, the waitress while handing each a menu, said, "I have rice, lichen, pancit, chicken legs and ..."

"Hold it," Ed interrupted the waitress. "You have your troubles and we got ours. Why don't you skip your sad story and order each of us bacon and eggs, toast and a cup of coffee?"

As soon as the waitress placed the order she returned to the spot where Ed and Linda were sitting and said, "You say you got troubles? What kind of troubles?"

"We do have a problem," Ed admitted. "My wife wants a German shepherd dog for security sake but the price I can get one for is 5,000 pesos. That's too much."

"I'll say it is. You are getting ripped off. I can get you one for 200."

"Am I ever gland we ran into you? How soon can you deliver the dog?" Linda asked.

"Let me make a phone call and I'll let you know," the waitress replied and went to a phone to make her call.

The dog was delivered within an hour. What the waitress did was to phone SPCA but that did not matter, what did, Linda felt she would be protected at a time Ed was away selling real estate. "Thank you, thank you," Linda said as Ed paid for the dog and placed the animal in the back seat of the car.

Ed and Linda were on the road again, and as Ed still couldn't swim, booked into the Regency Beach Resort on Boracay Island, staying there for 3 days.

At one time a secret hideaway for private individuals but now filled with international tourists who participated in aqua sports, shopped and party hopped. On the final day of their Boracay honeymoon there was an advisory from Environment Philippines advising Bella Norte Beach that it should brace its self as a vicious electrical storm was on its way.

Ed recalled the time he was still single and courting Louisa, when he was on a Boracay beach the first time and almost carried away by a typhoon. Sure enough several hours later as Ed and Linda saw clouds covering the sun and there was an electric storm with thunder and lightning and at same time whitecaps rolling towards shore, accompanied by a wind at 90 kilometers an hour.

Seeing the storm ahead of them, Ed and Linda picked up their belongings, climbed into their Honda and during a 3 hour dusty journey, arrived in Iloilo City where the air was warm and fragrant.

On arrival they booked into the Hotel Del Rio, and the following day took a tour of the urbanized community.

Included in the tour, they watched witches riding on broomsticks through the air. Not to be confused with a magic carpet, also a flying object, Ed as a former Canadian found this interesting and purchased a broom and took a flying lesson. "Broom riding," Ed said to Linda, that broom riding would be an excellent way to overcome Manila's heavy traffic and an excellent method of transportation, hopping from place to place taking real estate listings.

After spending a day and night in Iloilo City Ed and Linda drove to Cebu City to admire the scenery and find out why it was the fastest growing community in the Philippines and the location where in 1521Magellan was killed by his adversary, Lapu Lapu. As soon as Ed opened the car door, the dog, whose name was Dominic, jumped out and took after a cat. In spite of much whistling, calling, horn blowing and waiting for several hours, the dog did not return so the new bride and groom decided to place an ad in the Cebu *Daily News* newspaper.

"You are late for today's edition," the editor said as soon as the bride and groom walked into the newspaper office. "This issue of the paper goes to press in another fifteen minutes."

"I wish you could squeeze the ad some place," Linda pleaded. "This is a valuable dog and we are offering a 5000 peso reward."

"Write the ad up," the editor said. "If it's that important, we'll hold the presses another fifteen minutes." Linda wrote the ad, paid for it and with Ed headed back to their car.

Ed was about to start the engine when it occurred to Linda that she had not included the cellular phone number in the ad and both rushed to the newspaper office expecting everyone being busy. Instead there was no one around except the janitor. The presses weren't running and no one was in the office.

"Where's everybody?" Linda asked the janitor." I expected to see presses running and everybody working."

"Oh!" the janitor replied. "They stopped the presses and everybody took off 5 minutes ago. They are looking for someone's dog which if found, there's a 5000 peso reward."

Ed and Linda never did find the dog and within the city spotted a billboard that read: Bernardo's Auto Service. *Try Us Once and You'll Never Go Anywhere Else.*

Here the street was in such deplorable shape that Ed drove into a deep pothole which was filled with mud and water that splashed the car engine, killing it dead.

It cost fifty 2500 pesos to have the car towed to Bernardo's Auto Service, and another 5000 to get the engine repaired.

When Ed and Linda were ready to take off, Linda said to Bernardo, who repaired the engine, "Why don't you fill the hole with dirt?"

Bernardo's answer was, "It's hard to do during daytime because of the heavy traffic. You must remember that hundreds of vehicles pass through Cebu each day on their way to and from Boracay."

Linda then asked, "Then why don't you fill it during night time?"

Bernardo was candid, "I confess that business is slow these days and that's why I fill the hole with water."

As soon as Ed and Linda registered at the *Holiday Inn* they did what other tourists do by shopping at souvenir shops for something to bring home.

At one of the shops Ed purchased a beautiful T-shirt with an intricate design which included Cebuano words. Ed thought he would give the shirt Linda as a reminder of the honeymoon so he asked the clerk to translate the writing.

"Very easy," the clerk said, "It says smoking may be hazardous to your health."

Linda meanwhile purchased a slingshot with the words *I Visited Cebu* inscribed on the handle. This was no ordinary slingshot made out of cheep plastic from China but one made of Canadian metal. Instead of using stone pebbles this slingshot could use golf balls, which when fired, could travel 100 yards at speeds of up to thirty meters per second. Linda also purchased a blue budgie bird in a cage just in case Ed was out of town she had someone to talk too

Next, Ed and Linda were driving on a one-way street and met up with a runaway caribou that refused to leave their route. It seemed that a laser beam from a galaxy controlled this Philippine national animal.

The faster Ed went so would the caribou kicking up gravel. Suddenly a stone the size of a golf ball struck the windshield cracking it from top to bottom.

Can you imagine how alarmed Linda became? It's difficult to believe that Ed would not harm this animal.

The caribou eventually disappeared but not before Ed met a patrolman screaming, "Hey, there! Where do you think you're going?"

To the *Holiday Inn* but I must be late because all the cars are coming back."

As the policeman approached closer he asked, "Didn't you see the arrows?"

"Arrows. What arrows?"

Then the cop asked, "Do you know why I pulled you over?"

Linda, uptight, without thinking, said, "Because my husband couldn't catch the other cars."

"No," the cop said, "Why I pulled you over is because you are on a one-way street."

"But I was going one way," Ed said.

It was here that Linda interrupted the conversation and while pointing a finger at Ed said rather sarcastically, "See, didn't I tell you not to follow the carabao. Now what have you got to say?"

"The patrolman turned towards Ed and asked, "Who is that woman with you?"

"That's my bride, Linda. We are on our honeymoon."

"Well, sir, drive on," the patrolman said, "Looks like you are in enough trouble without me giving you a ticket. Enjoy your stay in Cebu City, the Queen of the South."

But things weren't enjoyable the following day when Ed met a Bearcat (Binturomg) near a public picnic site.

Ed expected the animal to be tame and was shocked when he was taking a snapshot, it attacked him.

Since there was no use arguing with a bearcat and there is no such a thing as bearcat politics or plea bargaining, Ed was cornered and had no option but to fall to his knees and pray. Ed was surprised, however, when the bearcat suddenly stopped attacking him and got on his knees also.

"That's marvelous," Ed said to the bearcat, "You joining me in prayer when I was giving up myself for being dead."

The bearcat made loud, grunting noises which translated from bearcat language into English meant, "Don't interrupt, sir, as I'm saying grace before I have you for my meal."

Seeing the difficulty Ed was in Linda picked up the slingshot she had purchased, inserted a golf ball and with all her strength stretched the elastic and let it go—zing! Within a split second the golf ball struck the hungry bearcat on the head, stunning it momentarily.

As soon as the bearcat scampered into the wilderness and Ed recovered from the shock of being attacked, he and Linda returned to the hotel where during the afternoon they decided to play a round of golf. Their game was progressing nicely until the 16th hole when the game was interrupted by two crocodiles known for their agility and notoriety. The crocodiles were fighting among themselves right on top of the ball. Both Linda and Ed were afraid to approach the fighting crocodiles because if they got near one of the crocodiles and maybe both, would attack them like one attacked a tourist in Palawan.

"So why don't you chase the crocodiles away with a golf cart?" Linda suggested and that's what Ed did but not before the larger crocodile tipped over the cart and bit Ed on his rear end.

Prior to that, Ed managed to go out of bounds on the 15th hole while Linda went out of the bounds on the 16th and then, they went into the 17th hole tied. The hole was a long par 3-195 yards. It seemed even longer on a hot summer day.

Ed had the honor to teeing-off first using a five iron and came within several feet of the pin. Linda planted her ball in the middle of a pond nearly hitting a goose. What was good for the goose wasn't for Linda and that did it.

After going through the motion of playing out the 18th hole, Ed and Linda

parked their carts, at the clubhouse and returned to the hotel where in the lobby, they ran into Ed's friend from Quezon City, Sammy Banko, who was registered in the same hotel after getting married on the same day as Linda and Ed did.

While Sammy and Ed were alone Sammy whispered to Ed, "Ed, boy, let's see who can perform our manly duties the most often tonight. I'll wager you a San Miguel beer six pack that I can do it more often with my bride Lisa, than you can with Linda."

Ed agreed to the challenge and that night he and Linda made love two different times, each time marking a stroke (11) on the bedroom wall.

The following morning Sammy entered Ed's and Linda's room and asked, "Well, how many times did you and Linda do it?"

Ed pointed to the two strokes on the wall (11), which surprised Sammy.

"Wow!" he cried out, "You surprise me. You did it eleven times. Do you want to know something?"

"What?"

"You beat Lisa and me by 3 times"

The following morning, when Linda rolled out of bed she excitedly asked Ed, "Where is our car, dear?"

"I parked it and the hotel parking lot last night."

"But it's not there."

"It has to be there," Ed said as he jumped out of the bed and then mentally retraced the evening when he last saw the car. "We were at the Basilica del So to pray and admire the San Nino image and the site where Lapu Lapu killed Magellan in the year 1521. It was midnight when we returned to the hotel."

Finally it registered, "Someone must have stolen our antique burgundy colored Honda."

"Cars don't get stolen in Cebu. This is a honeymoon town and not like Manila where teenagers cruise the alleys and rip off wheels for excitement."

"But it's gone. Now what do we do?"

"Call the police."

Instead of phoning, Ed took Linda by the arm and walked to the police office.

As soon as they explained what had happened the constable on duty said, "I know how you feel. That's what I went through when my car was stolen."

"A police car stolen?" Linda asked.

"That's right. Car theft these days are so routine in every Philippine city, that even policemen who take theft reports, have their vehicle stolen."

The officer then had Ed fill out a car-theft report in which he wrote," I parked my car at midnight and it wasn't there when Linda and I woke up this morning."

Glancing at the report the officer asked, "Was the tank full?"

"Three quarters."

"Then they could be driving around for a while."

Ed didn't get a sense of urgency that a crime-fighting approach was mobilized on his behalf and then was given a file number for the insurance company.

As Ed and Linda were making their exit the cop said. "If the car is found police will get in touch with you."

Ed and Linda returned to their hotel room where Ed phoned his insurance agent who said, "Because this involves theft of an entire vehicle, I'll hear from the insurance company and then phone you."

"You mean to say there's theft of parts of vehicles?" Linda asked.

"There is. I see where there's a lot you have to learn about car insurance."

That afternoon Ed called the police station and asked the dispatcher if his Honda had been located. The dispatcher punched the license number into a computer and announced, "Still outstanding, sir."

Ed and Linda decided it was a waste of time sitting around and waiting for the phone to ring so they walked the streets and alleys of Cebu to see if thieves had ditched the car.

They hadn't. In the evening Ed again checked with the police but the officer on duty said, "Still outstanding, sir."

Ed felt totally devastated until the insurance agent phoned and said, "Ed, the loss-of use clause in your policy pays for the use of a rental car."

And then the agent explained that if the car wasn't recovered in a week it probably would never be recovered. The agent also said that the insurance company would wait about a month before settling the claim. "Call if you hear anything."

In order to expedite the car recovery Linda suggested placing an ad in a newspaper and offering a reward.

"An excellent suggestion but I'll first check with the police," Ed said and when he and Linda did check, the officer on duty said, "First the very process of offering a reward for a stolen car will create its own stolen market, criminals stealing cars to claim the reward. Plus police won't supervise the rewards."

The officer went on to say that there was nothing to prevent Ed from placing an ad in a newspaper, television or radio but gave several things to consider.

"If joy riders have taken the car and wrapped it around a pole or a tree we would already known about it. If people are to recognize the car in a parking lot, you'll have to provide some identifying feature aside from the burgundy color. In your case, is there such a feature?"

"Other than the horn honking the sound of a rooster crowing and then there's the license plate."

"Forget the license plate. It won't be on the car."

Next, the officer explained that if Ed wanted to offer a reward he would have to deal with sleazebags who would phone and say something like, 'Give me 5000 pesos and I'll tell you where your car is,' And once you get this supposed lead you'll have to check it out yourself because police don't have he time going around after all the losers this type of an ad may attract."

By now Ed was convinced that his Honda would not be found until the following morning when police phoned and an officer on the other end said, "Sir, we have located your burgundy colored Honda."

The first question Linda asked was, "What shape is it in?"

"Some parts are missing and there's damage to the ignition. You'll also need a new paint job. Otherwise it doesn't appear severe."

"Any idea who stole the car?"

"We are not dealing with kids or joy riders. The thieves are professionals from Mindanao."

"How did you reach that conclusion? Did you find finger prints?"

"And a tip, from Calapan City police. It appears that three riders had their motorcycles run over at a restaurant. Each biker filed a damage report which had a signature. The signatures and finger prints on your vehicle which was dumped, matched."

"Dumped? Where?"

"It was found on an isolated road near Iloilo City."

Ed immediately phoned the insurance agent in Mandaluyong City who made arrangements to have the car towed to Bernardo's' Auto Go Service to have it repaired and painted. And Bernardo said, "Your car will be ready tomorrow evening."

When 'tomorrow evening' arrived, Ed went to have the car picked up, but unfortunately Bernardo said, "We are still waiting for parts from Manila." The following day the missing parts were replaced and a new paint job given. The problem however, was that Ed's 1993 Honda was an antique model and paint manufacturers discontinued making the color burgundy. Bernardo risked his life and painted the car a bright yellow instead. But this did not matter as far as Ed was concerned.

What did was that he had his car back and he and Linda could continue their honeymoon by visiting Linda's bride's maid, Maria, who lived in the poverty section of the Visayas mystical island province of Siquijor, inhabited mostly by farmers and fishermen.

Among the attractions in Siquitor are its beaches, caves, Bandilaan National Park, a butterfly sanctuary, a place full of witches, fireflies and other supernatural phenomena.

Ed and Linda checked into Maria's nipa hut as the sun began to set and the absolute beauty revealed when darkness came, as Ed, Linda, Maria and her parents watched the blinking lights of the fireflies. The enchanted beauty of these thousands of the nocturnal insects glowed around the mangrove trees.

"It's like Christmas time," Linda said as the flickers of lights took the shape of the trees. These marvelous creatures are wonders of nature as thousands of them were teaming up to the trees as they were flying, dancing and circling around the branches.

Ed and Linda found that people in this village are happy, work hard and keep their homes and children clean.

In the barrio where Maria lived stray dogs, chickens and pigs are allowed wonder in the yard. The hens, roosters and chicks' pecked rice drying in the sun until the sunset.

Ed and Linda also watched a sow which recently gave birth to twelve piglets which later would be sold or butchered and made into lechon.

This was followed by lizards about 3 inches in length climbing the walls and ceilings of Maria's home.

A short time later. a larger lizard that made its home in the coconut tree greeted people with its "kakachoo" sound and an owl that responded with a "Who, who" until midnight when the barking dogs took over until 4.a.m at which time the roosters took over by crowing.

By 6:00 Maria's grandmother nodded off over her knitting before saying,

"It's very, very hot." And then Maria's mother took over as she pumped water from a nearby well and began washing the family clothes. Maria's father meanwhile, collected fire wood in order to cook a meal. To be truthful Ed and Linda did not have a good sleep that night while sleeping on the living room floor blanket and the following day since the temperature was C38 degrees because of the humidity, having to change their attires 3 times each day, have two showers and as a last resort had to purchase *Avert Gel Bait* to get rid of the mosquitoes and tiny ants which seemed to be everywhere.

One can tell the time of day in Siquijor by the cries of the peddlers. Fish vendors greet one the earliest in the morning hawking whatever seafood of the season. Not just fish but also shrimp, crab, guso and even prawns and lobster. Between 8 and 9 came the peddler lady selling puto, cassava, paltoa, budbud and bibinka. She always enumerates the variety of rice cakes in her sing song voice.

Anyone too lazy to cook lunch can rely on the lumpia vendor who also sells warm ngohiong at this hour. Toward noon and the rest of the afternoon the fruit vendors came. On certain days one can get enough ripe mangos, fresh buka, pineapples, jackfruit, apples and avocado to whip up a salad.

Then there was the indefatigable lady Rona who passed Maria's home at least three times a day, gracefully balancing a heavy basket of native boiled corn on top of her head. The other regulars who came and went throughout the day were the tabo msn and the puto man, sometimes called "poot poof" after the horn that has become his trademark. The tinkling of the sorbetero's bell was always music to the children around 10:00 a. m. and 4:00 p. m.

There were two kinds of sobetero: one pushing the ice cream cart, the other lugging a box of frozen delights like buko and pinig ice cream.

Later at night the balut vendor made his appearance at around 9:00. He made his rounds until well past midnight to satisfy the craving insomniacs.

Food is not the only stuff these ambulant vendors sell. The shoe and umbrella repairman sauntered by once in a while to offer their services. They have a distinct amusing way of announcing themselves. They probably get tired repeating "Ayo sapatos" all day, so they shorten it to, "yos patos." The umbrella repairman comes out only when their services are most needed, which is during rainy days. There is no need to go downtown to have those dull scissors and knives sharpened.

A sharpener came, riding into the neighborhood on his bicycle. There is no occasion that is inappropriate for eating and it's not uncommon to eat with their hands or with a fork and spoon but not a knife.

One thing about Filipino food culture is that they always ask you to share their food.

If you have food on the plate, you are expected to share their food; no matter how hungry you are, with those who may be even hungrier which in this case there were three poverty stricken women asking for favors.

The 1st was an elderly convalescing woman who aside from the food asked for pesos so she could fill her medical prescription.

The 2nd asked for money so she could buy a casket for her baby who had died several days earlier, and the 3rd, was a middle-aged woman who needed money for her husband's funeral who was killed in a motorcycle accident.

Ed discovered that about half of Philippines 94-million people live in rural areas where poverty is most severe and most widespread.

In Siquijor, like in the rest of the Philippines Filipino family terms of endearment show themselves in their naming conventions.

Neighbors with names like: Bong Bong, Ting Ting, Pong, Ping, Toto Boy Girl, Pinky or simply Baby. Many Filipinos have multiple names and with added nicknames it is easy to get confused although they are seemingly flippant: Johnny Boy, Babes, Junior, Booboy, and Jun are the most common.

Maria had five sisters and their names were: *Candy, Carmel, Cookie, Peanut and Popcorn* and three brothers named *Lord Jim, Coke* and *Sprite.*

The remainder of the honeymoon was no more auspicious than first half when Ed noticed that Filipino bus, jeepny and taxi drivers and their driving and skills were the same as throughout the entire Philippine but when they were shown some traffic signs and symbols Ed scratched his head as they could not gather to guess even if they had at least 20 years of experience. For example they did not know what the triangular "yield" sign meant or that those colored traffic lines are signs too. And one may wonder why traffic conditions are always in a mess, their driving habit border on the criminal side and road courtesy is nonexistent.

At any rate to tour the island Ed and Linda used the tricycle (pot. pot) with an attached cabin on the side of it. A taxi was too expensive and they are a scourge of the streets. Ed felt they drive private motorists crazy: they scare the living daylights of the pedestrians and vendors whenever they swish by an inch short of the raised sidewalk.

Ed and Linda returned to Maria's squatter home a bit late. Why they were late is a contradiction for people well known for their hospitality. Filipino time sticks out like an eyesore. Their intention is there but for some reason they are often late, half an hour late, even an hour late. By the time Ed and Linda arrived back to Maria's home was to turn 23 the following day when the family received a balikbayan door to door box from a brother in America.

And what was the box filled with? Soap, shoes, toilet paper, shampoo, tooth paste, vitamins, noodles, used clothing, *Spam* along with corned beef and *Tang*. The manufacturing companies would have gone out of business long ago if it had not been for some eleven mullions Filipino's working abroad.

On the penultimate day of their honeymoon Linda went swimming and Ed enjoyed a milkshake. After having spent a week in rural Philippine, Ed and Linda went home to rest and enjoy their marriage.

FIFTEEN

As soon as Ed and Linda returned to Mandaluyong City, they discovered that during their absence, the cabin ceiling had sprung a major leak and there weren't enough catch basins in the city to prevent water from flooding the living room and the carpet, which had to be replaced. As soon as Ed finished replacing the carpet, he noticed a lump under it in the middle of the floor. Ed felt his shirt pocket for his cigarettes, but found they were missing. Ed wasn't about to tear up the carpet, so he stood on the lump jumping up and down, until the it disappeared and the new carpet was smooth. Satisfied that there was no lump, Ed gathered his tools and carried them to the car. As Ed opened the door, two things happened simultaneously. Ed found his cigarettes on the front seat, and on his shoulder, Linda's hand as she said, "Ed, have you seen my budgie bird which I bought while on our honeymoon?"

Irritated, Ed said, "I haven't, and do want to know something else?"

"What?"

"I don't like your budgie bird."

That night, Ed and Linda had a spat over the missing blue-colored bird, which had a mania for flying around the condo and scattering droppings everywhere. Several droppings had landed on Ed's shoulder, which struck Linda funny. During a love spat that followed, Linda quaking with fury screamed, "Ed, if you don't get me another budgie bird, I'll call the police."

"Unbelievable," Ed thought. "Married for two weeks and already she's taking control of my life. Who does Linda think she is? I have married Miss Right but didn't realize her first name was Always."

Linda's nagging got the better of Ed, so he slammed the door behind him, and while pointing his finger said, "Linda, I beg you get some therapy. Believe me I did not kill your budgie bird."

Ed then drove to his office at Best Realty, where he slept on a couch that night. In the meantime Linda called police and minutes later, her mother phoned and asked, "Linda. How was your honeymoon?"

"Oh, Mamma," Linda replied. "We had our car stolen but the honeymoon itself was wonderful. Boracay is such a romantic place but Mama, as soon as we returned home Ed and I had an argument and Ed used the most horrible language. I mean all those four-lettered words."

"Linda," her mother said. "Calm down, what could be so awful" What four-lettered words did he use?"

"Please don't make me tell you, "Linda sobbed. "I'm so embarrassed they're just too awful."

"Darling, you must tell me what four-letter words were used?"

Still sobbing Linda said, "Oh, Mama the words are dust, wash, iron and cook."

In the morning at the Best Realty office, to Ed's surprise, he was arrested as a cop said, "Ed Ramos you have the right to be silent but if you decide to say something you will be misquoted, then what you say will be used against you."

Ed was finger printed and charged with hunting birds without a license.

Ed was carted off to the Mandaluyong City Jail and placed in a holding cell, where 20 or so guys were exchanging drugs.

After spending a night Ed said to a guard, "Sleeping on a concrete floor with one eye open isn't much fun. One of the guys even said to me that if I didn't buy some of his drugs he would spit on my grave."

Hearing about Ed's arrest, his parents came rushing to the Police Headquarters but were told, "Sorry Mr. and Mrs. Ramos, but your son has been charged and must stand trial."

The defendant is presumed innocent until proven guilty beyond a reasonable doubt did not matter, what did, was that Linda's budgie bird was missing and Ed was the prime suspect. It was an open and shut case. At the time of the investigation the living room window was open and the entrance door was shut.

The following day, a kangaroo-type trial took place. There was no kangaroo present, however, but Judge Pinky Onod did resemble one, except that he had no tail and couldn't hop because of a sprained leg.

The prosecuting attorney Bong 'Boomer' Vargas was a short stubby lawyer who wore spectacles, kept picking his nose and often said, "Whatever" or "As President Marcos use to say."

On the stroke of 10:00 a.m. there was silence in the court room when the court clerk glanced towards Ed and said, "Ed Ramos, do you swear that the testimony you are about to give this court is the truth and the whole truth so help you God."

"I do."

As the two attorneys began debating the case, Ed's defense lawyer, Thomas Huff said to Vargas, the prosecutor, "You are a dirty shyster and before this case is over I'll show you the crooked ape you are."

Vargas retorted, "And you sir are a cheat and a liar."

"Come, come." Judge Onod, who was tall in stature with a mustache, broke in and said, "Let's proceed with the Ed Ramos trial now that you have identified each other."

And when the trial began and following a short testimony, the judge said to Ed, "How old are you?"

"24."

"Are you qualified to give a urine sample?"

"I can,"

"And what kind of a flower are you wearing in your lapel?"

"It's a tropical orchid, your honor."

Judge Onod was allergic to pollen, sneezed and then asked, "Mr. Ramos, do I know you from somewhere?"

"Yes, your honor. I gave your daughter guitar lessons."

Judge Onod pounded his gavel and emphatically said, "Thirty days in jail. Case closed."

An appeal for a lighter sentence was denied on the grounds that Ed had earlier faxed an uncomplimentary lawyer joke to the prosecutor. The joke was. What is the difference between a rooster crossing the road and a lawyer? The answer of course is. "Skid marks in front of the rooster."

In jail, when the Pastor Atupan arrived to visit Ed, the pastor suggested, "You should make up with Linda. I'm certain she will forgive you."

Ed then asked if there was a remote chance he could end up in Heaven, if he should die in jail.

"If you pray, you may, but until your prayers are answered you may have to spend some time in purgatory."

Ed would do anything to be free and sleep with Linda in the same bed. He was about to go on a hunger-strike when a remarkable development took place.

The jail guard flung the door wide open exclaiming, "Ed Ramos, there has been a terrible mistake! You are a free man. The budgie bird has been found!"

"Where? Where?"

"In the parking lot. Unfortunately a cat had eaten it partly."

"So I'm free?

"You are."

Relieved, Ed sank to his knees and kissed the floor of the holding cell and as he was preparing his exit his eyes were dull, his hair was turning grey for a man his age, and even his face seemed to have taken a graying hue that blended with the drab jail uniform he had worn.

"Although I'm free I feel as if God is calling me," Ed said to the guard and after shaking hands with him, made his quick exit.

The first thing Ed did once released was take a jeepny to Passay City where there are rows and rows of pet stores and purchased another blue colored budgie bird. Linda was pleased. From that day onward they hugged and kissed, adjusted to being married and slept in the same bed. The real estate market was booming but Pollsters indicated that it soon would be slumping and a world recession was about to take place.

205

Sixteen

Ed was married during the month of August. On a September warm day, two years later, he was at the Rizal Park outdoor swimming pool taking part in a charity Belly Flop contest with proceeds going to Meals on Wheels to renovate its kitchen.

A large crowd, each person paying 5000 pesos, gathered at the pool bleachers to embrace the sun and watch an event billed as the Manila*s Battle of the Bulges.*

Contestants drew numbers as to when to dive, flex their muscles and display their physique.

When a whistle was blown for Ed to make his dive, he climbed to the diving board, pulled in his stomach, puffed out his chest and a smile spread across his face. Once on the diving board in a blue colored swim suit he jumped up and down several times and then dove into the water as those present watched.

At the conclusion of the dive the announcer on the pubic address system said, "Ladies and gentlemen. I have some good news and some that is bad. The good news is that the judges have awarded Mr. Ramos's magnificent dive a perfect score."

There was a thunderous applause.

"And the bad news is that during the dive Ed couldn't swim well, it seems he drowned."

The audience moaned and groaned.

Hearing the PA announcer, Reverend Atupan rushed and with the help of a lifeguard dragged him out of the pool where he was resuscitated.

Seeing Ed in excruciating pain the Pastor leaned over Ed's shoulder and asked, "Ed, have you made peace with God?"

In a faint voice Ed replied, "I didn't know I had an argument with Him."

Then the Reverend continued, "Do you believe in the Father, Son and Holy Spirit?"

And these were the last words Ed had spoken on Planet Earth, "I'm dieing and you are asking me riddles."

Minutes later Dr. Perez, who was also one of the contestants felt Ed's pulse and then pronounced Ed dead.

A day after Ed had died his wife Linda, got into an argument with Ed's parents if her husband and their son should be buried or cremated.

They also argued what hymns to sing, use an organ or a flute, should the casket be open or closed, should a private service be held or one open to the public.

In the end it was agreed that Ed would be buried and to hold the funeral at the No Name Universal Church.

The casket would remain open. Among the hymns to be sung were *Rock of Ages, Hallelujah I'm Not a Bum* and *Lupang Hinirang* accompanied by an organ. After the burial at a municipal cemetery there would be a wake at the church basement and lunch served.

The obituary notice in the *Manila Bulletin* read: "Rather than flowers, the family suggests donations be made to Meals on Wheels."

Mandaluyong City bid farewell to Ed Ramos in a simple service remembering him as an upcoming realtor whose state was Manila and the Philippines.

Some arrived early to pay their respect. Sammy Helper, who knew Ed all his life, flew in from Tacloban and publicly said, "I have lost a true friend."

Outside the church several passers-by's enquiring about the service, reacted with difference and one even said, "So Ed Ramos is dead. Who cares? Let them make a potpourri from his fingernails and hair."

It is true that when Ed was alive there were people who said nasty things about him but as soon ad he died, they praised him.

Reverend Atupan said, "Ed Ramos the, Canadian, was the kindest and most generous young man I have ever known. heaven will not be the same with Ed there."

Shortly after 1:00 p. m. church bells rang and a motorcade delivered Linda and her and Ed's parents to the No Name Universal Church. They made their way in silence up a flight of stairs into the church and then the front pews where Ed's body lay in front of them in an open casket. Mourners listened to tributes as the mood of the service swung back and forth between grief and laughter. They all had to pause to shed tears or regain their composure as Pastor Atupan urged everyone to celebrate the real estate salesman who put Mandaulong City on the map of the Philippines and helped Manila Meals on Wheels out of debt.

"Linda, Ed loved you very much," Reverend Atupan continued, "We all know that, so don't cry. Think of Ed up there in Heaven with Saint Peter, Saint Michael, the guardian angel and Rabbi Libowitch, Ed's friend who died recently."

Reverend Atupan then read words from the *Bible* and there wasn't a dry eye in the entire church as he said, "Ed Ramos, this isn't the final chapter of your life. May your soul enter heaven and may you be reincarnated. Till then, rest in peace."

But Ed had little peace in heaven initially because when he arrived at the queue outside the Pearly Gates, there was a long line-up, and Ed hated line-ups even on Planet Earth.

Saint Peter while screening people spoke to the first, second and third and then eventually asked another, "Where are you from?"

"America," the elderly man in the lineup answered while waving the American flag.

"And what have you do to deserve admission to Heaven?" Saint Peter continued.

"I have helped President George Bush attack Iraq in order to get rid of Saddam Hussein."

"And many innocent civilians died because of the bombing," Saint Peter said and the Pearly Gates remained closed.

Saint Peter then turned to the man in front of Ed, and asked, "And where are you from?"

"Germany," the man replied.

"And what have you done to deserve admission into heaven?"

"I've been a lawyer all my life, sir, and taken part in many complex lawsuits."

"Saint Peter began to escort the lawyer inside the gates, when the lawyer began to protest that his untimely death had to be some sort of a mistake.

"I'm much too young to die. I'm only 38," he said.

Saint Peter agreed that 38 did seem a bit young to be entering the Pearly Gates and went to another room to check on the case.

When Saint Peter returned, he said to the German attorney, "I'm afraid the mistake may be your own doing, my son. We have verified your age on the bases of the number of hours you billed your clients, and you are at least 78t. You must go to hell."

Ed didn't wait for the question when it was his turn to be interviewed so he knelt in front of Saint Peter and said, "I'm from Metro Manila, Philippines. Do I have to go to hell too?"

Saint Peter took off his glasses, shook his head and said, "Ah Manila. That's where it gets very hot during summer and there are catastrophic typhoons, even during winter."

"And don't forget the mosquitoes and air pollution."

"Well, you have already been there." and along with a clergyman from Argentina was told to go inside the Pearly Gates.

"Reverend, here the keys to one of the nicest suites in heaven," Saint Peter said to the clergyman."

And to Ed, "And you Mr. Ramos, here are the keys to heaven's penthouse where angels don't sleep during the night and play harps and sing. It's a very nice place."

This upset Reverend Garcia who said, "Saint Peter, I don't understand. I dedicated my entire life preaching the word of God and . . . ."

"Listen Father," Saint Peter interrupted, "Clergymen are a dime a dozen here but this is the first honest real estate salesman we have seen in a long, long time."

The following Sunday, parishioners at the No Name Universal Church in Mandaluyong City, prayed to Saint Peter, the gate keeper, to have just a glimpse of Ed in heaven. Their wish was granted, but in their horror the following Sunday, they saw on a huge screen, Ed with a beautiful blonde on his lap.

"Ed! Ed!" they cried out. "How come you behave this way in heaven, when you didn't chase married women while in Manila?"

Ed replied, "Listen, you people below in the Philippines. The blond is not my reward. I'm her punishment."

A month after Ed entered Heaven; he was presented with a Chevrolet car by Saint Peter. This allowed Ed to travel all over heaven and meet his friends, until one day he met Rabbi Libowitch driving a Mercedes Benz with a chauffeur. This amazed Ed, and after sixty seconds of eternity said, "Discrimination!" and registered a protest with Saint Peter.

"Why would I get just a Chevy and Rabbi Libowitch a new Benz? We are both from the Philippines."

Saint Peter leaned over Ed's shoulder, and whispered in his ear, "Look. Rabbi Libowitch is related to the Boss."

While Ed and Saint Peter were engaged in a conversation, a Texas oilman who was allowed into Heaven appeared and got on Saint Peter's nerves. It seems that no matter what part of Paradise the Texan was shown it failed to measure up to the state of Texas. Finally Saint Peter took the Texan to the edge of heaven so he could look straight into hell and said, "Have you anything like this in Texas?"

"No," the Texan replied, "But I know some boys in Huston who can put it out."

As soon as Saint Peter was through dealing with the Texan, two politicians from Italy arrived at the Pearly Gates, but Saint Peter, because the two gents were implicated with the Mafia, refused to let them inside and in a thunder-like voice said, "Scram!'

As he said those words, an angel flew by and said to Saint Peter, "You can't do that. Please go get them back."

Saint Peter ran off and came back exhausted and while out of breath, said, "They are gone!"

"The two Italians?" the angel asked.

"No, the gates."

While in heaven, Ed Ramos became a celebrity and tried his hand at being a poet. Here are several limericks he wrote. A quick glance at these verses may encourage one to become a poet too. If it doesn't its understandable.

A realtor named Jane Moroso	I'm not certain about my next verse
Displayed her torso	As a method of which to converse

A crowd soon collected
But no one objected
Some even hollered, "More so!"

But it's clear to me
From what I can see
In Heaven that's how words are disbursed

There was a tenant named Claire
Who had a magnificent pair
That's what she thought
Until she got caught
In her boyfriend's underwear

I'll get it in a minute or two
I like doing things for you
I'm at your beck and call
But doggone it all
There are things I sometime must do

Amorous Sue
Had a date she knew

The coroner found
The couple had drowned
While paddling a canoe

There's a lady from Moline
Who writes limericks that are clean
It wasn't her aim
To continue this game
It's getting a bit obscene

An old Scottish realtor from Skye
Reckoned "Old realtors don't die"
Though without any doubt
When their heartbeat runs out
He will be unable to cry

A realtor in Saskatoon
Never learned how to eat with a spoon
He would fork up his soup
With a bending stoop
Too bad—he died so soon

There was a realtor named Fred
Who said as he climbed out of bed

A Cebu realtor named Rex
Eating beef he always rejects

"There's no heaven, I'm sure
But I hate to endure
The alternative if I wake up dead"

He lives on herbs
His appetite curbs
And slimmer and trimmer he gets

As a realtor I made many mistakes
In life those are sometimes the breaks
I got married and joined the crowd
Which made my mother proud
For the good sense that it makes

There was a realtor named Joe
Who lost his 'get up and go'
Almost without thinking
He began heavy drinking
And found his sales astonishingly slow

Occasionally when I'm blue
With nothing in particular to do
I stand on my head
At the foot of the bed
And then shove my nose in my shoe

My dog, Fido, can hardly see
One day I took him for a walk with me
When I felt something warm
I looked down with alarm
Fido thought my leg was a tree

When things go wrong, as they sometime will
My search for a lasting mate was uphill
When my funds were getting low and debts high
I wanted to smile but had to cry
So I kept taking a headache pill

My search in finding Linda had its twists and turns
And as everyone sometimes learns
Not to give up though the pace may seem slow

But then I received another rejection blow
Leaving my heart with scars and burns

Often I was frustrated and nearly gave up
When I thought I had captured the victors' cup
Another rejection came down
As I imagined my love mate wearing a wedding gown
In my dream she was sweeter than a toy Pomeranian pup

But at last my search came to an end on a moonlit starry
   night
I found Linda next day who now, she's is my Mrs. Right
I have learned to fight back when hardest hit
And when things are rough one must never quit
And go through emotions of anger, depression, rejection
   and fright

Ed also published a *Bible* Trivia game and one titled
Heavenoply

SEVENTEEN

Ed spent nine years in heaven, and while there, again met guardian angel Michael who stopped a little, thought a little and since angels do not sleep at night, he said to him, "Ed Ramos, there's a major economic crises on Planet Earth. Philippines need you. God will

incarnate you for your life time so you can help ease an economic crises, especially in Manila where there are spiraling home foreclosures and the only 'deposits' made on new cars, are those made by birds flying over them. And it has nothing to do with media allegations that the recession is caused because of the sun and the moon."

Ed who was always willing to help anyone with a problem received permission from God to return to the Planet Earth.

Ed then said, "I can't wait to return to the Philippines, see Linda and follow up on the recession that is taking place and assess the impact it is having on the City of Manila. Being in Heaven will inspire me and have an impact on the rest of my life.

In the mean time all the money I made while in Heaven I will donate to charity."

As soon as Ed arrived in Manila, they hugged and kissed, and Linda asked what Heaven was like.

"Awesome," Ed replied, "But to you want to know something?"

"What?"

"There's a shortage of chairs."

While readjusting to earth's gravity Ed was back in Manila as a real estate salesman and an economic consultant. After analyzing the serious credit crunch in the Philippines Ed came to the conclusion:

(1) If we spend money at the New Asia Mall it will go to China

(2) If we spend money on gasoline, it will go to the Arabs

(3) If we purchase a computer, the money will go to India

(4) If we purchase a good car, the money will go to Japan

(5) If we purchase rice the money will go Thailand

(6) If we purchase something else, the money will go to Taiwan

(7) If we purchase diamonds the money will go to Africa

(8) If we purchase a Schumatz Hagen the money will go to Germany

(9) If we purchase crystal the money will go to the Czech Republic

(10) If we need special surgery the money will go to the United States

"None of this will help the Philippine economy," Ed thought and suggested that in order to survive the crunch corporations should merge.

For example: Hale Business Systems, Mary Kay Cosmetics. Fuller Brush and W. R. Grace should merge to become—Hale Marry Fuller Grace. 3M and Goodyear should merge and become MMMGood. Fedex should merge with UPS to become FedUp. Fairchild Electronics and Honeywell Computers to become Fairwell Honeychild."

The bigwigs running the financial market took notice of Ed who then he did a door-to-door survey about the global recession and posed the question: "In Your Opinion How Bad is the Philippine economy, really."

The response was the following:

(1) Its so bad that African television stations are now showing "Sponsor a Philippine child," commercials

(2) Its so bad that the highest-paying job in the Philippines is jury duty

(3) Its so bad a polygamist was seen in Tarlac with only one wife

(4) Its so bad the American government is helping GM and Chrysler with a stimulus package

(5) Customers at Robinson's are now buying only one roll of toilet paper at a time

(6) MacDonald's is introducing the mini ¼-burger and is selling donuts

(7) Its so bad some hotels urge visitors to use only one strip of toilet paper

(8) Philippine foreign contract workers working abroad are sent back to their homeland

(9) At basketball games some fans have turned in their season tickets and instead singing the national anthem live now play a taped recording

(10) Its so bad that Practical nurses are replacing RN's

(11) President Arroyo is about to fire herself

(12) The Manila Casino Hyat has asked to be managed by Somali pirates

(13) Its so bad that 7 out of 10 homes in the Pina Santold subdivision are in foreclosure

(14) Its so bad that the light at the end of the tunnel has been turned off

(15) Its so bad that chickens that have stopped laying eggs and KFC is experiencing difficulty filling menu orders

(16) Its so bad that there is an increase in hostage-taking and home invasions

(17) Bottled water has become more expensive than a litre of gasoline

(18) Its so bad that Henry Sy and Lucio Tan now purchase their wardrobe from the Salvation Army Thrift Shop

(19) The picture is now worth only 200 words

(20) Its so bad that tourists cannot afford to see the tarsier monkey and the Chocolate Hills in Bohol

(21) Every penny counts so men are avoiding haircuts and growing beards

(22) Its so bad that IKEA is now selling funeral caskets.

(23) There are many signs that read: "Will Work free for Food and Lodging"

(24) Parishioners in the No Name Universal Church are placing slugs, instead of coins, in the collection baskets

(25) Its so bad that that now up to 5 people ride on the same motorcycle, without helmets

(26) Intel and Goodyear shut down plants in the Philippines.

(27) If the bank returns your cheque marked "Insufficient Funds" you call them and ask if they meant you or the bank

(28) It's so bad that Night Clubs in Manila are holding a 'Bailout Night' each Friday—Patrons with a pink slip get in free.

While Ed continued selling real estate and help solve the global economic crises by recommending austerity measures, Linda, having experience in husbandry and a swineherd helps Philippine Health Care find a cure for swine and chicken flu and research why so many honey bees are dying.

EIGHTEEN

Ed never felt this way before. With many years experience as a realtor and now a recession consultant, he did not demonstrate or attack Philippine establishment. "I'm kind of a realtor that doesn't cuss or fuss," Ed said to Linda showing displeasure.

"If I were you I would talk to the Mayor of Mandaluyong City, Benjamin Bubbles. His worship has been mayor for over 10 years and his father even more and should know something about handing out traffic tickets. I'm no lawyer but think one could even argue it in court," Linda said.

What happened was that shortly after Ed returned from heaven he was showing possible accommodation to a prospect whose home was foreclosed and needed help. Ed was caught in a laser speed gun trap and given a ticket for speeding. When Ed protested to the Chief of Police, who handed him the ticket, the Chief said, "Ed, we got you this time, we'll get the other salesmen next time," implying that all realtors in the Philippines were speeding demons.

Ed had received tickets before, so next morning, along Shaw Boulevard; the Chief was mystified how carefully everyone was driving. Motorists were head-on the speed limit and smiled at the Chief as they passed his laser tripod. Several blocks away Ed stood staging a one-man protest by holding a sign with bold letters that read: *Speed Trap Ahead.*

Minutes later the Chief said, "Ed you are distracting the attention of motorist and. confiscated the sign and gave Ed a 5000 peso ticket. Ed now had 2 tickets—1 for speeding and another for stunting.

The following day over a cup of coffee Ed said to Linda, "I guess I'll have to pay the two fines."

Linda disagreed, "Not before you see Mayor Benny Bubbles. Surely a citizen can stand besides a street holding up a sign. Is it not an attack on freedom of speech to criticize an expression of opinion on a piece of board? If radar traps exist to slow down traffic in order to fund City Hall, fight it, there's a principle involved," Linda said.

Ed took Linda's advice seriously and when he confronted Mayor Bubbles in his office the atmosphere was electric as the Mayor said, "Ed, fight it in court if you wish but long as I'm the mayor of Mandaluyong City, radar traps will continue on our streets. How else can the city pay for the upkeep of the cock fighting arenas, public swimming pools recreation facilities and the museum if not because of speed zones?"

"Your worship, if that is your position, I'll run for the Mayor's office myself," Ed said and went on. "I'm against speed traps for the sake of helping with the City Hall treasury. Furthermore there are no speed traps in heaven."

Mayor Bubbles burst out with laughter. His English wasn't the best and when the laughter stopped he continued, "Never, never. Watch, I'll win by a landscape. If Manduluyong City elects you as a mayor, there will be a lot of disappointments."

Ed shot back, "Despite your long term as a mayor you, may be surprised with the outcome."

By now Ed had grown several pumpkins in his back yard. Tiptoeing around the vines he carefully checked each for defects.

While bending his ear over the nearest guard that was as high as his stomach and wider that his car, Ed gave the pumpkin a solid smack and listened intently, like a doctor with a stethoscope.

"This pumpkin thumps pretty well," Ed said to Linda with a grin.

Linda's initial desire was for Ed to grow a pumpkin larger than the current record of 1.810 pounds and the weigh-in had begun in Manila's Large Pumpkin Contest whose theme was pumpkin, pumpkin, pumpkin and more pumpkins.

Although extremely busy as a realtor and now as a recession consultant, Ed managed to grow a pumpkin that weighed 900 pounds which won first prize.

The prize wasn't a ticket for free golfing in Singapore but a trip to Nova Scotia in Canada where they grow patches and patches of pumpkins., at times the largest in the world, and purchased a template at the Big Pumpkin Store in Halifax, which with the right tools, one could build a pumpkin canoe.

Once the template was purchased and Ed returned to the Philippines, he had students of the research department at the University of the City of Manila cut a hole for a lid and then slowly, cautiously, scoop up the seeds with a spoon, scrape the flesh from the inside, so the pumkin shell was an inch thick all the way around, thus constructing the first pumpkin canoe in the Philippines. With an oar and a sign added, Ed could climb inside and paddle the Pasig River back and forth, urging those facing his cabin to vote for him

On the day the election was called, there was a typhoon in the Philippines and 80 km wind and rain which wasn't pleasant if one wore a skirt or a hair piece.

The wind rattled the coconut trees and scattered leaves on the streets and sidewalks, a time Ed filed his nomination papers and to a group of supporters said, "I don't come bearing gifts. The only promise I make is that there will be no speed traps in Mandaluyong City."

In his mayoralty campaign no matter where Ed went, he was all eyes and ears taking notes of voter desires and their complaints. Many of those who retired in Mandaluyong City came from rural provinces and said they would vote for Ed not because when he visited Cavite City a television news clip showed a dog mistaking him as a fire hydrant but because as a salesman he was honest. Ed's visit with a couple from Mindanao was particularly interesting not that Manny Paquiao lived there but because Jonah Paler had just made bangoong and she gave him the recipe.

As a real estate salesman, Ed knew the city well and increased his hectic pace by visiting the Philippine Legion where his said to a group of veterans over a glass of beer, "You should have better pensions."

In days that followed Ed picked up votes after participating in a three-legged, sack jumping and spoon carrying contest during the annual Fiesta and cock fighting contest that followed. In the evening as the Fiesta continued and was filled with people and while a band played Ed and Linda spun around dancing until past midnight.

In the final week of the campaign Ed knocked on door for the second time striking up conversations with home makers and if there were any babies inside, he made every effort to kiss them too. Wherever there were two people, Ed was the third. Ed's advertisements in newspapers began to appear larger and larger and more frequent. He also doubled his distribution of leaflets, billboards and lawn signs and car bumper stickers.

During this time Mayor Bubbles was busy too. His newspaper ads appeared much larger and like Ed, advertised on the radio and television. That was the week Linda came to Ed's campaign headquarters to monitor the switchboard and answer calls from the public

"You should find it easy." Ed said, "When answering the phone just say, 'Ed Ramos campaign headquarters' and if you aren't sure about an enquiry, tell the caller I'll call back."

'I'll do my best," Linda said as Ed stepped out the door to do more electioneering.

The first caller that Linda had to deal with was a woman who wanted to know where to vote. As soon as Linda told her there was a dial tone. Seconds later the phone rang again and Linda answered, "Good afternoon, Ed Ramos's campaign headquarters."

"Is this the campaign manager?" a male voice asked.

"No, but maybe I can help you."

"OK. Tell Mr. Ramos I wouldn't vote for him even if he was the only candidate alive."

"Why is that?"

"Because I hate politicians and furthermore, when he had my home listed for sale, he never did sell it."

The phone cliqued again and Linda began licking envelopes. When the phone rang the next time she let it ring four times before she answered.

"Good afternoon dear," a female voice said at the other end. My name is Iris Ortiz, will you please tell Mr. Ramos that I will need a ride to the polling station on Election Day."

"Are you going to vote for Ed?"

"No, but I might as well save on gas for the incumbent mayor."

Following several more phone calls Linda began to regret that she had volunteered to work at the campaign headquarters and to Rosa Bitang who came to replace her, said, "Everything was all right with the exception that I may have lost Ed votes."

"Why is that?" Rosa asked.

"Because some of the callers were rude so I told them to go and jump into the Pasig River and . . . ."

In the final week of the campaign, Ed and Mayor Bubbles appeared at a public forum which was televised on TV 5. Ed debated that he was against speeding radar traps because on account of them, tourists did not stop in Mandaluyong City but continued traveling either to Makati or Pasig City. Mayor Bubbles meanwhile, stuck to his theory that speed traps were necessary in order to upkeep municipal public buildings and that Ed did not understand municipal politics and his lack of experience.

The following day, Ed used his pumpkin canoe and paddled the Pasig River that faced his cabin and then purchased 60 minutes of airtime on radio station Magic 89.9 and took calls from listeners. At the beginning, the callers asked serious questions about taxes, poverty and bus service. As the program progressed, however, it turned into a Comedy Hour.

"Hey, Ed" a listener phoned. "Do you have enough money for a rainy day should Mayor Bubbles defeat you?"

In reply Ed said, "I never shop on rainy days."

The same listener then said that he saw Ed campaigning at a Chowking restaurant and asked, "How did you find the meal?"

Ed's response was, "With a magnifying glass."

Another caller said, "Ed, "As a mayoralty candidate you don't seem to know which side of your bread is buttered," to which Ed replied, "What does it matter. I eat both sides."

When Ed looked towards the clock he realized that he just enough time to say, "Remember folks, tomorrow get out and vote for Ed Ramos."

On election Day Ed and Linda voted as soon as the polls opened and Ed's and Linda's parents came to campaign headquarters to help voters who needed a ride to the polling station and as soon as the polls closed went to the Edsa Shangri-La hotel contemplating a victory, while Ed went to City Hall to watch the counting of ballots by the returning officer and his staff.

Initially, incumbent Mayor Bubbles was in the lead, only a short time later to be passed by Ed. There were more changes in position than Imelda Marcos use to change shoes.

In the end Ed won the election with a plurality of 1782 votes and in his victory speech said, "Everyone that knows me knows that I'm a fighter. Let me say one more thing, I want to thank my wife Linda, for standing and sitting behind me during the election campaign."

Outgoing Mayor Bubbles took the defeat with dignity and after congratulating Ed on the upset victory said, "I don't know what happened. I assume there will be no more speed traps from this day onward."

"Absolutely," Ed said. "As soon as I'm installed into the mayor's office I'll have the speed traps discontinued."

Mayor Bubbles then said, "Ed, you never did mention during your campaign how city council is going o pay for the upkeep of our public buildings."

"Simple," Ed said, "Mandaluyong City will host the largest Fishing Derby the Philippines ever seen, and the proceeds will be more than necessary for the upkeep.

"Correct me, if I'm wrong but you must have meant build more arenas for cock fighting."

"I'll do nothing of the sort; I did say a fishing derby, which with council's approval, will be held during the first week in August. And do you want to know something else?

"You riding a broomstick won't be a pretty sight."

"This is no laughing matter. The fisherman who catches the largest fish will win one million American dollars."

"How about the second prize"

"Bottled water for eternity courtesy Nature Springs Drinking Water

"And the third?"

"All the pizza one can eat for a year, courtesy Pizza Hut."

"Give me a break," Mayor Bubbles said, "One million dollars? Mandaluyong City can't afford such a generous prize."

"But it can."

"Show me?"

"Through corporate sponsoring."

On the day Mayor-elect Ramos took office he was euphoric because city council unanimously agreed to hold an international fishing derby in the Manila Bay considered to be one of the best natural harbors in Southeast Asia if not the world.

News of the Derby first appeared on the front page of the *Inquirer* accompanied by a photograph of the city of Mandaluyoung.

The major wire services picked up the story and flashed it to it members around the world including BBC in Britain, CNN in America, ABC in Australia, CBC in Canada and Radio Moscow in Russia.

Those living in and out of the city, got excited as Mandaluyong was literally transformed by a pre-derby construction boom. The highways near Mandaluyong City were resurfaced, bridges given a new coat of paint and even the observation tower at Aquino International airport was renovated.

For those not familiar with the city of Mandaluyong and to stimulate interest in the Derby, the Chamber of Commerce issued a brochure implying that the city was a power house and a hot bed for entrepreneurs and that if foreign fishermen weren't familiar with the city one must first:

Learn to pronounce the name of the city. It's Man-Da-lu-yong by affixing the consonant "n" to the first syllable and not Manda and Loo Young."

It's one of the cities that is a city within Metro Manila. The city of approximately 280-thousand is bordered on the west by the countries capital, Manila, to the north by San Juan City, to the east by Quezon City and Pasig City. The city is sometimes known as *Mand* or *Tiger City* and as the *shopping Mall Capital of the Philippines.*

The Chamber also printed a road map showing directions to Manila Bay.

The maximum acceptable speed on Shaw Boulevard is 60 km an hour. Anything above is considered downright outrageous. Car horns are actually 'Road Rage' indicators. If, while driving, someone has actually their signals on, it's probably a factory defect.

All ladies with red hair driving a Mercedz Benz have the right of way. In asking directions you must know how to speak Tagalog, Spanish or Chinese. Forget the traffic rules you learned elsewhere. Mandaluyoung City has its own version—Hold on and pray.

If you suddenly stop at a yellow light you will be rear ended by a jeepney. The morning rush hour is from 6 a. m. to 11 a. m. The evening rush hour is from 1 p m to 7 p. m. Friday rush hours are 6 a.m. until midnight. For safety sake, watch out for overloaded jeepneys and buses.

Prior to the Derby opening, a survey was conducted by SurveyMonkey as to which is a better sport—Having Sex or Fishing? 90% answered that fishing indeed was better and gave reasons why:

The Ten Commandments don't say anything about fishing.

No matter how much you had to dink you still can fish.

It is perfectly acceptable to pay a professional to fish with you.

You don't have to go to a sleazy shop to in a sleazy neighborhood to buy fishing stuff.

Your fishing partner will never say, "Not again. We just fished last week. Is fishing all you think about?"

Nobody expects you to fish with the same partner for the rest of your life.

Nobody will ever tell you that you may go blind if you go fishing.

When you are fishing with a pro, you never have to wonder if they are really an undercover cop.

Nobody expects you to give up fishing if your partner loses interest in you.

Arrows were posted connecting Manila Bay with the Mandaluyoung City Hall where in the Maysilo Circle was the fish weigh-in site along with an information booth where one can avoid traffic circles, twists and turns and an alternate route to find where to eat, dine and relieve themselves just in case . . . .

The first sign to appear within the Circle was *Coca Cola Welcomes All Fishermen* to *Mandaluyoung City* and the *Coke* cans were white in color with a photo imprinted of various fish found in Manila Bay. More signs throughout the city read: *San Miguel* the official beer during the Derby.

Philamlif, the official insurance company, *Jollibee,* the official fast food restaurant. *Bangko Sentral ng Pilipinas,* the official bank and Shell the official gas station.

There were other official sponsors too and it seemed each corporation listed in Fortune Magazine was sponsoring one thing or another.

This included *Hewlett Packard* the official scanner and printer, *Commonwealth Foods* the official distributor healthy snacks, *United Laboratories* the official prescription centre in case of an accident, *Puma Spring and Rubber Industries,* the official supplier of footwear and apparel, *Raid* the official mosquito repellent and Toledo the official scale to weigh the fish on. *Duracell* agreed to be the official battery and Visa the official credit card.

Each sponsor agreed to pay P200.000 to have its name and logo displayed in and around Mandaluyoung City for the duration of the Derby.

The creative financing did not end there. Mayor Ramos concocted a deal with the private sector where City Council sold corporate names attached to City Hall Complex and its offices housed in different buildings and locations which included the City Gymnasium, Tennis Court and Clubhouse. Elsewhere in the city, public buildings are composed of barangay halls and multi-purpose structures, local health centers and public schools.

The creative financing did not end there. Mayor Ed Ramos concocted a deal with the private sector where City Council sold advertising on public buildings and services to private companies for a substantial fee during the Derby.

For P250.000 one could have the city fire engines, buses and LRT wrapped with advertisements. If 250.000 was too rich, one could have a company logo placed on the garbage trucks driving up and down back alleys.

Lawyers could advertise on police cars for P50.00 a day and for several more, they could ride in the cruiser and sign up clients as soon as they were handcuffed and interviewed. *Goodyear Tire* agreed to send its blimp for aerial shots of Manila Bay. City Council and all airlines signed an agreement whereby the airlines added fees to existing fees of P5.000 for late fight departures and arrivals, and if a passenger wanted to sit by a window they had to pay an extra 500.

There were also garbage can murals with pictures of celebrities that previously visited Manila and that included Pope John Paul 11, Mohammad Ali and the Beatles.

A different private company sponsored each can but if one sponsored 100 it was entitled to a 10% discount.

Of course, the Derby sponsorship wasn't just a wealthy corporation paying out a sum of money to become a sponsor so that it wouldn't have to pay federal taxes. It was people who paid P1000 each in order to personally meet with a participating fisherman and see who could tell the silliest fishing story. For an extra P500 a contestant autographed his/her fishing license with proceeds going to the Philippine "Stop Bullying" foundation.

Cash strapped Manila Public schools board agreed to initiate roof top advertising. The huge ads appeared visibly only from flying aircraft and students on ground level didn't see them. The revenue derived from this form of advertising was allocated to purchase badly needed equipment and increase teacher salaries.

As the date for the Derby drew nearer, there was a parade through Mandaluyoung City, a Miss Fish Derby pageant, a fashion show displaying the latest fishing apparel and fishing gear, a spelling Bee of fish names and paraphernalia associated with the fishing industry, and all-star cast of world retired fishermen from Europe, Africa, Asia, North America and South America and Australia in a fly casting tournament.

Finding accommodation in Manila became difficult to find as all hotels, motels campgrounds, High School, College and University dorms were reserved in advance.

Finding a hotel room was difficult as daily rates skyrocketed by P2000 and a glass of beer by P500. At the Edsa Shangri-La Hotel for example the general manager said, "Extra beds and cots have been placed in rooms. We have been sold out since an ad appeared in *Field and Stream* magazine. Derby fever has certainly taken Manila by storm. This is something popular and huge forcing us to add more rooms."

The manager of the New Horizon Hotel said something similar and continued, "We had requests for blocks of space ever since Mayor Ramos first announced the Derby. Not only have we booked fishermen from Asia, but the entire world."

One Manila entrepreneur advertised that he was willing to rent his home for P50.000 a day. As it turned out the house was in Cebu City. But that did not matter because wealthy Sheik Mustafa Mohammad from Saudi Arabia rented it and in his private jet flew to Cebu back and forth until the Derby was over.

Most of the contestants that entered the Derby were heads of state, news makers, sports and Hollywood celebrities.

There could have been criminals too but no one could tell by the fishing gear they used.

In the Philippines regular monsoons are part of an environmental equation but fortunately the weatherman forecast ideal conditions to catch the 'Big One'.

Local Filipino's who did not enter the Derby could watch highlights on TV5.

On August 4[th,] sport fishermen from throughout the world and it seemed some from the moon and planet Mars, gathered in Mandaluyong City thus giving the city and sponsors, a lot of publicity.

Next, on a sunny morning, Mayor Ramos stood on a platform in the Maysilo Circle and while waving his magic wand declared, "Let the Manila Bay Fishing Derby begin!"

Fishermen with fishing rods and landing nets boarded their boats and began fishing.

Tourists and visitors, meanwhile, crowded, into the city with bottles of rum hidden in their backpacks to enjoy the Derby, and turning the event into an atmosphere of a Fiesta.

As the Derby progressed, tonnes of fish were caught and in the process here are several amusing incidents:

The first incident which was extensively described by ABC-CBN News took place when a Hollywood starlet got into a fight with a pesky eagle. The actress had landed a tuna but the eagle had his eyes open on the fish too and followed it right into the boat where the bird nabbed the hook line and sinker.

The actress, who had just won an Academy Award, wasn't going to give up her prize without a struggle. As the eagle took off with the tuna and yards and yards of line, she hung on to the rod and succeeded in reeling the fish until the thief was within grabbing distance.

As the actress was struggling to pluck the fish from the pelican's bill she dropped the fish into the water below. The eagle quickly dove down into the water to take hold of what he considered was his meal. Easier said than done the pelican missed his target. Since the fish was still on the line the actress hauled it in as fast as she could, popped it into a basket and snapped on the lid.

The eagle infuriated and having been done out of meal, came from behind and gave the actress a spiteful peck on her posterior causing her to fall into the water knocking over the basket. As the lid flowed away, the eagle went into action. He seized the actress's fish, and taking no chances this time, swallowed it down then and there.

Another amusing incident took place when Pastor Atupan from the No Name Universal Church in Mandaluyoung City tried his luck at catching the largest fish but tragedy stuck when a sudden storm blew over and destroyed his boat. The Pastor barely escaped with his life. Being a religious man he picked up the *Bible* and read: "The lord gives and the Lord takes away I shall bare the cause"

When the storm was over the Pastor set out fishing again but as soon as he reached the Manila Bay shore a shark attacked him and in the process broke the Pastor's arm. From the Bible the Pastor read again, "The Lord gives and the Lord takes away. I shall bare the cause."

Pastor Atupan, oh how he loved to fish. He was a determined fisherman and wasn't about to withdraw from the Derby so with his good hand picked a hook, line and sinker and was on his way fly fishing. With the first toss of the hook the hook however got caught in the pants of his butt leaving the devout man in terrible pain.

Looking towards the sky the Pastor said, "Lord. What did I do wrong to deserve this?"

A Superior voice answered, "Pastor, there's something about you that browns me off."

"And what might that be?"

"Instead of participating in the Manila Bay Derby you should be paying more attention to your parishioners and convince them to put paper bills instead of coins into the collection baskets each Sunday."

A fisherman from India, Harjet Singh, launched his boat at 4 a.m. and after making himself comfortable accidentally dropped his chewing gum into the water. The moment the gum hit the surface a fish snapped it. A moment later he dropped more gum and another fish snapped it too.

As an experienced fisherman Mr. Singh continued dropping his chewing gum into the water and as fish came up he batted each over the head with has paddle and hauled them out one after another. He was disqualified because he used his paddle and not his hook.

Near the end of the Derby there was curiosity among several fishermen as to why a fisherman from Poland was catching only large fish. "The Derby is fixed," a fisherman from Japan protested and demanded the fish inspector from France find out what the Polish fisherman was using as bait.

When the inspector began his investigation he initially used his binoculars and spotting scopes but then when he dove into the bottom of Manila Bay found a perogi. As the inspector surfaced he concluded why the Pole was catching so many large fish because he used perogi as bait. The inspector concluded: "Upon close scrutiny I found Mr. Polanski attaches a cheese perogi to his hook, drops the hook into the water and as the perogi unfurls, the fish get excited and voila, latch onto the hook."

As soon as the inspector said those words a fisherman from Norway let out a scream that could be heard all the way to Quezon City. "Hey! I just caught something huge, really huge on my fish lure! Please help me to tow it to shore!"

Those watching the Norwegian and other fishermen tug and pull, onlookers were at awe when his wife ran down the dock with a large net, and Mayor Ed Ramos with a camera. Following the catch the whale shark was brought to Mandaluyong City Hall Maysilo Circle to be weighed at a time the site was overrun with reporters from throughout the world and as a military band played and chorus girls waged flags, Mayor Ed Ramos declared:" "Congratulations Ollie Jensen, you have latched on to the largest whale shark ever seen in Manila Bay and have won first prize. I now declare the first International Manila Bay Fishing Derby officially over."

A soon as the shark was weighed, Mr. Jensen said, "A whale shark is worth more alive than dead,"

The whale was brought back to Manila Bay and in the calm water let loose. A short time later Mr. Jenson accepted the 1-million and flew back to Oslo, Norway.

As soon as the Derby was over Survey Monkey conducted three research surveys among the foreign fishermen: (1) What they didn't like about Manila. (2) What they did like about Manila and (3) Why the foreign fishermen were often late to launch their fishing boats.

What Foreign Fishermen Didn't Like about Metro Manila

1 Traffic jams throughout the city and the honking of a car's horn a way of life

2   Some poverty stricken Filipinos make a cemetery their home
3   Mosquitoes everywhere
4   Everyone has a chicken, even in the city
5   Too much bribery, graft and corruption and people can pay to defy the law
6   Too many monsoons which cause flooding and mudslides
7   Every Caucasian fisherman is called Joe
8   The government suggest people pray for miracles
9   Many Filipinos believe in 'Filipino' time' no matter what
10 The personal computer is mainly used for games and Facebook
11 Believe that the Virgin Mary is always keeping an eye on you
12 Jeepenys and buses are overloaded and crossing the street involves running for your life
13 Hundreds of Koreans who can't speak English or Tagalo
14 To many earthquakes and hostage taking of foreigners
15 Many Filipinos bugged foreign fishermen to find work abroad in their country

What Foreign Fishermen Liked About Metro Manila

1   Filipinos have a sense of humor and laugh at themselves despite a crises in the country
2   Even the poverty-stricken use the latest cell phones and wear a fake Tommy Hilfiger or a Ralph Lauren
3   The number of large shopping malls where one can purchase a, 'I have been to the Philippines T-shirts

4   Observe whales and dolphins in Manila Bay
5   Wealthy foreigners could invest in building a casino or a shopping mall
6   Can do bungee jumping from almost any bridge
7   Mandaluyoung has some of the pretties women in the world
8   Manila has no nuclear power plants
9   Enjoy the Manila Bay sunset
10 The personal computer is mainly used for games and Facebook
11 Excellent snorkeling in coral waters
12 Filipinos are good ballroom dancers and karaoke singers
13 4 a. m. is not considered bedtime yet
14 Being the sister city of Dubai, United Arab Emirates
15 Every street corner has a basketball court, a Jollibee restaurant and a Shell gas station,

Why Foreign Fishermen Were Often Late to Launch their Boat

1   Long lineups at Jollibee and McDonalds
2   Chickens and stray dogs crossing the road
3   Temporarily lost keys to car or boat
4   Unexpected family emergency back home
5   Attending a blow-out sale is more important that being 10 minutes late
6   Lost their watch which was received in a door to door box from Dubai
7   First had to have a haircut
8   Staying up late enjoying a glass of rum or beer
9   Argued with other fishermen about the bait they were using

10 Roosters failed to crow in the morning
11 Afraid to be kidnapped
12 Forgot to flush the toilet
13 Waiting to see when there will be another coup d'état
14 Staying up late and enjoying a balut
15 'Wondering when the next Miss Earth Pageant will be held in the Philippines

Nineteen

Ed did not seek re-election as mayor of Mandaluyong City and in 2006 instead he purchased Best Realty from Rogelio Best and changed the agency name to Ed Ramos Realty, and at the same time was going to celebrate his 50th birthday. The agency purchase deal was complicated, and completed only after Ed offered a 10% commission discount to vendors should their property be sold within ninety days. This of course annoyed some of the rival agencies and even Linda said he should not do that. Negotiating the complex sale was difficult which in the end Ed said, "If you own the company you have to climb the corporate ladder. In my opinion it's the best deal since the Philippines was purchased by the Americans from Spain for 20 million dollars and more exciting than when Canada defeated America in the 1812 War. At any rate, Ed Ramos Realty has so expand its operation and move into a new office and direction."

After the dust was cleared Ed sat down at a table and with Linda discussed items that were critical in the future success of the company. These items included: additional staff. a cellular phone and a measuring tape for each salesman, a pair of grey colored pants and a blue blazer with an Ed Ramos crest on it, a talking alarm clock so the salesman wakes on time, a pair of rubber boots in case of a heavy rain, a shiatsu pup so the wife has someone to talk to when the husband is away from home, a digital camera and as for the new office

Location, it was in the SM Megamall EDSA where the parking was adequate and rent a bit higher. But to Ed that did not matter, what did was that the mall was the largest in Asia and the traffic in the mall was heavier with prospective buyers wanting to buy and vendors to sell.

The new office at SM Megamall was huge with wooden floors lacquered in shining white and a modern kitchen with a coffee maker to enjoy coffee during a break, a microwave oven to warm up the rice and other Filipino food and a refrigerator to keep beer cool. The office also had a stylish stone bathroom, a twenty foot oval table in the conference room, well lit cubicles for individual salesmen and a twenty four hour alarm system. Computers and monitors were everywhere. Wires to faxes, copiers and scanners ran over the floor in no apparent design. The wall in the lobby was covered with photos of Ed Ramos Realty salesmen.

Now Ed needed someone to help run the office so Linda advertised in the *Inquirer, Twitter, MySpace and Facebook* and within a week received more than 50 applications.

Ed interviewed a bunch of great candidates but none greater that his own housekeeper Christian Udio.

Christian was enthusiastic, tireless, had a sense of humor and previous experience as a clerk in the with Lucio Tan conglomerate in processing Chowking restaurants. This for Ed was a blessing.

Christian accepted permanent full-time employment with company benefits which included a lucrative pension plan, free health and dental benefits and the ability to spend a three week holiday with her family in Tomas Oppus, Southern Leyte. With Christian onboard it made everything feel different, Not better or worse just a lot more serious.

As soon as the April showers turned to May flowers and the grass had riz, Linda and Christian often wondered where Ed is. Ed was a promoter and when he wasn't in Metro Manila he would be Singapore or Hong Kong trying to float a loan but because of inexperience, finding a mortgage loan was difficult until he went to the Banco de Oro Universal Bank and asked the receptionist, "May I please see the bank manager," and she replied, "Certainly, I'll go and fetch him?"

Once the bank manger arrived he introduced himself as Peter Wong, a 45-year old Filipino of Chinese heritage and invited Ed into his office. Once inside, Mr. Wong closed the door behind him, and for extra measure, tuned the key in the lock. Once seated, Wong said, "Now, Mr. Ramos, that we are alone, how can I help you?"

"I need to open an account in your bank and request a mortgage loan."

"For what amount?"

"2000.000 pesos."

Ed fidgeted in his chair while the bank manager reviewed a mortgage application and then said, "Mr. Ramos, your assets seem to be in order. How about your liabilities?"

Ed said that he could lie with the best of them. The manager took that to mean that Ed was a successful entrepreneur and the mortgage was approved without difficulty.

There's no human impulse greater for a realtor than the urge to own his/her own real estate. Ed wanted to purchase revenue producing properties for him and Linda and the first property he purchased was a 26 unit apartment building called Sunset Place in the poverty stricken district of Mandaluyong City where parents had to choose between putting food on the table or a child's education and the cross was more popular than the switchblade.

City police recently published a month of criminal activities in the area and were called to investigate 12 stolen vehicles, 11 fights in bars, 10 false security alarms 9 B and E's, 8 purse snatchings, 7 marital disturbances, 6 obscene phone calls, 5 purse snatchings, 4 stabbings, 3 child abductions, 2 homicides and rescue of a cat which refused to come down a tree.

Shortly after the mortgage was approved, Ed named Christian as the manager and her first experience as a landlord began when a tenant moved into a one-bedroom unit and hosted a warm-up party whose theme was: "As many friends in the small unit as possible."

This was a major success and confirmed by the number of policemen ultimately involved following a phone call to 911 and fistfights, broken glass and furniture which preceded the call.

Christian was out to be a Kind Lady type of a landlord and listened to tenants' complaints acknowledging them immediately.

As it turned out besides being a landlord Christian soon became a plumber, which was unfortunate because the building was equipped with antiquated fixtures. Also inappropriate items kept mysteriously lodged in the toilet. Christian would respond to the toilet alarms in the middle of the night using a mechanical snake, retrieving the plugged toilet items. Items like: female sanitary pads, fish heads, bowling shoes and stripped marijuana plants. When Christian would show the items to the tenants they always appeared to be amazed and blamed the lodged items on other tenants.

On the 15th of each month Christian would usually be hit for a loan by some of the tenants. Most of the reasons were for:

1   To buy rice
2   Bus fare
3   Repair a bicycle
4   Buy gasoline
5   Attend a cock fight
6   Pay for a drug prescription
7   Bail a relative out of jail
8   Buy school supplies
9   Buy fish from a vendor
10 For a fee at an Internet Café

One may say Christian had a sense of humor, and so did one of the tenants. This occurred when an amateur musician was making horrendous sounds with his saxophone and Christian knocked on his door. As soon as the door opened Christian yanked the saxophone from the tenant's hands and said. "Don't you know there's an elderly lady in the suite next to you?"

The tenant replied, "I don't think so. Would you mind humming a few bars and then I'll be able to play it for you."

Then there was the tenant in # 21who phoned Christian in the middle of night complaining that the smoke detector in his room was so sensitive that it had gone off for the umpteenth time.

"Rodolfo Prima, maybe it's because of the smoke from your cigarette that is causing it to go off. When did it go off the last time?" Christian asked,

Prima answered, "The last time the smoke detector went off was when I farted."

It's not the first time that Mr. Prima came to Christian's attention. A week earlier while Christian was in Cebu on a business trip, he had an accident when he tried to open his apartment door as he was about to go to work at his bank and the key broke in the lock.

After resorting in vain to screw drivers and pliers he decided to call a locksmith who arrived promptly and as Prima looked through the peep hole said, "My key broke off inside the lock.

"To change it, it will take at least an hour and I'll have to charge you at least 3000 pesos," replied the locksmith.

"I don't have any money with me at the moment but when I go to the bank I'll pay you."

"I'm very sorry sir," the locksmith articulated with instructive courtesy. "I'm afraid that as a charter member of the Mandaluyong City locksmith union and one who helped to draw up the last Collective Agreement, I'm prohibited from unlocking your door unless I'm paid in advance."

"You are joking of course."

"The subject of the Locksmith's Union is no joking matter. In drawing up the Collective Agreement no detail had been overlooked and clause number 7 says Gold shall open doors, and doors shall adore it."

"Please," Prima pleaded. "Be reasonable. "Open the door for me and since I have no cash on hand I'll use my credit card."

"I'm sorry sir. Our company doesn't accept credit cards and further more there are ethics involved. Have a good day."

And with that the locksmith made his exit.

Bewildered Prima called the bank where he worked as a teller and informed his supervisor that he probably wouldn't be able to come to work this day and called another locksmith, and just in case, said to himself, "I'm not going to say I have no money until after he opens the door for me."

Prima then searched the *Yellow Pages* in the city directory and dialed a number.

"What address?" a guarded receptionist asked.

". . . . Street. Sunset Place. Apartment number 21."

The receptionist hesitated and asked Mr. Prima to repeat the address and then said, "The place where you are calling from is Sunset Place?"

"It is."

"Impossible. The locksmith union prohibits us from doing any work at that address."

And before another word was said the receptionist hung up.

So Prima went to the *Yellow Pages* again and made another dozen calls to other locksmiths and the instant they heard the address and the name of the apartment building they refused to do the job. To find a solution elsewhere Prima called the janitor, Ray Joson, and he replied, "In the first place, I don't know how to open door locks, and in the second, even if I did know, I wouldn't do it because my job is cleaning the place and not letting suspicious birds out of their cages."

Prima then called the bank in hope his supervisor could come and open the door.

"Bad luck," the supervisor said. "So you can't get out of your apartment? You just never run out of excuses not to come to work."

At this point Prima had a homicide urge. He hung up, called the bank again and asked for a co-worker, Jun Cariano, that he knew well and a bit brighter than his supervisor.

Sure enough Cariano seemed interested in finding a solution and asked, "Tell me, was it the key or the lock that had broken?"

"The key. Half of it is inside the lock. The doorknob won't turn left or right."

"Did you try to get the piece that is stuck inside out with a set or pliers or a screw driver?"

"I tried both but it's impossible."

"Then you'll have to call a locksmith."

"I already did but they want to be paid in advance."

"So pay them and there you are."

"But don't you understand. I have no money with me."

"You sure have problems. Sorry but I can't help you."

And so ended that day, but on the 2nd Prima got up early to make more phone calls. But something he found quiet frequent, not only the intercom but also the telephone was out of order. Problem: how to request repair service without a telephone to place a call? Prima went onto the balcony and began shouting at people walking along the street which was deafening with honking vehicles. At most, an occasional person would raise his head distractedly and then continue.

Next on his computer Prima composed the following message and had it printed: Madam or Sir: My key has broken off in the lock. This is the second day that that I'm locked inside my apartment. If you find this note please help me. I'm at the Sunset Place Apartment unit # 21.

Prima made sheets of paper into little airplanes and threw them over the railing and they fluttered a long time. Some with the help of the wind flew as far as Shaw Boulevard and some were run over by non-stop vehicles, some landed on awnings of outdoor buildings but one dropped on the nearby sidewalk where diminutive gentlemen picked it up and read it.

Prima then looked towards the sidewalk shading his eyes with his left hand putting on a friendly face, but the gentleman tore up the paper into many pieces and with an irate gesture threw them into the gutter.

Seconds turned into minutes and minutes into hours but Prima continuing throwing paper planes from the balcony, but they were either not read or if they were, weren't taken seriously.

By late afternoon, an envelope was slipped under Prima's apartment door. The telephone company had cut off its service for non-payment. Then is succession electricity was cut off also and that is when Prima got irate and with his fist kept banging on the door alerting Christian who just returned from Cebu. Taking notice of the problem, Christian called a locksmith, paid in advance, a new key was cut and the door opened.

Christian kept a monthly Sunset Place tenant/landlord diary which highlighted each day of the month with an interesting event or two for the record. Here is a sample of Christian's diary for the month of June.

DATE—JUNE   HIGHLIGHT

1   People's Army, the armed wing of the Communist Party, attacked last night
2   Temperature 38C—very hot
3   Tenant in # 1 used a trap door in the kitchen floor as a bathroom
4   A disturbance erupts in # 4—Cops charge common law husband
5   Tenant in #23 unable to pay his rent
6   Fish vendor forgets his cell phone
7   Tenant in #11 has his bicycle stolen
8   Four year child found sleeping in the laundry room dryer
9   Temporary power outage in area
10 Tenant in # 24 given an eviction notice
11 Sunset Place has a mosquito attack. I slap, slap, slap
12 Celebrate Philippines Independence Day—Freedom from Spain in 1898
13 Someone steals flowers from Sunset Place landscape

14 Remove chicken droppings from apartment entrance door

15 Bats found in Sunset Place attic

16 Graffiti removed from back entrance door—Several vulgar words

17 Another rain storm in Mandaluyong City

18 A transient found in the apartment dumpster searching for food

19 # 17 at 62 years of age, still wears a bikini instead of conventional clothing

20 First day of summer

21 I find large crayon marks in the first floor hallway

22 On television I watch a Philippine earthquake

23 Tenant in # 5 complains about the high cost of gasoline

24 Tenant in # 7 says she saw a UFO flying towards Baguio

25 Tenant in # 9 believing God is on her side engaged war on poverty by bombing the soup kitchen

26 Someone used a hallway corner on the third floor as a toilet

27 I have a meeting with apartment owner, Ed Ramos

28 Found many empty beer bottles in # 16

29 # 6 says as a youngster she worked at a Chowking restaurant in Davao

30 # 7 shouts, "Booo" every time one mentions the name Gloria Arroyo

As a landlord Christian kept a record of complaints received about Sunset Place

For the month of August. They were:

1 The washing machine in the laundry room is on the blink again

2   The toilet is blocked and we can't bath the children until it is cleared

3   I'm writing on behalf of my sink which I running way from the wall

4   Will you please send someone to mend our cracked sidewalk

5   Will you please send someone to look at my water? It's a funny color

6   We are letting you know that there is a strange smell coming from next door

7   What time is the 5:30 bus leaving for Bagio?

8   I want to complain about the farmer across the street. At 4:00 am his cock wakes us up

9   I request permission to remove my drawers in the kitchen

10 The tenant next door has a large erection in his back garden which is unsightly and dangerous

DATE; NOVEMBER   COMMENT

1	Yesterday Halloween	72 Kids knock on door trick or treating
2	All Saints Day yesterday	I light a candle on grannies grave
3	Purchase a new umbrella	Old one worn out
4	Fool moon tonight	Tenant in # 11 expects baby
5	A bus-sized meteor narrowly missed Planet Earth yesterday	
6	On TV watched a severe storm blow away a nipa hut in Southern Leyte	
7	Tenant in # 23 concerned about Global warming	
9	Purchase a new computer	
10	Health Inspector visits Sunset Place	

11 Eleven month of the year, 11th day of the month and 11th hour of the day

12 Ed gives me several tips on how to use YouTube, Twitter and Facebook

13 I'm in a dilemma if to evict # 2 or just give him a warning

14 Make a payment on the computer I purchased

15 Tenant in # 22 complains about washing machine broken in the laundry room

16 I must be getting dementia—forgot to put out the garbage last night

17 So windy overnight that it uprooted several coconut trees.

18 Have spare time so I read poems by Jose Garcia Villa

19 Ha, ha Ed Ramos says there are more important things than cock fighting

20 Tenant in # 17 buys a new motor tricycle

21 Tenant in #23 says she saw a frog on her bed. It's not a frog but a large bed bug

22 Tenant in #12 says she's moving to Palawan

23 Weather forecast for tomorrow 29C

24 Tenant in #26 says Tenant in #27 is smoking marijuana

25 Time to paint #03

26 Tenant in #29 has his bicycle stolen

27 Tenant in #20 says he lost his keys. I help him out with the emergency

28 Kids playing soccer beak window in # 03

29 Tenant in 05 says she has no money to have a prescription filled. I help her out

30 Celebrate Banificio Day with Linda and Ed

AND

<u>DATE—DECEMBER</u>   <u>COMMEMT</u>

1   Time to Christmas decorate Sunset Place as tenants have been singing Christmas songs since last October

2   Vicious rain storm over night. Several nipa huts blown away

3   I figure out that to deliver his gifts in one night Santa would have to make 888.6 visits per second, sleighing at 3000 times the speed of sound. At that speed Santa and his reindeer would burst into flames simultaneously

4   Cleaning lady wins 5000 pesos during a Christmas basketball raffle

5   Balcony lights rigged up

6   Big Pre-Christmas sale at Robinson's Department Store

7   Fifteen shopping days left before Christmas

8   Tenant in # 2 wants a motorbike for Christmas

9   Tenant in #3 wants a shotgun to keep #2 quiet

10 Rumor spreads that Christmas and Chanukah will amalgamate

11 Donate to the Salvation Army

12 I notice that tenant in # 23 keeps more beer in stock than food

13 Tenant in # 22 plays Christmas carols until 3 am

14 Postman begins Christmas deliveries to Sunset Place. Tenant in #5 receives a partridge on pear tree. # 19 two turtledoves and #17 3 French hens' and # 7, 4 Calling birds (Noisy things)

15 What a surprise as Postman delivers 5 golden rings to # 13. Honestly the squawking birds are getting on my nerves

16 Postman is back with more birds. Delivers 6 huge geese to # 3 and 7 laying swans to # 2. Several tenants complaining about the birds, their eggs and doo doo on some of the floors. I'm a nervous wreck.

17 On this day the Postman makes a special delivery of 8 maids who milk 8 cows in # 1 which is a two-bedroom unit. The cows were dancing and the maids singing *Jingle Bells* throughout most of the night.

18 I hear 9 pipers. They never stopped chasing the maids. The cows are upset and stepping on the birds. Feathers all over.

19 I watch as 10 Lords visit unit 22 and then leap out the second story balcony. A major health problem exists

20 Twelve marching drummers enter Sunset Place with the Health Inspector who following a thorough inspection says, "Christian, you have 24 hours to clean up or else I'll condemn the building."

21 I do as told

22 Take part in a midnight shopping spree. Buy presents for Linda and Ed

23 Get hair and fingernails done

24 Christmas Eve. Attend the midnight service at the No Name Universal Church

25 Ed, Linda and I enjoy a turkey dinner. Ed and Linda fight over the wishbone

26 Take part in a Boxing Day a super-duper special where buy one and get the second free

27 Tenant in # 14 complains that a second hand smoke from Santa's pipe is affecting his health.

28 Enjoy reading *book by* Jose Rizal, *Noli Me Tangere (Touch Me Not)* that Ed and Linda gave me as their Christmas present.

29 On this day, nothing fits me, not even my blouse. The cookies I nibble and the eggnog I drank at Christmas parties had gone to my waist

30 A Postman with a hernia shows up with a sack full of bills shouting "Dear tenants of Sunset Place. Your credit cards have been filled and you charged way. Visa, Master Charge and American Express. You have charged away all."

31 Attend the midnight New Year bash at the Hyatt Hotel Manila and at midnight from the balcony sip on wine and watch fire crackers light up the sky.

Its noisiest time of the year and Filipinos go all out setting off fire crackers. Pots and pans are clanged to scare away evil spirits. Several men shoot guns in the air and think they can get away with it. Cars, trucks and jeepenys are vroomed and horns are tooted to cause as much noise as possible. We watch as empty cans are dragged all around, whistles are blown and at exactly at midnight each jump as high as we can, a tradition, that we can grow tall and then wish each other other, "Bisperas ng Bagong Taon." (Happy New Year).

Early in January, after a tenant was evicted Christian found the unit trashed and hired a plumber to replace a damaged sink. While the plumber was working she went to MacDonald's for lunch. When Christian returned an hour later she found the basement apartment knee deep in water and phoned Emergency Control and Carpet Cleaning. When the van arrived the operator used a long vacuum hose, sucked up the water and then steam cleaned the carpets.

The operator was unable to repair the sink because while hosing the vacuum cleaner sucked the water and the screw driver and asked Linda to fetch him another. Christian was more familiar with sprits than tools, brought the plumber a glass, a can of orange juice and a bottle of vodka, placed them on the kitchen counter and disappeared.

By 5 p. m. the plumber got slightly inebriated and instead of working overtime or going home climbed into the Sunset Place attic and fell asleep not noticing the bats hanging from the rafters.

For three consecutive days the plumber did not show up to repair the sink. Thinking that he had quit Christian decided to do the plumbing herself. As she was installing a new sink she detected a strange odor coming from the direction of the attic.

Christian had never smelled anything like this before so she grabbed a ladder, opened the door leading to the attic barely squeezing inside, and searched with a flashlight. Christian already knew there were bats inside but was surprised the plumber didn't breathe.

There was no use resuscitating him so she called police but the policeman that answered the phone argued that it wasn't in the Police Policy manual to determine if the person was dead or alive. "It's the work of the coroner," the cop said. When Christian phoned the coroner's office was told that the coroner was about to strike for higher wages and was working to rule.

It was several more days before the coroner did arrive to view the body but in that time the bats had their Last Supper by devouring most of the plumber and an autopsy wasn't necessary. The coroner reported the death as SPDS—Sudden Plumbers Death Syndrome.

This is a syndrome of unexplained death among plumbers who ingest screwdrivers while at work.

The report was unchallenged except by hundreds of bats that flew out of the attic and dropped dead in the middle of the parking lot.

There were no last words. Christian never did find out what caused the bats to suddenly commit a mass suicide but thought, "The bats must have belonged to a cult."

The following night that the bats died, there was a solar eclipse of the moon in the Philippines and most of the Sunset Place tenants were outside watching the phenomena when suddenly Mr. Prima had an urgent call to the bathroom and minutes later, there was an explosion.

A careful Fire Marshall's report showed that the tenant in # 21, Rodolfo Prima, while watching the eclipse had a sudden urge to go to the bathroom, where he found a cockroach in the toilet bowl. Seeing that the roach was alive, Prima took a can of insect repellant and sprayed the bowl, making certain the insect was dead. What happened next, Mandaluyong City will never forget. Prima had tossed a burning cigarette into the toilet bowl. The cigarette made contact with the powerful repellant, and there was explosion followed by a fire. Prima escaped serious injury but this was the end of Ed's first revenue producing property.

As for Ed Ramos with the insurance covering Sunset Place, he used the 1000's of pesos to make a down payment on Ramos Tower, soon to be part of the Mandaluyong City skyline.

Twenty

Ed was surprised when he logged on his on *Facebook* page *and* noticed that Christian had already posted an invitation to his 50ᵗʰ birthday party that read: On April 15ᵗʰ Uncle Ed will be fifty years old and if you are planning to attend his birthday party please do not bring gifts of underwear, neckties or T-shirts. You are encouraged to bring adobo, bagoong, lechon and pancit instead. If you are unable to bring the above you may as an alternative bring $50 or 2500 pesos which will be given to a charity whereby poor children in Tomas Oppus, Southern Leyte can go to school. And please no rice as there's a current rice shortage in the Philippines. You'll have to enjoy potato salad instead.

Christian received 100 responses that they would attend the party but Daisy Ang who was employed by Popular Pinoy iHomes, a rival company, said that she couldn't bring the above but some balut.

Christian commented: "Daisy. Don't be funny, the suggested balut is an aphrodisiac and Uncle Ed has no need of the above for the present time, later maybe. If you really want to attend the party and are lacking food or money, I suggest you contact my former employer billionaire Lucio Tan and he might be interested in helping you, especially when the money will go to a charity.

Daisy commented: Christian, I made contact with Mr. Tan and he's unable to help because he is in the middle of recession renovating Chowking and Jollibee restaurants and opening new ones in Dubai, Unite Arab Emirates.

I also made contact with another billionaire, Henry Sy, and he too is building more Megamalls in Asia and thus can't help me. What should I do?"

Christian commented: Problems, problems. The wealthy make money while the poor make babies. Here's what you do. Contact President Gloria Arroyo and she may help.

Daisy commented: President Arroyo wasn't available to contact because she is preparing for another election. Her secretary however, said said that no donation would be forthcoming because she has problems of her own with the Muslim insurgency and the People's Army in Mindanao, recent earthquakes, floods and mudslides. The recovery cost is prohibitive.

But I have an idea. At age 50 Uncle Ed probably could use a walking cane, a walker or *Viagra*.

Christian commented: Daisy, I think you need a holiday. I'm told that Uncle Ed tried *Viagra* when he was 40 but Linda, his wife, got angry and threw the pills into a neighbor's yard where the chickens swallowed the pills one after another and were laying hard boiled eggs. So let's go to the top and contact Pope Benedict 11 in the Vatican. 80% of the Filipinos like you are Catholic so the pontiff may consider your request. But please do not make an error and contact the Queen of the United Kingdom because she may want to buy the Philippines like United States did in 1898.

Daisy commented: Christian. I've been chatting on *Facebook* too much and do need a holiday but here's good news. Pope Benedict is busy dealing with his own Church sex scandals throughout the world but his secretary suggested that I attend the the No Name Universal Church service and a special collection will take place to help with my problem.

Christian Commented: Awesome. I always believed a prayer could solve problems.
Keep me posted.

Daisy Commented: I attended the No Name Universal service and a special collection on my behalf took place which is great. I now can attend Uncle Ed's birthday party. I'm keeping the 2500 pesos so that I can attend Uncle Ed's birthday party and the rest I already sent to Tomas Oppus so the children can go to school and get an education which I never had. And do want to know something? There's 70% unemployment in Southern Leyte and parents have to make a tough decision if to put food on the table or the child's education. Twelve kids that I sponsor had no shoes and a day later each wanted a laptop and a cell phone.

On April 14th a tropical storm was taking place covering Metro Manila and the worse was still to come when on the 15th an earthquake shook parts of Laguna and 100's of flights were canceled or diverted from the Nimoy Aquino International Airport but at the Edsa Shanri-La Manila Hotel ballroom, Christian kept her promise and said to anyone who cared to listen, "Through bad weather and even bad time Uncle Ed's birthday party must go on."

Christian acknowledged the presence at the big bash that of the Canadian ambassador, the mayor of Mandaluyoung City and their wives along with leading socialites and business executives who earlier had paid for his and Linda's wedding expenses.

And adding to the excitement was Linda who would lead those present in karaoke singing and gorgeous Daisy doing magical card tricks. Soon there was the rhythmic pounding of the drums, shuffling of feet and waving hands as revelers in their Sunday best clothing were in a merriment mood wishing Ed a "Happy Birthday" while enjoying tuba wine, shoktong, beer and rum.

The Fiesta-like occasion featured a tapestry of Filipino food, karaoke singing and dancing.

For putting the party together Christian was given a, 'Thank You', applause. Raffles, promotions and giveaways were a persistent counterpoint as the crowd swelled, eager for the night's performance by *Freddie Agular* and to meet Ed in person.

As the evening entertainment progressed, excitement rose as scattered buzzes of excitement began to mount from the mouths of those lathed in sweets and from authentic Filipino food (buffet style).

Near the end the evening, there was cheering, shouting and hand clapping and a sense of coming as Ed's birthday cake with 50 lit candles was brought out which Ed had difficulty blowing out. Near 1 a. m. individuals shook Ed's hand wishing him another 50 years of good health, wealth and happiness and then went home.

With the food that was left over Christian donated it to the Mandaluyoung City Food Bank.

TWENTY-ONE

Since Ed was the sole proprietor of Ed Ramos Realty, he had to do a lot of travelling and one day while waiting at the Nimoy Aquino International Airport to catch a flight to the city of Davao in Mindanao to discuss an investment with a client, he noticed a computer scale that gave one's weight and fortune for 50 pesos. In order to make the trip tax deductable as humanly possible Ed paid 50 pesos into the slot machine and the computer screen displayed: "You weigh 150 pounds. You are married and on your way to Davao City."

Ed was amazed, and after watching 3 other people step up to the scale and their weight, marital status and destination correctly identified, he ran into the men's washroom, changed his clothes and put on a pair of dark glasses and stepped on the scale again and paid another 50 pesos.

This time he computer read: You still weigh 150 pounds. You still are married. You are on your way to Davao City. And idiot, you have just missed your flight.

When Ed caught the next flight, he downed a martini next to a portly gentleman from Baguio who was ignoring the *No Smoking* sign and lit a king-size cigar. He asked Ed, "Sir, will the smoke bother you?"

"Not if throwing up, won't bother you," Ed replied.

The passenger put out his cigar but then while flying over the mountains a young boy was making a nuisance of himself bouncing a ball inside the jet. Ed became annoyed and said to the child, "Listen kid why don't you go outside and play?"

By this time Ed had several more martinis' courtesy Philippines Airlines, when an elderly woman sitting nearby smelled his breath and said to him, "Sir, I think you're going to hell."

Ed jumped out of his seat, and raising his arms towards the sky, exclaimed, "Good heaven. I must be on the wrong jet!"

It was during April in 2006 that following his trip to Davao, that Linda and Christian accompanied Ed to Toronto, Canada for the International Realtors' Convention. Before their flight they each had a bath and a haircut and not to embarrass anyone wore a clean pair of under pants in the event there was a plane crash. Although the plane didn't crash, the three passengers sat in the back of the jet and had a diarrhea attack.

During flight to Toronto Ed said to Linda that since the Ed Ramos Realty business was booming she could have anything she wanted while he was attending the convention.

As soon as the plane arrived at the Pearson International Airport, Linda said to her husband, "Ed, darling, that was a wonderful flight. I really enjoyed the Philippine Airline plane we were riding in."

Ed purchased the 737 Boeing jet on the spot and changed the Philippine Airline logo to 'Linda Ramos's private jet' which meant that from this day onward Linda would have fewer headaches due to carry-on luggage. To ease the space crunch found on commercial airlines Linda wouldn't have to join the frantic scramble for overhead storage or someone else's suitcases stuffed in her space.

As a frequent traveler Linda wouldn't have to risk back injury trying to hoist heavy suitcases over her head or annoy fellow passengers with a couple of bags and no place to put them.

Best of all, Linda wouldn't have to get her luggage off the carousel, line up when she wanted to go to the bathroom or eat cold airline food while 30,000 feet in the air.

The following day, while watching a baseball game between the Toronto Blue Jays and New York Yankees, Linda sidled up to Ed and said, "The Skydome we are in, a retractable roof, what a beautiful building."

Ed purchased the Skydome outright and as a bonus the CN Tower next to it.

A day later, while shopping at the Eaton Centre Linda said, "Ed, do you think you can buy me a Mickey Mouse outfit?"

"Sure thing," Ed replied and purchased his wife the Toronto Maple Leafs of the National Hockey League.

Next day, the International Realtor's Convention started on time and during the mid-week break, Linda and Christian continued shopping and doing a Cultural Survey among Canadian, American, British, Australian and Filipino realtors. Ed on the other hand along with realtors from India and United Arab Emirates, decided to go into the country and see what other parts of Ontario were like.

But near Niagara Falls, the three realtors got caught in a severe thunder storm; visibility became so poor that they couldn't drive another kilometer. Seeing a farmhouse nearby, they asked the farmer to put them up for the night.

"Sure thing," farmer Bing Lodi, said and then apologized, "I live in a small cabin and there's room only for two. One of you will have to sleep in the barn."

The realtor from India, Harjet Singh, volunteered, but minutes later there was knock on cabin door and Singh said to the two other realtors,."I can't stay in the barn because there's a cow inside, and to sleep near one, is against my religion."

"That's all right," said Hasoon Mustafa, the realtor from the United Arab Emirates, "I'll sleep in the barn."

Minutes later, there was a knock on the cabin door, again and realtor Mustafa said, "I'm sorry, there's a pig in the barn. Sleeping near one is against my religion."

So Ed volunteered but several minutes later, there again was a knock on the cabin door. The realtors from India and UAE opened it and in front of them stood the cow and the pig.

Needless to say the realtors from India and Israel had little sleep that night. As for Ed, he slept well but when he woke up in the morning, accidently stepped into 2 separate manure piles.

As soon as the storm was over, the 3 visitors, after visiting Niagara Falls, Welland and St. Catherines, headed back to Toronto where as a highlight of the convention Ed was scheduled to speak about the surging real estate market in the Philippines. As Ed was about to make his speech he had lost his false teeth which embarrassed him.

The convention chairman sitting next to Ed, said, "Try these?"

After trying a pair Ed, frustrated, said, "Too tight."

"I have another pair, try these."

After trying a pair, Ed said, 'Too loose."

After trying several more "Try these" Ed finally found a pair that fitted perfectly and after a short pause began his speech by saying, "It's a pleasure to see you all here tonight at the International Convention of Realtors'—the big shots, the little shots and those who have just come back from the cocktail bar, the half shots."

Following the speech, the exasperated Ed, thanked the chairman sitting next to him during an embarrassing moment. "Thank you for coming to my aid, but please tell me, where is your office, because while in Toronto I might as well see a dentist?"

Ed was surprised when the chairman said. "But I'm not a dentist."

"What are you then?"

"I'm an undertaker at Bedford Funeral Services."

The convention concluded with the presentation of the coveted *World Best Seller Award* signifying that the realtor in his particular country had sold more real estate the year before than his competitors.

Records showed that Ed Ramos was not only the top seller in the Philippines but also Planet Earth, and for his efforts, was awarded the first prize, an opportunity to ask God three questions of personal nature.

As soon as technicians made the connection with heaven, Ed's first question was, "Will I, Ed Ramos, retire a happy realtor?"

"Yes," replied the Almighty "But not in your life time"

"Will I have a poetry book published?"

"Let me check."

There was a short pause.

"You had one published when you were in heaven the first time."

Ed's final question was, "Can I become a president of the Philippines?"

"Not in my lifetime," God answered, "Why don't you try and win a congressional seat instead?"

Ed reflected for several seconds and then said. "Thank you Lord, I might."

TWENTY-TWO

A Presidential election in the Philippines was called for June 10, 2006 so Ed asked Linda if she could be his campaign manager, to which she agreed, but on condition that if he won the election, she would not accompany him to Manila, but stay in Batangas City to which Ed agreed, but said, "You and I disagree now and then, but if you won't come with me and live in Manila, winning the election won't mean a thing, if you aren't with me."

Linda also agreed to be his ghost writer and that he would seek election as an Independent.

"Awesome," Ed said. "I'll have a 250,000 peso budget and 50,000 for printing signs and bumper stickers.

"And the remaining 200,000?"

"For incidentals. Of course these figures are subject to change, but the point is that an election is a golden opportunity for me to make international contacts, and expand our business on an international level."

So why did Ed choose Linda as his manager? Because Linda having planted a garden and pulled all sort of weeds from the lawn, she was familiar with grass roots which one needs in order to win an election.

On arrival home in Mandaluyong City, Ed asked Linda, "How did you and Christian make out with the Cultural Difference Survey while in Canada?"

"Fine, just fine. We noticed significant differences between the Brits, Americans, Australians, Canadians and Filipinos."

"What kind of differences?"

Linda while looking on her survey charts said:

Aussies: Believe you should look out for your mate

Brits: Believe that you should look out for those who belong to your club

Americans: Believe that people should look out and take care of themselves

Canadians: Believe that it's the government responsibility

Filipinos: Believe that they have lost faith in their government to do anything

----

Aussies: Dislike being mistaken for Brits when abroad

Brits: Can't possibly be mistaken for anyone else

Americans: Encourage being mistaken for Canadians

Canadians: Indignant about being Americans when abroad

Filipinos: Don't care, so long as they can find employment abroad

----

Aussies: Are extremely patriotic to their beer

Brits: Don't sing at all but prefer a brass band

Americans: Are flag-waving, anthem singing, and obsessively patriotic to the point of blindness

Canadians: Can't agree on the words of their national anthem

Filipinos: Can sing their anthem in Tagalog but can't sing it in English

----

Aussies: Export all their TV programs which no one
    watches, to Britain
Brits: Pay a tax for just 4 channels
Americans: Spend most of their lives glued to the idiot box
Canadians: Don't watch Canadian TV unless they are
    American programs
Filipinos: They watch CBS-CBM with a chance to win
    1-million pesos

Aussies: Are interested only in swimming, rugby and tennis
Brits:: Win in sports only during the Olympics
Americans: Love to watch sports on television
Canadians: All love to watch hockey, hockey and hockey
Filipinos love basketball and cock fighting

Aussies: Chatter incessantly on how they beat the Brits
Brits: Chatter incessantly about cricket, soccer and rugby
Americans: Chatter incessantly about football, baseball and
    basketball
Canadians: Chatter incessantly about the Federal
    government
Filipinos Chatter incessantly how to find an employer
    abroad

Aussies: Add 'Mate' and a heavy accent to everything they say
Brits: Pronounce their words differently, but still call it
    English

Americans: Spell their words differently and call it English
Canadians: Spell like the Brits, pronounce like Americans
Filipinos: Speak Tagalog but think its English

Aussies: Drink anything with alcohol in it
Brits: Drink warm beer
Americans: Drink weak beer
Canadians: Drink strong beer
Filipinos: Drink little beer but plenty of home-made
    coconut wine (tuba)

Aussies: Produced comedians like Paul Hogan, Steve
    Abbott
Brits: Are proudly justified of their comedians
Americans: Think that Brit comedians are Americans
Canadians: Have produced comedians like Art Linkletter,
    Jim Carrey and Dan Akroyd
Filipinos: have produced comedians like Marcos, Estrada
    and Arroyo

Aussies: Don't understand what inclement weather means
Brits: Endure oppressively wet and dreary winters and are
    proud of it
Americans: Have to watch for tornados and hurricanes
Canadians: Endure bitterly cold winters, and are proud of it
Filipinos: Have earthquakes and monsoons' to contend with
    and are happy

Ed was delighted with the Cultural Difference Survey Linda and Christian had done

Some of the finer points Ed could use while campaigning during the election.

TWENTY-THREE

Although initially it was thought that Ed wasn't a natural born Filipino and thus according to the constitution, prohibited becoming a congressmen, unless he proved his birth date.

Two weeks later, Ed produced a birth certificate proving that he was born in Batangas City and his parents at the time were living in Canada but holidaying in the Philippines.

Since Mandaluyong City was well represented by the current Representative and most likely unbeatable, Ed instead, decided to ease the existing recession and seek the political Congressional seat in his former stamping ground of Batangas City. According to the latest census, the city has a population of nearly 296 000 people where the major concern of the day can best be described in one sentence—Sudden Exploding fish in Batangas Bay.

At least voters should have expressed concern, because through carelessness of some kind or another, the Philippine premier tourist attraction had suddenly been badly thrashed because of the exploding fish.

And residents, in and outside, the city were literally weeping over this, a phenomena that took place most often during sunset. One fisherman gave an account of such an explosion in the *Daily Post.*

Next to the article, was a photo of a humungous fish which had a large gouged hole in the middle. The fish could have been a star in a low budgeted horror movie entitled *Filipino Fish in Jeopardy.*

So, Ed sold his condo in Mandaluyoung City and bought house in Batangas City which featured a walled perimeter with guarded gates and a security system. The house was near a beach and where one could go golfing, boating, surfing, scuba diving and snorkeling and a short distance from Taal Volcano and Lake, another tourist attraction. The house was also near a shopping mall, a recreation facility and nearby lookalike homes.

As a declared candidate, Ed was familiar with the sights and sounds of the constituency and to anyone who cared to listen, said, "I intend to be upright, honest and straight foreword during my election campaign. I won't be like other politicians who make promises that cannot be fulfilled. You won't see me slinging mud at anyone. I state that my priority is to find out what is causing the fish to explode. The rest of my platform will be announced to the media tomorrow."

The following day Ed held a media news conference and released his 10-point platform.

1 Do a study of fish exploding in Batangas Bay
2 Help Batangas City construct more places of worship than cock fighting arenas
3 A free trampoline for each public playground
4 Provide a computer for each elementary school
5 Make the coconut tree the Philippine national tree
6 Make Pig Latin the third Filipino language
7 Help Meals on Wheels to assist the poor and unemployed
8 Establish more reliable weather forecasting
9 Bonificio Day not moved from Wednesday to a Monday
10 Go after Batangas City smoking belchers

At the conclusion of the news conference, Ed said, "It deeply concerns me that none of the potential candidates, especially Liberal Ryan Noble and Ernesto Cheato of the Christian-Muslim Democratic Party, has the courage to speak on the daily fish explosions or other subjects I'm going to push forward."

Why did Ed run as an Independent aside his interest in the exploding fish? When Ed first voted Liberal and then for the Philippine Christian-Muslim Democrats, both parties seemed similar to him, with no difference, and both sides in Congress and outside, made derogatory remarks about each other.

There were gaffes in the campaign, some funny, some fatal.

There was the time Ed spoke to the Filipino Women Equal Rights Movement and did not follow Linda's script that she had written and instead said to the ladies present: "You women must unite because I'll be candid, as long as you are split in the middle you'll always find men on top of you."

But the NUCD-UMDP Party too, distinguished itself with triple gaffes. There was the early revelation that their candidate Ernesto Cheato, as a lawyer, defended an Abu Sayaff terrorist, who believed part of Mindanao should be a separate country.

Then card carrying members came forward to link Cheato with the New People's Army with the aim of overthrowing the government. Officials then blatantly admitted they knew about Cheato's radical views before an article appeared in the *Inquirer*, but no one notified their leader President Gloria Arroyo.

Then with the deadline fast approaching, lawyer Cheato, won the candidacy, but next day was charged with overpaying Legal Aid. Hearing this, President Arroyo stepped in and fired Cheato as a party candidate but he ungraciously refused to withdraw.

And then the President ordered the riding Association to pick another individual, which it did. It picked Cheato's campaign manager but in the end, she refused to file her nomination papers by deadline and Mr. Cheato ran as an Independent. The NUCD-UMDP had no candidate but Cheato's people pulled several boners too. They warned through newspaper and television ads that if a Liberal government was elected, voters in Batangas City would have to pay a large amount in taxes and sent out fake tax notices to all constituency homes. The unsubstantiated claims came in envelopes with a "Notice of Assessment" printed on them. The claim was that over the next 5 years Liberal programs would cost an individual tax payer in excess of 25.000 pesos per person.

There was a P. S. "Just think how many Jollibee hamburgers you could get for that amount of money."

And Pastor Atupan of the No Name Universal Church made a faux pas too when during his Sunday service said, "It's time for some change."

Hearing the Pastor, all the Liberals, except those with sore knees, walked out vowing not to attend his next service unless the Pastor apologized and even then, would place slugs into the collection basket instead of pesos.

Unfortunately for the Cheato group, the Provincial Assessment Authority had just mailed out the *real* tax notices.

The difference in this particular Batangas City riding compared to the rest of the Philippines was that there were 2 Independent candidates, Ed Ramos and Ernesto Cheato and the incumbent Liberal Ryan Noble and no NUCD-UNDP in a country that was ruled by the middle of the road party and Gloria Arroyo as president.

Liberal Noble as a sitting member of the Congress for 12 years was an experienced politician.

Although Liberals called him, "The old work horse" Cheato's supporters called him a "Womanizer."

Noble operated several Fast Food restaurants. That of course isn't saying a great deal. He also operated several pizza restaurants throughout Batangas City but lost them when he failed to make franchise payments. Then Linda and Christian did some nosing around and what they discovered surprised Ed. Besides having several pizza restaurants foreclosed they discovered that Noble:

1   When the Liberals were in power, he was going to be named as an ambassador to Canada, but wasn't fluent in English or French

2   Never had an inclination to attend the annual Independence Day celebration although he enjoyed taking part in the annual fiesta

3   Constantly complained about the courts and the Feminist Movement

4   Employed 2 nannies, but did not pay them the prevailing wage

5   His favorite expression was, "As President Cora Aquino use to say."

6   Knew that Philippines got independence from America but didn't on which date

Then Linda and Christian did a similar expose on Ernesto Cheato. Their finding, aside helping terrorists to plead innocence he was:

1   A left hander putting him in the same category as Napoleon Bonaparte and Jack the Ripper.

2   As a college student, stuffed pepper spray in a basketball cheerleader's pompon

3   Had a joint bank account. A deposit account for his
     wife and a checking account for himself
4   As an adult, killed a rooster that was crowing at 4
     o'clock in the morning
5   Was a charter member of the Get Rid of President
     Arroyo fan club
6   While in college smoked a marijuana cigarette

Halfway through the campaign, Ed went up and down
Batangas City streets, shaking hands, kissing babies and
handing out candy.

Following the ritual he would go to his campaign
headquarters, close the door behind him and discuss
strategy with Linda and Christian where one day he said,
"I'm not as young as I use to be but still, my main concern
is the fish exploding in Batangas Bay."

While Noble and Cheato were planning their
campaign, Linda lined up a series of appearances for Ed
which included a St, Brigit College class where he said to
the students:

"Education is great and College sex is dandy. Linda's
survey shows however, that four out of five college students
still prefer candy. And before you enjoy that candy make
sure that you do your homework. And no matter what
career you choose, you aren't going to be successful if you
have a stupid haircut, a tattoo on your body or a piercing
ring in your nose."

The college students were greatly impressed with
Ed's speech. This was confirmed by the questions they
asked afterward: "Why can't scientists make birth control
retroactive? While walking, why in most instances, is the
right foot at a 100 degree angle? Do mosquitoes sleep?
Which do you prefer a Pepsi or a Coke? And, "What is the
greatest joke you ever heard?"

And one student louder than the rest asked, "Sir, do you know any lawyer jokes?"

"I do," Ed replied, and told a story how Pinky Onod couldn't make it as a lawyer so he got an appointment as a judge."

Like at the college students those at the Batangas State University were also greatly impressed with Ed's speech. This was shown by the questions they asked afterwards, several of which were: "Is the Bible free of error and contradiction? For example, Gen 32; 30 states ". . . for I have seen God face to face, and my life is preserved," However, John1:8 states, "No man hath seen God at any time." "Why do scientists use rats instead of lawyers for laboratory experiments?, Should the book *The Origin and Growth of Whiskers* be mandatory reading in the Physiology 101 class? And, why sharks don't want to attack President Gloria Arroyo?"

Ed was accompanied to the university by a reporter from the *Daily News,* who wrote an article about Ed that he brewed his own beer and may not have a proper license. When Ed read the article, he shook his head to Linda said, "This is another example of media's desire to dig up sensational dirt about me."

Linda nodded her head and answered," One expects that kind of scrutiny. We live in an age where voters do not believe politicians or the media."

Ed continued, "I admit however, I must condition myself to dirty laundry tactics and for example that I made mistakes in my lifetime by fishing without a license, and not paying a traffic fine after I went through a STOP sign recently.

"But this is water under the bridge and while St. Patrick may have killed all the snakes in Ireland, I say it's time to get rid of all the liars in Manila. Now is the time to get on the Ed Ramos bandwagon."

Election time was an exciting event in Batangas City, where each candidate had handbills printed and distributed, 4X8 plywood signs placed in strategic locations and Vote for . . . . signs on lawns, fences and corporate buildings.

There were car bumper stickers too which read: 'Don't Trust a Politician" "No More Patronage, Bribes and Corruption" and "Why Waste your Vote this time?"

By now, Ed felt his chances of winning the election were increasing, following a strategy meeting and Ed had returned home, sank into a comfortable chair and said, "Linda, honey, the campaign is going fine, I now believe I might sweep the constituency."

Linda who was working on a report why fish were exploding in Batangas Bay, glanced at her husband and wearily said, "Great, then why don't you start with the living room floor?"

After Ed swept the floor, he enjoyed a cup of tea with Linda, and asked how her Exploding Fish Research was coming along?

"Fine, I think flashes during menopause have something to do with the explosions."

"You mean to say fish have menopause like women?"

"That still has to be researched."

Ed was worrying about the subject too because Linda was experiencing hot flashes, and at times was cantankerous and he had read that there were 3.5 million women in the Philippines near fifty and that the number was expected to top 5 million by the year 2015, when more women would be going through menopause than any time in Philippine history.

"Just think, if all that heat is concentrated in one time at one location, say Batangas City, what big explosion that would be."

Linda nodded her head and then sparing no expense interviewed Rabbi Libowitch's wife, Nora, who confirmed that menopause indeed could have an effect on global warming and cause fish to explode. "Personally at the moment I can cover either polar cap with steam."

The comment seemed conclusive having come from the wife of a rabbi, but the exploding fish of this magnitude, Linda had to have other input so she phoned a friend in India whom she got to know during the International Realtor's Convention in Toronto and spoke to her husband.

The husband said, quote, "Mahabeen is going through menopause right now and believe me it's not pretty. The temperature in a lake near Calcutta had shot up five degrees since the other women her age had power surges at the same time. Who knows, maybe the same thing is happening in the Philippines."

After interviewing menopause authorities in New York, London and Singapore, Linda's research was still inconclusive so she rented a mini-suberine like the one that found the *Titanic* in the bottom of the Atlantic Ocean, and along with a scientist from the University of Batangas, Dr. Jose Hillo, traversed the bottom of Batangas Bay back and forth. Dr. Hillo called this routine, "A bold new age in ocean exploration."

Of course the scientist could say that, but Linda couldn't say anything of that nature, because the back and forth movement made her dizzy.

As soon as Linda recovered from her dizziness, the mini sub was at the bottom of Batangas Bay where the couple collected soil and water samples, all in pursuit of exploring climate and pollution and what both had effect of the fish in Batangas Bay.

There was a plethora of reasons based not only a religious belief, but also on scientific, why the fish suddenly kept exploding but as soon as the fish were cut open at a laboratory, a concentration of toxic waste was found inside the fish tissue. Rumor spread that roughly 1.5 billion liters of partly treated effluent had spilled into the Bay from the city treatment plant, and officials had no idea how to solve the problem and hadn't shown a sense of urgency to fix it.

The other theory was that because poverty stricken residents, along with tourists, used the beach to dispose their garbage, which combined with the mercury and magnesium from natural sources, were the exploding culprit. To this point all theories were full of holes and inconclusive, so less than a stone's throw away at the No Name Universal Church, Pastor Atupan urged his parishioners and the entire Batangas City population to pray for a quick solution.

To assist with the exploding crises, the Batangas province ordered the Department of Environment & Natural Resources to find a quick solution and hired a scientist at the Philippines Water Solutions to do a study, and when he did, the response was alarming.

The scientist, Emmanuel Garcia, in his report stated that the North and South Pole Ice Sheets will disappear by 2020 and the ocean will rise 80 meters because of Global warming, and because of the rise in temperature the 7.107 Philippine islands with a population of 94-million, high tide or low tide, doesn't matter, may disappear. And the "Don't worry about the fish exploding; Get ready to move to the high mountains and Pastor Atupan's assertion that God's coming will spend half of his time in Jerusalem, and the other half in the Philippines, isn't definite, because my research shows that 50 years from now, only a handful of people on Planet Earth will believe that God exists.

A week before the election the three candidates appeared at public forum sponsored the Chamber of Commerce and televised by TV Patrol Southern Tagalog and simultaneously carried on radio by DZMM.

Numbers were drawn who would speak 1st, 2nd and 3rd.

Noble spoke 1st and fought to win the election based on his past experience and to serve Batangas City and the Philippines. Without paying additional taxes.

He also begged the electorate not to judge him on his past record as a congressman whose actions he could not control, especially the contracts that were doled out to relatives, friends and companies that contributed to the election campaign. And above all, the influence wealthy companies had on the government.

When it was Cheato's turn to speak he accused Noble of false promises and slammed what he termed, "Lies and innuendos."

Cheato also spoke about the large coconut tree he has grown in his back yard and promised to make Batangas City the coconut capital of the Philippines.

When it was Ed's turn to speak, he took exception to the poll Cheato's party had released and said, "Choice is of paramount concern to voters. The survey you conducted is rife with bias. Linda's poll will be released tomorrow."

Initially Ed thought both Noble and Cheato were impressive orators and formidable candidates and it appeared like a 2-way race between one and the other. The down feeling changed however after Ed said, "You are a political plum the result of careful grafting. Your machine is well oiled and it's no wander your group of supporters have so much friction."

Ed's assessment of the 2 opponents must of had struck favor with the voters, because after the forum, Linda's poll showed Ed's popularity rising with leaps and bounds.

"There's a surge, an uprising, a groundswell," Linda went on to describe the latest poll which appeared on television and was 19 out of 20 times correct and had a margin of error of 4.5 percent.

Then came the weekend before the election date, and Ed's excitement about being the next congressman was short lived when Noble leaked a report to the media, true or false, that he was carrying the constituency. It's difficult to comprehend how any man or even a woman could carry such a large parcel of land, but Noble did say, "Linda is plumb wrong with her survey because surveys are for losers."

What Cheato said at the time was that he had to cancel an interview on radio because of recurring laryngitis. "Why my vocal chords aren't working as well as Ramos's or Noble's is because I'm answering questions from the public and they aren't."

Finally, came the great day when Ed's volunteers phoned each household on the polling list reminding them to: "Vote for Ed Ramos."

As soon as the polling stations closed at 8:00 p. m, many of Ed's supporters were still inside the polling stations casting their ballots. Many had forsaken to do their nightly chores, to make certain Ed would win the election.

Ed, Linda and their strategists watched returns come in by watching television and listening to the radio at the same time.

While the NUCD-UNDP were winning federally, in the Batangas City riding, a 3 way race developed with Noble in the lead then Cheato and then Ed. In the 2nd bulletin Noble was in the lead and Ed was 2nd, and Cheato 3rd. The 3 candidates kept changing positions more often than Imelda Marcos changed shoes. This lasted for 6 hours until the Returning Officer officially declared: "Ed Ramos wins the election with a plurality of 1237 votes. A recount is unnecessary."

Here's a scoop on Ed winning the election. Noble said after the votes were counted, why Ed won the election was because due to the full moon on the day the election was held and commented, "People in Batangas City were under the spell of the moon and voted like zombies."

What Cheato said was, "Why I lost was because of an all-day traffic jam in the city."

At any rate one should have been at the Days Hotel Batangas ballroom that night when Ed and Linda walked inside and a 5 piece band struck up the *tune For He's a Jolly Good Fellow*. After, Ed smiling, with Linda by his side, and supporters cheering, gave his "Thank You" speech, and then pumped his fists into the air and said, "Friends, it's time to boogie."

Ed then grabbed Linda by the arm and the couple took to the dance floor. Soon a keg of Ed's home brewed beer was opened amid a burst of applause. Then, some who voted against Ed, joined those who did. Several even came up to Ed who weren't members of any party but Reformers.

Even the local undertaker, Ryan 'Boom Boom' Pinong, came to shake Ed's hand and apologized, saying his conscience was bothering him because he licked envelopes for the Liberal party.

Pinong wondered if his wife could get the job as the next census taker. To others who approached Ed and said it was only at the last minute that they decided to vote for him and wanted a civil service opportunity, Ed had a standard reply which was, "I had to kiss your ass so you would vote for me, now you can kiss mine if you want me to find you employment."

From then on, Ed didn't have to say much, aside his maiden speech. For the next 3 years as a Governor, Ed did not have to say a word while enjoying numerous perks. At any rate Ed winning the governorship in Batangas City was aside being the world's greatest real estate salesman, and now a rookie Philippine Governor, was one of his greatest achievements.

In Manila, the back white wall of Governor Ramos's office hung a picture of himself, the national the eagle, eating a monkey, and the national animal, the cariboa, pulling a plow in a rice field.

Behind his desk were the Philippine and Batangas City flags and at one end of his desk was an aquarium with tropical fish. It was a week after Ed got elected that he attended a school that outlined rules and procedures to fallow while Congress is in session.

Another week elapsed, before Congressman Ed began receiving mail and requests to be a guest speaker. He had already received copies of the *Inquirer* and *Batangas City Post*.

He also began receiving mail from lobbying groups along with pens, ashtrays, calendars and coffee mugs with logos on them and free I. Q. and stress tests.

During the 3rd week there was no hoopla, no posters or bumper stickers but aplenty of pomp and and circumstance as President Arroyo opened a new session of parliament and later, Ed made his maiden speech.

Ed did not speak about the maidens that were plentiful in his constituency but asked the Congress what the government was going to do about the sudden fish explosions in Batangas Bay.

Ed then handed the speaker an updated copy of Linda's Report on the fish explosions and with head tilted to one side, arms akimbo, eyes wide open asked Congress several questions which were:

When will fish stop exploding in Batangas Bay?

Why do so many people want to move Andres Bonificio Day to a Monday?

Is there enough pesos in the budget to provide a trampoline in every public playground in Batangas City and when Congress will establish more reliable weather stations?

As soon as Ed returned to his office, his secretary, Nena Ana, reminded the Congressman to send a newsletter to his constituents. She said, "It won't cost you a peso and leave an impression back home that you are extremely busy."

Next day, another letter came and addressed simply to the Stupidest Congressman in the Philippines.

"One would get angry even before it's opened," Ms. Ana said.

"Oh, I wouldn't get angry over a letter like that, but it does upset me when I realize the Post Office knew where to deliver it."

After several months in Manila, Ed began receiving mail from other constituencies. He enjoyed reading several in particular. The first was from Olympia Actuel, chairman of the Action Committee to Eliminate Poverty in Batangas province which helps those who have known nothing, but disenfranchisement, and wanted Ed to become an honorary chairman during a campaign to raise additional funding.

When Ed opened another letter, the signature was difficult to read but after putting it under a magnifying glass deciphered that it came from Linda who applied for funding honoring the 3 Batangas City, witches that were, along with Jose Rizal, hung in 1896.

Ed was opposed to such monuments but hoping Linda would join him and live in Manila the request was passed on to the Finance Committee which looked after such funding.

As soon as Ed finished reading the mail he rushed to the Philippine Historical Archives and read up on the witch hangings, and indeed found artifacts and literature about the Witches. The minister of Justice at the time had addressed his townspeople and said, "History imposes us tonight a difficult balance and task. We are here to commemorate something we are willing to forget."

The residents of Batangas City long absorbed the shock which had sent three innocent Christians including Linda's grandparents, to hang on the gallows and hoped the incident would have been forgotten but it wasn't until Linda revived it.

As recently as the time Manny Pacquio won his first fight in Las Vegas, Linda's family petitioned the Philippine government to declare the witches innocent.

Despite Ed living in Manila and Linda in Batangas City, their relationship was excellent and unfaltering. Linda spent much of her time entertaining Dominic but there were days too that she entertained her friends.

One evening Linda met with Lisa Ayop and Cherry Avila at the Casa Corazon Resort bar, and while sipping on a cocktail discussed their respective husbands.

Lisa was a loveable character who went prematurely gray so she dyed her hair to a range of festive colors. This particular evening she was a copper blond. Lisa always smelled exotic, not because of the under arm deodorant that she used but a combination of expensive perfume and cigarette smoke.

Cherry on the other hand, had a knack of making people feel as if they had known her for ever. She always wore fashionable clothing, knew the latest dance step and how to play the guitar, but never attended a Rock concert. Cherry was a brunette, bubbly and obscenity-sporting. After a second round of cocktails Liza said, "My husband is fantastic, for my birthday he bought me an expensive mink coat."

"And mine for my birthday bought me a yacht," Cherry said.

Then Linda continued, "Since Ed became a governor, he's so busy that he forgot to buy me anything and his tummy has grown so large that three hundred cockroaches can stand on it side by side."

After a long silence Lisa said, Listen girls. I was lying. My husband didn't buy me a mink coat but one made out of cloth."

Cherry followed, "Well, since you are telling the truth, Lisa, you might as well know that my husband didn't buy me a yacht but a rowboat."

As Liza and Cherry stared at each other Linda cut in and said, "Okay so I will tell you the truth too. That part about three hundred cockroaches standing side by side on Ed's stomach isn't true. There were only two hundred and ninety nine."

The following Saturday night, Linda, Liza and Cherry were enjoying cocktails at the Casa Corazon Resort Bar for the 2nd time, but this time, they were trying to impress each other how much money their husbands made.

Liza began by saying, "My husband just bought me a necklace and an earring set for our wedding anniversary which cost 1 million pesos, but I had to return the set because I'm allergic to platinum."

"I understand exactly what you mean," Cherry said, "For our wedding anniversary my husband bought me a mink coat, but I had to return it because I'm allergic to fur."

Just then Linda fainted, and when she recovered, Lisa and Cherry asked what made her faint.

Linda sighed, "I guess I'm allergic to hot air."

Despite living separated, Ed and Linda did exchange gifts. To mark their wedding anniversary, Ed went to Cesar's Jewelry Shop on Mabini Street. Seeing a musical box, which wound up played the tune *I Love You Truly*. Ed said to the clerk, "That's a gift my wife in Batangas City will like, but for one thing, Linda doesn't like the blue color."

"No problem," the clerk said, "We have some that are red," and wrapped the gift with appropriate paper. The day the musical box arrived in Batangas City, Linda was ecstatic until she opened it, and after she wound it, it played the tune," *The Old Grey Mare Ain't What She Use to Be.*"

Linda wasn't exactly perfect when it came in choosing gifts. For becoming a Congressman she wanted to buy Ed a gift honoring his new status and went to Plaza Mabini and said to the saleslady, "I'd like to buy a hat for Congressman Ed Remus who resides in Manila."

"No problem. What size?"

"I think Ed takes size 17."

"17?" the saleslady gasped. "You must be mistaken. Hats don't come in that size."

"Don't tell me that. I didn't marry a freak of nature but a Congressman. I know Ed's shirt collar is size 15, and his head is certainly larger than his neck."

As soon as Linda purchased the hat and sent it away, she returned home and with Dominic crawled into bed.

As Linda gazed at Dominic, she remembered that it wasn't his looks that attracted her to Dominic when she first met him. It was at the Days Inn Hotel that Linda came alone, sat on a stool and found that Dominic had replaced Fido as a security guard.

As soon as Dominic spotted Linda, he leapt from behind the counter, and sat on a vacant stool next to her. Dominic didn't offer to buy Linda a drink but after one glance in Linda's direction, she did not suggest that he was an unacceptable replacement for Ed. A minute later Dominic planted a kiss on Linda's cheek and she returned the touch with a smile. Neither Dominic nor Linda felt the need to speak and sat in silence, each thinking what would happen next. Linda kept enjoying her cocktail and Dominic his milk.

When the bartender cried out, "Last call, we're closing with the next half hour," Linda and Dominic jumped into a car and left together for home where Dominic envied Linda whose hair was turning gray and who still riding a mechanical bull each day as an exercise routine.

Linda never questioned Dominic's background, but the truth must be known, since Dominic came from a large family and eventually became an orphan. Dominic began to drift, often trying to stay ahead of the law, which was difficult to do in those days. Eventually Dominic showed up at Days Inn Hotel in Batangas City and hired as a security guard. All Dominic wanted all his life was someone to love, regular food and perhaps a family of his own. And so that night, Linda allowed Dominic to sleep in the same bed as she did. This led to a 2nd night and then a 3rd until they discovered that they really loved each other and even Ed's return would not break them apart.

By loving Dominic Linda wasn't breaking rules in a contemporary society, even when he attempts to commit adultery with all the D's in the Batangas City telephone directory.

Dominic can anticipate almost to the second when Linda will have breakfast ready for him. First he hears the sound of milk pouring into a bowl and Linda hollers, "Hey Dominic, my pet, it's time for breakfast!"

At that point, Dominic heads straight for the kitchen where Linda says, "Good morning Dominic."

As Dominic walks closer to Linda she pushes the bowl towards him and then Dominic begins to wag his tail and lap his milk.

It's a myth that a German shepherd dog that is lost may not eventually find the rightful owner.

TWENTY-FOUR

As soon as parliament adjourned for the summer recess, Ed returned to Batangas City where he visited as many of his constituents as he could. One of the first people Ed met was Olympia Actuel, chairman of the Action to Eliminate Poverty Committee in Batangas province and said to her, "How is the Meals on Wheels campaign coming along?"

"Amazingly well, we have already paid for one EnreBus and desperately need another where the mobile bus with a kitchen inside offers meals on wheels and aspiring chefs instruct for free culinary skills to the poor and the unemployed. It's an excellent program with cooking skills the poor and unemployed after passing their fourteen month culinary certificate, can gain employment in hotels and restaurants."

"And the cost for the mobile bus with a kitchen inside?" Governor Ed asked.

"120-million pesos."

'I'll tell you something," Governor Ed continued, "To raise that amount in Batangas City isn't easy these days so here's a suggestion. I realize that I'm much older than the last time and now can swim so why doesn't the Action Committee roast me and see what happens?"

"Governor Ed, that's a wonderful idea. I'll speak to the committee members and have tickets printed right away. On what date do you suggest that the Governor Rd Ramos roast be held?"

Ed looked at his appointment calendar which he always carried in his wallet and after studying the optional dates said, "How about a week from this Saturday?'

"Fine I'll have the Action Committee start planning right away."

Not having a physical examination in the past 5 years. Governor Ramos dropped in to see Dr. Perez at the Medical Clinic. While waiting in the lobby Governor Ed picked up a copy the Medical Dictionary and was surprised that in the medical community, like in the real estate industry, some words had to be translated in order to be understood by ordinary people. Here is an example of some of the words and what Ed thought they meant:

WORD	MEANING
Artery	Study of painting
Bacteria	Back door to a cafeteria
Barium	What doctor's do when treatment fails
Cat scan	Searching for Kitty
Caesarean Section	Municipality in Rome
Illegal	A sick bird
Diabetes Dead	because of a bee sting
Colic	A sheep dog
Coma	A punctuation mark
Congenital	Friendly
D & C	Where Washington is
Diarrhea	A journal of events
Dilate	To live long
Enema	Not a friend
Genital	Non-Jewish
Varicose	Located nearby
Labor pain	Get hurt at work

Impotent	Distinguished
Prostrate	Flat on your back
Rectum	Damn near kill 'em
Urine	Opposite to you're out
Seizure	Roman Empire
Illegal	A sick bird

When it was his turn to see Perez, Ed immediately said, "Doctor, since I became Governor I have developed a problem."

"What kind of a problem?"

"It's my sex drive."

"Come, come?" Dr. Perez said, "Your sex drive is in your head."

"That's the problem. Can you please lower it a bit?"

As an examination went on, Dr. Perez took Ed's wrist to feel his pulse and then said, "Stick out your tongue."

"There, you are sound as a nut and your ticker is in fairly good shape. Now drop your pants and lean over the table."

"Yes, doctor," Governor Ed, said and did what was told. Ed never called a doctor by his first name as he had no wish to be on a first name basis with someone who referred to his tongue as a nut, heart as an a ticker and further more stuck his middle finger all the way up Ed's rectum. At the end of the examination Perez thought Ed should have a wart removed from his neck and went on, "Governor Ed, in addition to the wart you'll have to quit smoking, drinking and having sex or else you'll have a heart attack soon."

A week passed and Governor Ed went to see Dr. Perez again. "Look, doc," he said, "I'm so miserable to Linda that I might as well be dead. Please, can I smoke just a little?"

"Very well, just a filter a day."

Another day passed and Governor Ed went to see Dr. Perez again, "Look, doc," he said, "I miss my home-made beer, please . . . ." "All right, just a bottle a day."

Another day passed and Governor Ed approached Dr. Perez for the 3rd time and said,

"Listen. Doc, I simply must have sex."

"Fine," replied the MD, "And remember only with Linda, no excitement."

The following day, Governor Ed met with Pastor Atupan over a cup of herbal tea and outlined his age problem and said, "Even Linda sometimes calls me an old geezer at a time when she knows I have made arrangements to leave her everything I own when I die.'

"And what happens should Linda die?"

"Linda can will our wealth to her favorite charity."

Pastor Atupan was getting on in age also and said, "Governor Ed, let me tell you a story about a pig ad a cow. The pig too was complaining to the cow that people always talked about the cow's genteelness and kind eyes while pigs name came as an insult.

The pig admitted that the cow gave milk, cream, butter and cheese pork chops, pickled feet and even headcheese. The pig could not see why the cows were esteemed so much. It was here in the story, that the cow replied that maybe it was because cow' give while they are still alive and pigs are beneficial only after they are dead."

"Good point." Governor Ed said, "That is why I'm so happy that Linda and I are able to contribute to society while we are still alive. I'm looking forward to volunteer on behalf of the Action Committee to help the poor and unemployed."

The following afternoon, Governor Ed was admitted to the Golden Gate General Hospital to remove a wart, which was beginning to look like a cauliflower.

Following the minor surgery Ed was in the recovery room. Seeing a patient next to him he sighed, "Thank God it's over."

"Don't be so sure," the patient next to him moaned. "They left a sponge in me and had to open me a second time."

And the patient on the other side said, "They had to open me too in order find their instruments."

Just then Dr. Perez who had just operated on Governor Ed stuck his head into the room and asked," Has anyone seen my hat?"

No one did.

Meanwhile, the tension of being a Congressman's wife, led Linda to seek psychiatric help and to Dr. Cresencio Yu said, "I'm irritable most of the time and find it difficult to get along with my friends." Linda and Dr. Yu talked at considerable length about aging and prescribed a tranquilizer for her nervous condition. The following day Linda returned for her session with the psychiatrist who asked, "Linda, have you noticed any difference in your condition?"

"Not that I can notice," Linda said. "But I do notice that everybody else, including my husband, has calmed down and have been more polite than before."

The psychiatrist suggested why Linda was feeling that way was because aging could be a woman's nightmare unless she had the right attitude. "At your age you have become an invisible woman."

"With that part I agree," Linda said and gave an example that whenever she was in downtown Batangas City shopping, her dog Dominic was the focus of attention. "It seems that I'm fading away. My life is changing."

"There are at times when I speak to my shadow, think Happy Hours is a nap, my memory is shorter and my complaining last longer, I look for my glasses only to find that I'm wearing them."

"In a society that worships beauty and youth, wrinkles and gray hair can be tickets to obscurity," the psychiatrist said and suggested to add spice to her life Linda should consider riding a mechanical bull at least once a day.

"I do that already," Linda said.

"Well, here's something more challenging. I understand you have your own private jet."

"I do."

"Then why don't you join a skydiving club?"

"I was a member once."

"And what happened?"

"You may not believe this doc. I pulled the parachute cord and nothing happened until I was about 60 meters from the ground and saw a Filipino going up."

"And what happened?"

"So I shouted, "Hey, there do you know anything about parachutes?"

"And."

"No, ata," the Filipino answered and asked if I knew anything about barbecues."

"Did you get hurt when you landed?" the psychiatrist kept probing.

"Fortunately not, because I landed on a trampoline and bounced back into the aircraft."

The following day, Governor Ramos was released from the hospital and it was time for the Meals on Wheels Roast which took place in the ballroom of the Hotel Portofino and many prominent residents turned out for the formal dinner which featured Heaven of Health Asian food including iced tea, seafood soup with sautéed vegetables, pork/shrimp adobo and blue marlin.

The men wore tuxedos, women long dresses and Ed was escorted by the Mayor and 2 Miss Batangas City candidates to the head table.

Pastor Atupan said grace and Linda was the first to roast Ed when she said, "When Ed first thought about seeking the governorship he said the Philippine parliament was filled with a whole bunch of corrupt fools."

Other prominent Batangas province celebrities and businessmen took turns in roasting Ed and each time the audience burst out in laughter. Ed never laughed so hard in his entire life. In the end the master of ceremonies thanked everyone for roasting and poking fun at Ed and helping Meals on Wheels support the poor and the unemployed.

There stood Ed to a thunderous applause, a man of the old school who had goose bumps on top o f goose bumps, Batangas City patriot, an achiever, a bread winner with tears of joy running down his cheeks. It was the only time Linda saw her husband display such an emotion in public and was proud of his achievements in real estate and politics.

The following day, Ed met Olympia at her office and Governor Ed asked, "How did we do with the roast?"

"Rather well, but we are still 500,000 pesos short of our objective."

Governor Ramos stopped, paused and scratched his head and then said, "I'll tell you something. To reach your objective and since its Christmas season, that won't be easy but now that I can swim, I'm willing to volunteer to have another Belly Flop contest."

A week later, a huge crowd, each paid a handsomely for a ticket to watch Ed and 12 other prominent Batangas City celebrities and newsmakers for the event billed as the Batangas City Battle of the Bulges at the City Swimming Pool bleachers. Contestants drew numbers as to when they would dive. Congressman Ed drew # 1 was the first to climb the diving board, flex his muscles and display his physique.

As soon as a whistle was blown for Ed to make his dive he jumped up and down on the diving board and then made his dive and when he did, the announcer on the public address system said, "Ladies and gentlemen, I have some good news and some bad news. The good news is that the judges have awarded Governor Ed Ramos's dive a perfect score"

There was a thunderous applause.

"And the bad news is that while making the dive Governor Ramos had a heart attack."

Hearing the outcome a lifeguard dragged Ed out of the pool where he was resuscitated. Seeing Ed in excruciating pain Dr. Perez and Pastor Atupan rushed to his side and Dr. Perez said, "Governor Ramos I warned you to stop smoking; drinking and having sex but you didn't listen."

Minutes later, Dr. Perez, who was one of the contestants, felt Governor Ramos's pulse and pronounced Ed dead and said, "That's too bad because Governor Ed was about to receive an honorary doctorate degree from the University of Batangas."

Ed was dead and the Batangas City was electrified with the painful tragedy.

Linda couldn't believe that her husband had passed away for the second time as it seemed just minutes ago that his lips were touching hers. Several days later, as the bagpipes played loudly and the drums beat slowly at the No Name Universal Church 6 congressmen picked up the coffin covered with white linen and a hearse took Ed to the San Fernando Funeral Home Crematory where his ashes turned to dust and in a flash POOF—Ed went straight to the Pearly Gates where Saint Peter, the Gate Keeper was waiting to interview him.

In the hours that followed, Linda returned home and grieved like she never grieved before saying over and over, "Ed, I have no one now since you have left me," and threw herself on to her bed sobbing so loudly that it could be heard next door. Minutes later, while dressed in black and lying on her bed, she was joined at her bedside by Pastor Autopan, her bank manager, Peter Wong, and her lawyer Thomas Huff.

Several hours later, Linda died also and with Ed, appeared at the Pearly Gates where Saint Peter said, "Entrance into Heaven isn't easy. In honor of the holy season, you must each possess something that symbolizes Christmas to let you inside heaven."

Ed fumbled through his pockets and pulled out a lighter. He flicked it on and said, "It represents a candle."

"Just a minute," Saint Peter said, "Your face is familiar. You have been in heaven before."

"I have."

"Have you done anything wrong since then?"

"No, Saint Peter. Because of the severe economic conditions I made a lot of angry people happy."

"You may go through the Pearly Gates," Saint Peter said.

When it was Linda's turn, Saint Peter asked, Mrs. Ramos, what makes you think that you deserve entry into heaven that symbolizes Christmas?"

Linda genuflected and then said, "I probated my will and all the earthly assets which I inherited from my husband, I have donated to the Action Committee in Batangas City to enjoy a prosperous Christmas and eliminate poverty and unemployment."

Seconds later, Linda was united with her husband in heaven.

NIGHT WIND

As the night wind cries its soft an endless theme
I sit by the window absorbed figuring out our dream
Each month you send me a door to door balacan box
That includes food, toiletries and socks
As the night wind reminds me that many applied but you
were the one chosen

I miss you my darling, and when I'm lonely and blue
I scratch my head and wonder where are you?
When things go wrong as sometimes they do
I wish I was with you.
As the night wind reminds me that many applied but you
are the one chosen

And when our funds are getting low and debts high
I want to smile but instead I sigh
Often I'm frustrated waiting for you and nearly give up
At a time I'm married to a victor's cup.
As the night winds reminds me that many applied but you
were the one chosen

You are not me and I'm not you, except when you hold my
hand
You from abroad and across the sea in a foreign land
I pray and sometimes cry
You are abroad and I wonder why

As the night wind reminds me that many have applied but
    you were the one chosen

Darling, I know you still love me and I love you
And we'll make it through
Through the good times and the bad
You're the only and best husband I ever had
As the night wind reminds me that many have applied buy
    you were the one chosen

Joe Remesz (2013)